THE UNIVERSITY OF WINNIPEG
LIBRARY

<u>THE ASHDOWN COLLECTION OF CANADIANA</u>

THIS SPECIAL COLLECTION
OF
CANADIAN HISTORY AND LITERATURE
COMMEMORATES THE NAME
OF

HARRY C. ASHDOWN, 1886-1971,

A DISTINGUISHED MEMBER OF
THE BOARD OF REGENTS FROM 1929 to 1967,
WHOSE GENEROUS BEQUEST
TO THE UNIVERSITY LIBRARY
PROVIDED THE INCENTIVE FOR
THE ESTABLISHMENT OF THE COLLECTION

UPROOTED HEATHER

1.

UPROOTED HEATHER

A Story of the Selkirk Settlers
by
WEMYSS CAVAICK

MITCHELL PRESS LIMITED
Vancouver, Canada

Printed in Canada
MITCHELL PRESS LIMITED
Vancouver, B.C.

"Where are they now? Tell us where are thy sons and daughters,
Sutherland sad mother! No more in thy bosom they dwell;
Far, far away, they found a new home o'er the waters.
Yearning for thee with love no language can tell,
Nimrods and hunters are now lords of the mount and forest.
Men but encumbered the soil where their forefathers trod,
Tho' for their country, when its need was the sorest,
Forth they must wander, their hope not in man, but in God."

Contents

CHAPTER ONE

O God! O God! Do Not Forsake the Children of Our Tribe!

"The ghosts of the lately dead were near, and swam on the gloomy clouds: And far distant, in the dark silence of Lena, the feeble voices of death were faintly heard."

FINGAL*

THE spring of the fateful year 1746 was a mild one. The snow, having vanished before the warm April showers, brought a renewal in the valley of the age-old custom of tilling and planting the workable land.

In one of the fields, Murdoch MacKay paused at his hoeing, his eyes drawn to the snow-capped summit of Ben Horn, a rugged peak that towered above its smaller companions. "It's strange," he remarked to his wife, now come to stand beside him and share his respite, "the mist seems to be clinging around Big Ben like a funeral shroud!"

Nora's toil-worn fingers tensed on her husband's muscular arm. "It's unusual, Murdoch — looks as if some supernatural power is holding it there."

Hardly had she finished speaking than an unnatural stillness settled over the valley. The birds ceased their evening twittering. The light spring zephyr died away. Even the rushing sound of the Brora River, as it cascaded over Blackwater Falls, was strangely

---

* All verse captions used as chapter headings are translations of the Highland Gaelic poet Ossian.

muted. All nature seemed to be standing still as if awaiting the arrival of some mysterious event.

"There's an eeriness about all this!" declared MacKay when he saw a mantle of ugly black clouds surge abruptly across the western horizon to beat out the blood-red glare of the setting sun. Apprehensively he recalled that the shroud had been there the day that he and his brother John, against the advice of their mother, had set out to gaff for a salmon in the deep pool below the falls. John had lunged for a big one but as he struck out, he slipped and fell into the rushing Brora River and was drowned. As he brushed the horror of that day from his mind, MacKay remembered that the ominous cloud was also there the day he was called in from the fields to the stern Sergeant George MacLeod of the 42nd Highlanders. George had brought the news, two months old by then, that MacKay's son Donald had given his life in battle.

As she watched the strange manifestations in the heavens Nora's heart beat faster. She moved closer and took her husband's trembling hand.

"We'd better get inside, Murdoch," she whispered.

Before her husband could reply the wind came shrieking down the valley and through the unsheltered ravines. Jets of wild fire forked from peak to peak along the rim of the mountains.

Breathless, MacKay and his wife struggled through the door of their straw-thatched dwelling. The haste of their entry brought their little Fiona running from the kitchen.

"What happened?" she cried in a quivering voice.

Her mother could not answer. She clasped her to her bosom as a torrential rain and wind buffeted the cottage until it rocked on its very foundations. The gale hissed and roared through the well-bound thatch and wound its dismal horn in the mud and stone chimney-top as though in sudden fury at its stubborn resistance.

MacKay, deafened by the crashing thunder, imagined voices; Nora saw scores of blood-covered phantoms flitting across the room. In silent fear, Fiona surrendered herself completely to her mother's terror-stricken embrace.

When the storm had spent itself, a welcome calmness settled over the expectant valley.

"Nora," MacKay whispered hesitantly. "Nora, did you hear the voices?"

"Voices! What voices?" sobbed Nora, lifting her face from

2

the coarse woollen plaid that hung over MacKay's shoulder.

"I heard a voice. I thought it said, 'Oh God! Oh God! do not forsake the children of our tribe!'"

Nora shuddered. "I heard no voices. But I did see bloody spectres flying earthward. What did the voices mean, Murdoch?"

"It must have been a sign."

MacKay recalled the latest news circulating among the crofters of Sutherland. A mighty English army under the Duke of Cumberland was following close on the heels of Prince Charles and the Jacobites; the Highlanders were retreating north toward Inverness, just eighty miles south of MacKay's storm-battered dwelling.

"The bloody spectres I saw must have been the spirits of the dead Highlanders taking the low road home," Nora whispered. "The voice you heard could have been the Great Spirit calling upon us to give our dead countrymen free passage to their eternal rest."

"Such strange manifestations are beyond our ken," acknowledged MacKay. "What we saw and feared may portend something good or something evil — we'll know at the proper time. Meanwhile, let's have supper and to bed early, for tomorrow brings a trip to the mill — perhaps all will be explained."

Like many of the crofters of Strath Brora, MacKay had heard of the sudden arrival of Charles Edward Stuart from France. The young Prince had returned to the land of his forefathers proclaiming liberty and justice if the Highlanders would only unite to destroy the English tyrant. As this welter of events passed through his mind they caused MacKay to stir uncomfortably in his chair as he sipped at his mug of fiery liquor. He placed great store in premonitions and second sight — all Highlanders did. Thus, Nora's forebodings, the voices and visions troubled him deeply. "God knows what will happen to us should Charles be defeated," he muttered under his breath.

Next morning, April 24th, 1746, the MacKays were up early.

The day broke calm and showed scant reminder in the valley of the previous day's turmoil.

MacKay whistled light-heartedly as he harnessed his old mare Rosey in preparation for the semi-annual trip to the meal-mill, operated by the Earl of Sutherland near Dunrobin Castle. For this occasion, throughout the winter months, MacKay had carefully preserved a quantity of oats which he would exchange for oatmeal at the mill.

3

Fiona had been fluttering around the cottage since before dawn for this was a very special day. Today she would accompany her father to the Mound and while awaiting his return from the mill, she would spend the day gathering shell-fish and dulse.

The dim light in the cottage disclosed a young girl, tall for her years, with cornflower blue eyes and pleasing auburn hair. Her parents lovingly referred to her as the 'spurtle' — the round one. Her eyes shone and her face flushed with excitement at the prospects of the day ahead.

She had barely finished her porridge when her father halted the mare at the door of the cottage. He threw the crab basket onto the grain sacks, and as Fiona scrambled up on the wagon after a parting kiss to Nora he headed Rosey up the rocky track.

The way to the mill was no hazard for the mare; she was quite capable of going there and back with little guidance. Thus, Fiona and her father were able to chat light-heartedly, oblivious of everything save the delights of the spring morning while Rosey herself found the road and plodded her way to the seacoast.

The Mound was a quiet little spot, resting in the cleft of a hill where a trickling burn flowed across the roadway to meet the tossing Firth. Here if the season was right and the tide went out far enough, the crab and cockle beds were exposed.

Fiona had arrived in good time. As Rosey stopped to refresh herself at the stream, Fiona planted a kiss on her father's cheek, grabbed her basket, and leaped to the ground.

"You'd better take your plaid and shawl," MacKay admonished. They'll keep you warm when the sun goes down. Watch for the incoming tide and don't cut your feet on the rocks."

"I won't, father, don't worry!"

Fiona watched from the roadside until Rosey and her father had disappeared over the hill. Then she skipped across the soft sand to the shoreline where she removed her deerskin slippers, wrapped them in her plaid and tucked them safely in a cleft of rock.

For a moment she glanced around the scene of spring beauty. Clouds floated like tufts of fleece in the brilliant blue of the sky. The breeze came sighing across Mickle Ferry, and rippled the waters until the whole sea glinted like a vast flashing shoal of herring. Anxiously she made her way among the rocks toward the crab and cockle beds that the ebbing tide had exposed.

When her basket was full, she dragged it across the sand and left it beside her shoes and plaid. For a little while she watched

4

the crabs clawing and scraping at each other with locked pincers but, satisfied they could not escape, she looped up her apron and quickly filled it with whelks and cockles.

The little girl was well pleased as she thought how happy her mother would be to have the fresh seafood. When she had finished she wrapped her woollen plaid around her slim shoulders and amused herself by watching the wheeling gulls and listening to the incoming tide crashing on the rocks.

Ordinarily Fiona never worried when her father did not return before sunset, but in the gathering twilight the happenings of the previous night disturbed her. She watched the speeding sea birds head west to roost on the cliffs of Dornoch and shivered despite her shawl. With a tinge of anxiety, she set out for a walk along the shore.

Fiona loved all living things. Her eyes sparkled at the sight of the rabbit, hare, grouse or pheasant which were regular visitors to MacKay's yard. Her little body had been toughened by the hunt for the bird's nest and the chase after the baby rabbits which found it so difficult to make their way through the gorse and heather to their burrow on the hillside of Sciberscross.

As she strolled on, she thought of her dog Heather, her friend in all her ramblings. She remembered that the story of Heather's heritage went a long way back to the last wolf to be killed in Scotland.

The story began when Murdoch MacKay as a young man travelled with horse and cart throughout Sutherland, buying and selling lambs, pigs and calves. One day at Midgarty, on the East coast of Sutherland, he came upon a tribe of starving Gipsies who called upon him for help. Murdoch wasn't slow to comply for he feared the strange power of these people. He killed a calf which he could little spare and after feeding the tawny-skinned wanderers he was about to move on when the Chief spoke:

"Stranger, we would have starved had it not been for your kindness. But the Gipsy code does not permit us to accept charity. You must be rewarded. You must accept some tin ware or some beads for your woman. You cannot refuse us."

MacKay glanced around and his eye lighted on a scrawny, grizzly-haired cur that lay on a bed of heather.

"What about that whelp?" he asked.

"Yes, stranger," said the Chief. "You may take her. She's got a pedigree to match her looks. You know that the last wolf killed in Scotland was killed up the glen from here in Strath

Dionard. A few days ago I traded some pots and pans with a cattle drover by the name of Polson. I took the dog in exchange— we were going to eat her for dinner tonight if you hadn't come along. Polson took the Gipsy's oath and swore that one of his ancestors had killed the last wolf and its five cubs."

He pointed a mutilated arm at the emaciated cur. "This bitch is a descendant of the Strath Dionard wolf. Maybe if you give her something to eat she'll live."

MacKay made a gipsy bargain and took the dog home.

Many generations later, Fiona's Heather still carried the grizzly-haired, wolf-like traits of her ancestors. This was especially evident when it came to protecting the MacKay family against predators.

Now as she walked along the beach Fiona missed her companion trotting at her side. She was about to bend down to throw a stick into the surf, when she paused. Something had changed the old wreck that had been cast on the beach many years before. She remembered the overturned hulk because one day when it rained she had crawled under it for shelter. Now a ragged plaid hung over the keel. As she drew nearer, Fiona was startled to see a little foot, then a bare leg showing from behind the derelict. Fiona stopped. The stillness of the leg in the last rays of day and its bleached whiteness told her that something was wrong. Instinctively she feared death, and could not face its prospect. Had she not better wait for her father and Rosey?

With a last look she began to retreat. Suddenly, the leg twitched and she heard a fretful groan come from under the boat. Panic stricken, she turned quickly away from the strange discovery but had gone only a few steps when her young mind reasoned that someone was hurt — like the lambs and the rabbits, he needed her help.

"Hello! she called. "Hello, there! Hello! Do you hear me?" There was no answer. Timidly she approached the figure huddled on the sand. His ragged tartan plaid had caught on the keel and the loose end had fallen over one naked shoulder. It was a lean, gaunt little boy of her own age. His face was white, his lips blue and he looked more dead than alive. Sand matted his red hair. His kilt was torn and deep scratches marked his thighs. Dried blood caked around a gash on his left foot.

Dropping on one knee, she tenderly raised the boy's head from the sand, removed the plaid from his shoulders and wrapped her warm shawl around his still body. With his hand clenched firmly in her own she pleaded, "Speak to me. Can you hear me, boy?"

6

The full moon rose and its mellow light bathed their two small figures; her hands continued to massage the benumbed boy. Praying all the while that he would not die, Fiona rubbed the cold fingers over and over again in an effort to restore warmth.

The lingering evening shadows disappeared, and the silver beams from the full moon flooded the shoreline with their mellow radiance. Fiona was so engrossed in her efforts that she failed to hear the clip-clop of Rosey's hooves or the creaking of the wooden wheels of her father's cart until it was opposite the wrecked boat. She leaped to her feet and hastened across the sand. "Hurry, father. Come! Hurry!"

MacKay drew Rosey to a halt and dropped the reins. "What is it, lass?" he asked as he stepped down.

"A boy — there's an unconscious boy lying on the beach! Come! Come quickly, father!"

MacKay hurried after his daughter as she raced ahead to the wreck. He knelt down and took the boy's limp hand in his own.

"Hurry to the cart and bring me my jug and some milk."

Fiona stared as though in a trance.

"Hurry," he insisted, "we may still save him!"

MacKay rubbed the arms and legs vigorously. The lad groaned and stirred. Lifting the jug MacKay forced some of its fiery contents between the pallid lips. The boy choked and spluttered.

"Easy lad, easy," soothed MacKay in a reassuring voice. "You're going to be all right."

The boy's eyelids opened but he did not stir. Fiona could discern fear and bewilderment and her eyes welled with tears.

Weakly the boy struggled to get up but MacKay restrained him gently. "Take it easy, lad. You're among friends."

Fiona cried with relief. "You've saved him, father, you've saved him."

"Pour the boy a horn of milk."

Fiona held the horn to the boy's bloodless lips. Drinking was difficult for the weak lad and some of the milk settled in a pool on his tattered homespun kilt.

"What's your name, boy?" asked MacKay.

The little stranger, staring apprehensively, slowly replied, "Duncan."

"Where do you come from?"

There was no answer.

"You're wearing a strange tartan, Duncan," observed Fiona. "What is it?"

7

MacKay had been so busy reviving Duncan that he had not noticed the lad's clothing. In the bright moonlight he became aware of the tartan. His blood chilled. It was the outlawed Mac-Donald!

While waiting at the mill he and Sam Gow had walked through the glen to Dunrobin castle. They had been anxious to know if any bulletins had been posted on the fate of Bonnie Prince Charlie and his Jacobite forces. Tacked to the outside gate they had found a fateful announcement. It stated simply that a strong English Army under the Duke of Cumberland had routed Charles Edward Stuart and his Highlanders at Culloden Moor ten miles from Inverness. It went on to say that the English soldiers were rounding up the Jacobites, confiscating their possessions and burning their homes, and that anyone suspected of being such a traitor should be reported to the Earl's taxman or to Dunrobin castle. The penalty for harbouring would be the confiscation of the offender's possessions, his hanging or banishment to a colony overseas.

As MacKay knelt in the moonlight on the soft sand beside the Jacobite boy clad in the rebel MacDonald tartan, the fatal notice flashed before his eyes.

"We must leave him here," he muttered and stood up.

Fiona leaped to her feet. "What do you mean, father? What are you saying?"

Patiently MacKay explained the risk involved but its full meaning escaped his young daughter.

"We can't leave him here, father. He'll die."

MacKay shook his head in perplexity. "Fiona, it's too dangerous. If we're caught harbouring a rebel, terrible things will happen to us."

Murdoch MacKay was a dour, stubborn man. He had been born and raised to farm an inhospitable land and had worked on the croft since he was five years of age. There had been no childhood in his life — only a hard and dismal struggle to exist. He had fought to save his few oats and vegetables through late springs and early winters. Ever present, listening to every word and watching every action was Roberts, the hunchbacked taxman. On him the old Earl had placed the responsibility of keeping him informed as to the mood and employment of all his tenants. As MacKay listened to his daughter, he began to boil with rage at the cruelty that had crushed to near death the orphan who lay at his feet.

"But how can I take the lad to Blackwater?" he thought. "He

8

must be a Jacobite. If we're caught, the price we'll have to pay will be the destruction of all we have worked for."

Before he could give utterance to his thoughts, Fiona's ashen face, bewildered eyes and twitching mouth appeared before him. "Father," she almost screamed, "we *must* take Duncan home with us. If not, I'll stay here with him on the beach until he is well enough to take care of himself." Nearing hysteria, she dropped beside the boy and took him in her small slender arms. "Please father, please," she sobbed. "Don't leave him here!"

MacKay knelt down and lifted his quivering girl to her feet. His voice was strained and he spoke gravely. "Fiona, because of my love for you and your mother we cannot do this. Your mother and I hungered and slaved to build Blackwater to what it is today. You have no idea, child, what it cost in heartaches to provide the comfort that brightens our home. Taking this unknown boy to Blackwater could bring an end to all we've worked so hard for. The notice at the Castle said clearly — deportation or hanging is the punishment for that which you now insist that I do!"

"Father," whispered Fiona, snuggling close in his arms, "when we took our vows in the little church in Rogart, we pledged before God to help our fellow man. Surely, father, you wouldn't now turn traitor to a cause for which you have taken an oath?"

"Daughter, you know I try to obey God's laws and I love you and your mother dearly but surely you wouldn't want me to run afoul of the inquisitive taxman, Roberts. I know you are right but I am sorely distressed." He paused as though fearful to whisper the decision he had reached. "However, it's night time and the road is lonely. We'll take Duncan to Blackwater and give him a few days shelter then send him on his way. This I will do."

Having come to a decision MacKay gathered Duncan in his arms and carried him to the cart.

He tucked the silent boy among the bags of oatmeal and threw a plaid over him. Climbing wearily to the seat beside his daughter, he picked up the reins and urged Rosey homeward.

9

CHAPTER TWO

Terror of Drummossie

*The thistle shook, there, its lonely head: the moss whistled
to the wind. Desolate is the dwelling of Moina; silence is
in the house of her fathers.*

CARTHO

As the wagon jostled over the rough road, Duncan became aware of his great exhaustion, but the whisky and milk, the warmth of the heavy rug and perhaps the creaking of the cart itself combined to restore his vitality. Despite his suffering he became painfully conscious of his surroundings as the little group moved steadily into the valley.

Every stone, every grain of sand, seemed to set up an eternal throbbing all through his fear-racked body. His legs stabbed painfully. How long could he stand it? He must get onto his feet somehow. He must get off this swaying, bumping machine of torture on which he lay.

The road skirted majestic hills covered with heather, broom and sparse clumps of Scotch pine. A full Highland moon sifting through the waving branches of the nearby trees, flickered on his face and across the backs of the two people hunched in the seat above his head. Arching his neck, he could vaguely distinguish the broad back of the man and the smaller outline of the girl. Above the whining of the cart's wooden axle he could faintly hear odd snatches of their conversation.

"Could we really get into trouble for sheltering him?" asked the smaller shadow with the moon glinting on her golden hair.

She had a gentle voice, a soft voice, and Duncan warmed to the feeling that perhaps they had ages at least in common.

"We could, indeed," said the heavier shadow. He sighed and sang out a command to the pony as it stumbled over the deep ruts in the highway, "Whish-hi-hi!"

The heavier voice of the man was strangely mellow and expressive. It had a lilt and a touch of friendliness which was comforting to one who had so little in life to cling to. In the painful darkness Duncan heard the voice continue.

"There's no doubt he's a Jacobite. I should turn him in. It is my duty."

"Father, you're not angry with me? We couldn't leave the boy on the beach."

The man appeared to hesitate for a moment. "There was really nothing else we could do. To leave him there would have been inhuman."

The cart bumped again and Duncan winced with pain. His foot hurt, his head ached and he felt a wave of sickness pass over him. As memory returned, he re-lived the horrors that he had seen and the terrors he had in some way managed to escape.

He could see the hill beside Culloden Moor, where he had been drawn to watch the battle. The Highland battalions were manoeuvring for position. The weather was wild and the bitter, sleety wind from the west lashed at his face until his forehead ached with a painful numbness and the finger tips which jutted out from under his coarse woollen mitts were blue and lifeless. He squirmed in his sickness as he remembered how he put his fingers alternately into his mouth to blow on them to restore circulation. The drops which grew incessantly at the point of his nose could hardly be brushed off before they were re-forming again in icy blobs.

He could hear the faint incisive wail of the bagpipes ebb and flow through the storm as their stirring martial music brought the ranks of Prince Charles' army into formation. Dimly through the sleet he could see the yellow tartan of the MacLeods and the red of the Chisholms as they ranked up on the right of the Prince, and away in the distance the red and yellow of the Camerons and the burnished steel of Atholl. His father was among the MacDonalds who had knelt and prayed a short distance from him to receive the Holy Sacrament.

Less than a mile away, on his left, the Duke of Cumberland's mighty army was advancing. He heard their cannon roar. The whirl of the cannon balls was muffled by the hissing sleet as they fell with a dull thud into the soggy marshes and churned the peat up in fountains of mud. The pipes of the clans skirled above the din. The Highlanders advanced. Their wild, defiant cries echoed across Drummossie and up to the heather-covered hills where he crouched in terror. His heart ached for his people as the guns of the English artillery silenced the puny Jacobite cannon and tore the ranks of the defiant Highlanders into bloody shreds. He watched as the clansmen cast their muskets aside, grabbed their claymores, and charged into the red-coated infantry of Cumberland's army.

Before Duncan could realize what was happening, the Highland Army was in retreat. The English Dragoons were eliminating isolated remnants of the clans and somewhere on that littered field of dead and dying was his father, Colonel Duncan Grant, in his blood-stained tartan. An uncontrollable, high-pitched wail broke from Duncan's tortured lips as he clamped his wet hands over his face to hide the stain of Drummossie. He ran, he crouched, he fell, then he got up and ran again. He skirted the piles of dead and dying. As though by a miracle he was drawn straight to the very spot where his father lay. "Run for it, son," the dying Colonel gasped through swollen lips. "There's no hope now. Cumberland has sworn to kill . . . " The last breath whistled from his throat and his head lolled lifelessly in the bloody gore and the mud of the moor.

Duncan turned and fled. Fear and hate gave wings to his nimble feet. Red-coat stragglers mopping up the battlefield, shooting and bayonetting the wounded Highlanders, saw the lad dash through the heather. Their musket balls zinged off the rocks and furrowed the ground beside him as they tried to bring him down. But he was small and fleet. Frantically he raced across the moor toward his home, but the redcoats had been there before him. As he collapsed in sheer despair among the thick bracken, he was in time to see the final act of depravity and horror unfold before him.

"There's a flock of MacDonald spawn hiding there," shouted one of the soldiers. As he spoke, a wounded Highlander staggered from the smoke-filled doorway. To a chorus of jeering laughter and a volley of English musket fire, the soldier was cut down and crumpled as an untidy pile of lifeless MacDonald tartan on the wet moss.

Duncan was petrified with fear. As he crouched on the moor he heard a scream of agony from inside his burning home. Then

12

he saw his grandfather supporting his feeble old granny from the burning pyre. They collapsed in screaming pain and merciful oblivion swept over them.

Duncan knew that his mother must still be in the house and with childish recklessness he was about to rush to her aid when the weakened roof gave way with a roar of smoke and rending wood. Sparks and flame shot into the air and Duncan sprawled sobbing on the snow-covered ground. The song of the spinning-wheel, the laughter of the glen and the friendly banter of the croft had gone from his life. He was alone.

Cautiously, in the eerie light of dawn, he approached the ruins and poked around in the ashes. The sleet sizzled on the hot embers while the rushing, eddying wind made him a constant target for the acrid smoke of death which enveloped him and brought tears to his smarting eyes. There was no sign of his mother as he turned away — a grown man.

In the twilight of oblivion in the bottom of the cart, he could see again the burial parties of aged men and women sorrowfully gathering up their dead from the battlefield while Cumberland's soldiers beat and flogged them mercilessly with packstraps and the flat of their swords. He recalled how he had staggered through the countryside by night avoiding the flaming cottages which were the funeral pyre of many a kinsman.

Scrounging in an abandoned cottage he had found some food which kept him from starving as he moved steadily north from Drummossie Moor.

By the time he reached the seacoast he was certain that only the hand of God could be directing his steps and embuing him with the courage and hope he still felt.

His food dwindled. The coastline became a deserted, rocky shore-line where there was scarcely a cottage and only a few people lived. A cold wind began to whip in from the sea and a storm broke, more suddenly than he had ever witnessed, or even imagined. Dark clouds scurried over the horizon. Thunder crashed and lightning flashed brighter than the sun. Duncan stumbled and collapsed on the sand. He got to his knees and crawled forward. He had never seen such violence. The terror of Drummossie may have been driven out by hunger and exhaustion but it now returned to plague him and when a particularly brilliant lightning flash lit up an abandoned boat, he staggered toward it. He collapsed beneath the boat, suddenly aware of a voice: 'O God! O God! Do not forsake the children of our tribe.'

The howl and roar struck him with terror. The thunderous wind threatened to tear the flimsy shelter from over him. Erratic flashes of lightning reminded him of the horrible flames of death, and in the sighing wind he heard the moan of sorrow from the bloody moor of Drummossie.

He had to get out. He had to wrench himself free from this dreadful shroud which encircled him. He had to . . .

With a moan of despair Duncan jerked upwards from his bed in the cart. His unseeing eyes opened wide and stared glassily in the glimmering light of the moon. His small pallid face was contorted by a spasm of uncontrollable fear and his blue lips were opened wide in a wail of terror.

He was brought to his senses by powerful hands shaking him. "Canny boy! Canny! You're all right now," he heard a voice say. As he opened his eyes he saw Murdoch MacKay bending over him and the anxious face of a young girl peering from behind his shoulder. "You've been having a nightmare, lad; you were screaming so hard we thought you'd never stop. Easy now! Easy!"

The cart had been stopped on the road. The horrible swaying and bumping had ended and at last Duncan's aching limbs were at peace and the cold velvet darkness of the Highland spring night cast a cooling dew on his fevered head. He eased himself up between the meal sacks and heard a grunt of approval from MacKay. "That's better now. As long as we're stopped, we might as well have a bit of food."

Fiona could see by the way Duncan looked from one to the other that he was still distrustful. He tore at a cold chicken leg like a hungry animal. He was in a quandary; the horror he had lived through had shattered his faith and his father's last words rang in his ear, "Run for it, run. Cumberland has promised to kill every Jacobite in the Highlands". The thought brought a moment's renewed panic and he was trying to decide on the best way to escape when he heard the soft voice of the girl.

"Isn't that a beautiful moon?" Fiona whispered to reassure him. "Did you ever see so many bright stars? The northern streamers have been dancing across the sky all the way from the beach."

"You're making things hard on yourself, laddie," said MacKay. "Whatever has befallen you God alone knows, but there's no need for fear now. You're among friends." He explained how Fiona had found him unconscious on the beach. He told the

14

lad they were taking him to their home in Sciberscross and again he asked for Duncan's last name and his clan but Duncan looked his questioner glassily in the eye and spoke not a word.

"Listen to me, lad. We want to help you. You're now in the land of Sutherland. If you're seen in that strange tartan an explanation will be necessary. If you're a Jacobite or of their kin your presence in my home will place us all in danger. For your own protection as well as ours, I want you to answer truthfully if you are a Jacobite."

"I am, sir," replied Duncan. Then, having made his confession, he broke into violent sobbing.

"It's all right, son. It's all right now," MacKay repeated as he consoled the boy. "You're safe with us for a while."

Thus, with mixed emotions, the trio started upon the last leg of the return trip to Blackwater croft. Though tired from the excitement Fiona was childishly eager at the prospect of the surprise that awaited her mother. MacKay remained torn between two irreconcilable beliefs, first, the certainty that he could not have left the boy on the beach, but secondly, that by taking the Jacobite to his home, he had jeopardized his whole family. As he neared Blackwater croft in the early dawn, he pulled Rosey to a halt. "I want you to run on ahead, Fiona. Warn your mother that we have a sick lad in the cart. Keep a sharp lookout and if you see anyone near the house, leave the front door open. If all is clear let Heather loose. She'll come to meet us. Go now."

It was Nora MacKay's custom to keep a tallow candle burning in the window whenever her husband was out late. The glittering flame was nearly down to the holder and anxiety had kept her from sleep. Keeping busy was the only way to allay her fears so she worked away at the butter churn. She was about to light another candle when Heather, lying at the hearth, barked suddenly as Fiona burst into the room.

"What's all the fuss about?" Nora asked.

"Mother," gasped Fiona, her eyes gleaming with excitement, "we have a strange lad in the cart. He's very sick. I found him on the beach. We only know that his name is Duncan. Father will explain everything later." Fiona clipped a leash on Heather's collar and, leaving her bewildered mother, she hurried outside and quickly surveyed the yard. Finding no one around she released the wolf-hound and it raced off toward the waiting cart.

MacKay backed the cart against the door of the white-washed cottage, gathered Duncan in his arms and carried him in the house.

"Hurry, Nora! Let's get some warmth back into this poor lad. I'll put him in Fiona's bed for now."

The next few minutes were hectic. MacKay left the cottage to unload the meal and shell-fish into the barn and to stable Rosey. When he returned to the cottage Nora had wrapped hot rocks in cloth and placed them in the bed where Duncan lay under the heaviest quilts she could find. Fiona, utterly exhausted, was put to bed in a bunk in the kitchen.

When all was quiet, MacKay sat down with his pipe and related to his wife the story of how Fiona had discovered Duncan.

"Perhaps I've acted too hastily," he concluded after explaining the significance of the ominous notice on the castle wall. "The lad's an admitted Jacobite. If I did my duty, I'd advise the Earl's men that he is here."

"You'll do no such thing," declared Nora. "Didn't you notice anything about him? Didn't he remind you of someone?"

MacKay had been vaguely conscious of some resemblance ever since he looked down on Duncan on the beach. Now Nora put his impression into words. "Doesn't he look exactly like our Donald when he was eight, the same red hair, the same blue eyes and the same handsome look on his face? I could almost have sworn it was my Donald you were tucking into Fiona's bed."

MacKay was silent. Now, in the light of the taper he could see the similarity between Duncan and the young son who had scampered around the house and croft so long ago. Then, too soon, the boy had been called to military service and had never returned.

"Do you think it's a sign?" he asked.

"I'm sure it is," Nora replied. "You remember how granny predicted that a strange boy would come into our glen to settle among us and raise three children."

"Yes, but is this the boy?"

"I can't tell you that, Murdoch MacKay. But I believe God is giving us back our son."

MacKay shuddered, and looked apprehensively around. He noticed the faint morning light filtering through the cottage windows. "It will soon be sunrise. There may be searching parties out. If the lad's found here, we'll all be hanged."

"He won't be found," retorted Nora. "You did what was right— no Christian would have done otherwise. No one knows my relatives in Tain. All we have to do is introduce the lad as one of our kin. I'll burn his kilt and plaid."

16

He grunted noncommittally as Nora gathered up the boy's clothes and fed them to the peat fire. As the last of the Mac-Donald tartan curled up and smouldered to ashes, he felt relieved.

Some distance from the cottage at the west end of the croft, John Roberts, the Earl's hunchbacked little taxman, out for a bucket of fresh water from MacKay's field well, stopped and sniffed inquisitively at the clear morning air. "Burning wool," he mumbled, "who can afford to burn wool in the Highlands where nothing's wasted?" He tested the wind with a wet finger. It seemed for all the world as if the odor was coming from Blackwater croft. "I'd better find out what they're doing at Murdo MacKay's".

CHAPTER THREE

Respite

"When the haughty come to my halls, my eyes behold them not. But my arm is stretched forth to the unhappy. My sword defends the weak."

CALTHON AND COLMAL

THE SUN was well above the hills when MacKay strolled across the yard to take care of the livestock. Despite his wife's apparently foolproof plan, he was unable to dispel his uneasiness. Remembering that the jug of brew was under the seat of the cart, he brought it into the barn, uncorked it and took a long swig. The first draught of the spirits did little to ease his apprehension. He was about to have another when a shadow darkened the shaft of sunlight coming through the barn door. MacKay instantly dropped the flagon into Rosey's manger. He had started toward the door when he recognized the voice of the Earl's weasel-faced taxman.

"Are you in there, MacKay?" Roberts asked in a thin, high voice, squinting to adjust his eyes to the darkness of the shed.

MacKay licked his lips and wiped his mouth. "I'm here, John."

The taxman gazed at him curiously holding his head cocked to one side and looking out the corner of his eye.

"Was it trouble on the road that kept you so late last night, MacKay?"

"There was no trouble. Others were waiting to grind their grain and Nora's nephew from Tain was to meet me at the mill. I had to wait for him."

"That's strange, I've never heard Nora speak of her folks at Tain."

"Have you not? It's her sister's boy. She hasn't been well, so the lad's going to stay for a while at Blackwater."

"How old is he then?"

"Just over eight, I think."

"And his name?"

"Duncan."

The taxman looked at MacKay. "When I was at the well this morning I smelled burning wool. That wouldn't have anything to do with the boy, would it now?"

With the blood pounding in his ears MacKay struggled to keep his voice calm. "How could it have anything to do with the boy?" he scoffed. "He certainly doesn't have wool to burn."

"And would the lad be of our faith?"

"That he is, John."

Apparently satisfied, Roberts asked. "Did you hear any news of Cumberland and his men, or of the popish Prince Charles and his Jacobite army?"

Relieved at the chance to change the subject, MacKay related the information he had gathered about the battle of Culloden and the defeat of the Jacobites.

The taxman's features brightened. He rubbed his hands briskly. "Nothing would give me greater pleasure than to personally demonstrate my loyalty to King George by apprehending a few Jacobites." He lifted a talon-like finger and waved it emphatically. "Don't forget, MacKay, it's the lawful duty of you and me and all the peoples in the glen to support King George and the House of Sutherland."

MacKay nodded. "Aye, that it is."

The garrulous taxman continued, his hunched frame silhouetted in the doorway. "I had a word with the Earl's factor yesterday. He says it won't be long before the King's men catch the foreign Pretender." Roberts grimaced vindictively. "It will be a salutary lesson to all traitors when the hangman's noose tightens around his princely neck." When there was no comment, Roberts peered more closely. "Have you any strong convictions on the matter, Murdoch?"

MacKay smiled reassuringly. "You know where I stand, John." Desperately trying to avoid further interrogation, he stepped back and reached into the manger for his jug. He uncorked it and held it out to his unwelcome visitor. "It's a chilly morning, John. You could do with an eye-opener."

Caught off balance by the sudden offer, Roberts stared at the

19

jug for a moment. He shook his head. "Not so early. Perhaps I'll have a dram tonight when I pick up my poke of meal. I must hurry over to Sam's. I'm late, so I'll be on my way." With a farewell nod he turned and disappeared around the opening of the barn door.

MacKay hurried to the cottage and closed the door. "Nora," he declared, "the taxman smelled the burning wool."

Nora turned pale as she looked up from her kitchen work. "Does he suspect anything?"

"I don't know. He wondered if it had anything to do with the boy. We are in grave danger."

"Did you tell him we were burning some rug cuttings?"

"No, I changed the subject." He glanced at the alcove that served as Fiona's bedroom. "Is the lad up yet?"

"No, he's sleeping. So is Fiona. The poor things are fair beat after all the excitement."

MacKay crossed swiftly to his wife's side. "I'm sure the taxman suspects there's something amiss. Maybe we had better turn Duncan in, Nora?"

"We will not!"

"You don't understand the seriousness of our actions! The notice said that the penalty for concealing a Jacobite was imprisonment, banishment or death. Only God knows what will happen to us if we're caught."

Nora shrugged her shoulders. "Now Murdoch MacKay, if you've purged your mind of all your morbid thoughts I'll thank you to put this milk in the scullery."

"You must understand," insisted MacKay. "Lad or no lad, he's still a Jacobite."

"He's still our kin. He's still a Highlander," she retorted. "And Jacobite or not, I'll not turn him over to the foreign King's men." She stared at her husband determinedly. "Before you worry yourself to death, MacKay, it might be well to discuss this matter with your friend, the Dominie."

MacKay reflected and looked relieved. "Aye, that's what I'll do. Angus Gunn's a scholarly man. He'll know what to do. I'll pay him a visit after supper."

Later that evening MacKay reached the Dominie's cottage, a long low biggin with a thatched roof. As MacKay approached the thick mud and stone walls he passed a lone oak tree lifeless and decayed. When the tempests raged, wild sounds like demoniacal music wailed through its withered limbs. Angus half jokingly

20

maintained that the moaning and soughing of the wind were the voices of his ancestors calling him back to Strathnaver.

In most parishes in the Highlands, the dominie was the unofficial proctor and confidential adviser to the people. The crofters had little or no education and with long days of labour in the field there was little time to read books. So when trouble arose they turned to men like Angus who read books, knew clan history intimately and were understanding and sympathetic listeners. Angus Gunn had come as a teacher to Sciberscross from Strathnaver eight years before. He was a little older than Murdoch MacKay, but they soon became friends. Both were direct descendants of the original settlers in Sutherland and in great measure both had inherited the traditional Highland qualities of independence, sincerity, and reserve.

The Dominie's cottage was more than a home. Attached to it was a classroom with rough-hewn benches for the pupils and in a lean-to shed beyond, was kept a cow which supplied milk for children who could not bring their own. These children in return cleaned out the classroom, the Dominie's quarters, and the byre before going home for the day.

A large pile of weather-bleached peat blocks was stacked against the south wall of the classroom, the accumulation of several years. As was the custom, each pupil brought one peat block for each day of school and if a child missed a day for any reason, the block for that day had still to be delivered. When the fire in the rough stone fireplace had to be renewed pupils were assigned the task of turning over the peat or adding a new block. This was a welcome task since the far corners of the room were cold and miserable even on the best of summer days.

Angus Gunn believed that if he taught the children resourcefulness, it would prove most profitable and practical. He stressed initiative rather than the three R's and taught his pupils the importance of the four attributes of imagination, observation, memorization and the love of accomplishment. To make the children accept his fundamental teaching the Dominie applied some strange ruses.

To him imagination was the well-spring of all human effort for without it nothing could be created, nothing would be accomplished. Imagination was the font of human thought, and thinking was an exercise of the mind which was necessary in all walks of life. His pupils got a shock of pleasure as he put his exercises in imagination into operation. In the midst of a lesson he would put down his chalk, peer fixedly over his desk at his pupils and with sparkling eyes and excited voice, say intensely, "Look out, children, a wild stag just came through the door. Do you see him? He's cornered. His head's down. He's rutting the floor with his hoofs. He's looking for a way out — ten minutes to write a story on how we are going to get rid of him." Such a challenge wakened everyone and this was the first step in the development of imagination and his children loved it. It gave the rude classroom a spirit of liveliness which the pupils were to carry with them for the rest of their lives.

'Observation' he trained in the wide world beyond his classroom so that his pupils quickly learned to watch for the tell-tale marks of the deer or distinguish the humble droppings of the sheep from those of the stag and to envisage a whole living environment surrounding a growing bluebell or a flowering buttercup. The crofters would often see the tall, gaunt figure of the Dominie picking his way through the whins as he led his snake-like line of pupils down into the valley of the Brora, where they would watch the salmon rise to the fly and try to corner the little brown fresh-water newts as they darted off under the granite rocks. They had to remember these things. They had to memorize the type of fly, its colours and distinguishing characters. They had to re-member how to recognize wild flowers, plants and animal species.

This part of their training came only second in the Dominie's mind to their memorization of the Holy Book. So well did he love the high-sounding words of the Book, that his deep voice could be heard intoning from some one hundred yards away on the road to Brora.

To many it seemed that the process of memorization was spe-cifically to learn and remember the moral precepts and principles of the Holy Book. But to Angus Gunn it was more — memory was the storehouse on which man drew to help him reach the proper decisions on his way through life. Without it, decisions were hollow and worthless.

But it was 'love of accomplishment' that the Dominie wanted to inspire most of all. He saw life as a challenge to each and every individual. The only true life was in using utmost effort to meet the challenge which at first seemed unbearable; the great satisfaction to man was in attaining the seemingly impossible.

Angus Gunn knew each of his pupils as an individual. He knew their strengths and weaknesses and, what is more, he knew how to design a challenge which would inspire each to maximum effort. Hardly a day passed, winter or summer, that he did not arrange a few boxing lessons in the cow pasture. To Angus Gunn, the challenge of fisticuffs was like tempering the steel of the claymore.

As MacKay approached the schoolhouse, the Dominie came from the cowshed, raising the lantern high above his head and peering into the shadows.

"It's just me, Angus. It's Murdoch," called MacKay as he stepped into the lantern's light.

They shook hands.

"Murdoch, what ails you?" queried the Dominie. Despite the spareness of his frame, he had a loud, resonant but well modulated voice. From beneath two bushy eyebrows his deep set eyes flashed smilingly over his aquiline nose. "Your hand is as cold and clammy as a mackerel."

"There's trouble at Blackwater. I'd rather speak of it behind closed doors."

Once inside the cottage the Dominie remarked, "Before you start talking, MacKay, we'd better have a dram to loosen up that stilted tongue of yours."

"That's just what I need, Dominie."

For some time the two cronies sat before the flickering peat fire, sipping the strong brew. MacKay broke the silence. He told Angus Gunn about the proclamation at the mill, about finding Duncan on the beach and about his early morning encounter with the suspicious taxman. The Dominie listened quietly and thoughtfully swirled his drink in his cup. Only when MacKay had finished did he raise his head and fix him with a kindly gaze.

"You've done right, MacKay," he declared dropping his left eyelid in a wink. "Isn't it strange but I recall Nora often talking about her sister and husband Hamish who live at Tain."

The Dominie smiled at his surprised friend. "If I remember correctly Hamish was killed with His Majesty's forces. He always was a loyal and staunch supporter of the King."

Each encouraging word brought a brighter gleam to MacKay's eye. He was unable to decide, however, whether it was the Dominie's presence or his home brew that brought the mist to his vision as he watched his friend pouring another bumper of grog.

"I'll make this a stiff one, MacKay, because the next few hours may decide whether it's the dungeon at Dunrobin or the gibbet at Inverness for all of us."

23

Anxious to get on his way with the good news, MacKay rose to accept the parting cup. "You'll excuse my impatience, Dominie, but I should get back to Blackwater before the taxman arrives to pick up his poke of meal. Bless you, my friend. I don't know what I could have done had I not come to you for advice. I do want to thank you . . ."

"The hour isn't late," the Dominie interrupted with a smile and an admonishing wave of his hand. "I'll come with you and help entertain our taxman friend. At the same time I can have a word with Hamish's lad."

While MacKay and Angus Gunn quaffed their second cup they were unaware that taxman Roberts was sidling through the un-latched door of the tallow-lit cottage at Blackwater Croft.

The crofters were taught from infancy to bridle their passions, behave submissively to their superiors and to live within the bounds of the most rigid code of behaviour. While the roving bands of plundering Highlanders could strike terror into the lowland people to the south, there were few instances of murder, assault, robbery and other crimes in their own land. So when Roberts entered without knocking, Nora and Fiona were uneasy but not surprised.

"Good evening, Mr. Roberts," exclaimed Nora.

The taxman took off his hat and bowed politely. Against the black of his velvet collar his face was a white mask. His tight breeches, high laced boots and long coat made him look for all the world like a little sparrow as he stood peering intently around the room. His head popped in and out as he strained to penetrate the shadows.

"Greetings, Nora." Then, nodding to Fiona, "Is MacKay at home?"

"He's gone to the Dominie's, Mister Roberts. I'll tell him that you were here. Meantime, let me get your poke of meal so you can be on your way."

Nora would have done anything to get rid of the man but it was not to be. He had already made his way over to the fireplace and stood eyeing the peat and the hearthstone as though challenging them to tell him what wool material had been burned there in the early morning.

"Where's the boy?" he shot, swinging half around and fixing a penetrating eye on Nora.

Nora was taken aback. She had expected the question but not in this way. She had primed herself to answer it calmly and

24

honestly, but she was taken completely off guard. The gimlet eyes, staring unflinchingly at her, seemed to lay bare her every thought.

"He's not here . . . I mean he is here, but he's not in the room," she stammered. Her fingers trembled as she attempted to stitch the buttons on the jacket she was making for Duncan. At the far side of the table Fiona looked through the guttering candle-light at the little hunch-back. Behind the thin partition in Fiona's room, Duncan lay on the cot staring at the ceiling illuminated by the flickering tallow and wondering what kind of person possessed such an abrupt, high-pitched, demanding voice and what business had brought him there.

"Where is he?"

"The lad's asleep in Fiona's bed behind the curtain. Please don't disturb him. He was very tired and went to bed early."

Roberts paused on his way to the portal of Fiona's room and looked at Nora. "Let me have a candle so I can have a look at him. I suppose there is quite a family resemblance, is there?"

"How do you mean, Mr. Roberts?" asked Nora.

"Well, he's a nephew of yours, isn't he?"

Nora gathered herself together. The rocking of her arm chair took on a rhythmical beat and her strong fingers carefully and steadily pushed the needle in and out through the bone buttons. She regained her composure and looked through the billow of peat reek which wafted out from the fireplace. She spoke with quiet determination. "Aye, he is."

Roberts uttered his last few words whilst watching carefully to see what Nora's reaction would be. She and her husband were known to him and to the valley as God-fearing people, but in these days when father was turned against son and brother against brother, who knew how deeply the passion of freedom burned? It was Roberts' duty to read the feelings of the Laird's tenants and this duty he would do to the best of his ability.

"The Pretender fled the battleground, like the coward that he is," Roberts went on. "But the Duke of Cumberland's men are pursuing him and they're certain they can trap him before he gets a chance to sail for France."

But Nora showed no outward signs that she was disturbed. "Aye, I heard," she nodded.

Fiona did not like Roberts. She had a child-like distaste for his hunched back. She was afraid of him because she felt some evil spirit lived in the ugly hump and his sharp piercing voice and pig-like eyes were signs of this evil straining to get out. She would have nothing to do with him and was sure to skirt his cottage widely whenever occasion took her near it. In the last few years she had come to realize that he did more than just collect the rent. He was the eyes and ears of the Earl — the 'go-between' of the crofters and Dunrobin Castle. He had the power of life and death in the valley. He didn't have a friend.

"It's strange, Nora, but I've never heard you speak of those relations. Generally the people of the glen would be knowing all about their neighbours and their relations. In these troublesome times the folk at the Castle would be very interested in strangers from Ross-shire. It wouldn't be a Jacobite you are protecting, would it?"

Nora raised her head and noted that suspicion was lurking in Roberts' weasel-like eyes and that a leer of disbelief played around his mouth. Now fully aware that any mis-step she might make would increase the taxman's suspicions, she resolved to be bold. "There are many things you haven't heard me speak of, Mr. Roberts. The lad is my sister's son — he is no Jacobite. But I wouldn't disturb him this night to satisfy your foul suspicion or for all the taxmen in Scotland. You have no right to question my word. You should be ashamed of yourself."

Roberts shifted his feet. "Now, now, Nora, there's no need to get sharp with me."

"I'll get sharp with anyone who questions my word," retorted Nora. "We came to this glen many years before you knew there was such a place. We have always treated you with due respect but that doesn't mean we have to tell you everything that goes on too." Nora had now taken the offensive — and pressed home her advantage. "There's probably lots of things I haven't heard about you, Mr. Roberts. I've always been taught it's best not to pry into other people's affairs. Unless you have proof that there's something wrong in my house, I'd suggest that you sit down and behave sociably until my husband returns."

Roberts was confused. He hesitated and was about to reply; instead he leaned over the table and unrolled one of the scrolls he carried under his arm.

"You may be interested in the wording of this proclamation, Nora," he said, clearing his voice pompously in an effort to recover a little of his lost dignity. "As the Earl's taxman, it's my responsibility to see that everyone in the parish is made aware of what's taking place."

26

He started to read in as majestic a voice as he could muster. "Be it known . . . " but before the first three words were off his lips the sound of footsteps was heard on the path and the latch clicked on the door.

"Oh, you are here, Mr. Roberts!" exclaimed MacKay, as he strode into the room and rubbed his cold hands together vigorously. "It's a cold night but a clear one. Come on in, Dominie, and warm yourself by the fire!"

Roberts was ignored. Angus Gunn greeted Nora and then spoke to Fiona. "Well there, little lady, how do you like your cousin from Tain?"

"I haven't had much chance to talk to him, sir. I was catching up with the work I couldn't do yesterday and Duncan went to bed right after eating. He was so tired that I'm sure he'll sleep through until morning."

"When he's up and about, I want to see both of you in class," said the Dominie sternly. He turned to MacKay and put his hand on his shoulder. "This looks like a profitable day for me—I'll get two peat blocks from the MacKay croft now instead of one." The smile in his voice and the twinkle in his eye belied the importance to him and to the school of the daily fee payable by his pupils.

MacKay grinned and reached over to the kitchen shelf that held his jug.

"We'll have a wee nip of whisky to celebrate the lad's safe arrival." He looked at the taxman. "You'll have one with us, Mr. Roberts?"

The taxman smacked his lips. "I'll have a hot toddy."

While MacKay prepared the drinks, Roberts unrolled his proclamations. "I've been instructed to post these official notices throughout the parish before noon tomorrow," he announced importantly.

The Dominie paid no attention and turned to Nora. "If I remember right, Duncan was your sister's son. Wasn't her husband killed with his regiment?"

"Yes," replied Nora. "She's had a heavy load to bear. That's why we arranged to take Duncan."

The taxman, feeling rather crest-fallen in the face of Angus Gunn's calm self-assurance, slunk further into his chair before the fire and busied himself with the hot toddy. He realised that the small talk was pointedly ignoring him and he became drowsy as the hour wore on. He was startled when MacKay's big clock struck eleven and he jumped to his feet. "Look at the hour!" he exclaimed. "Get my sack of meal and I'll be on my way. It's long past my bedtime."

Behind the thin partition Duncan had heard every word. The short silence which had followed the altercation between Nora and Roberts had hung like a pall over him. He was terrified. His very breathing seemed to shatter the pregnant silence. But as the conversation drifted away from his own problems and its interest became more centered on the general life of the croft, Duncan dozed. He awoke with a start as the door slammed.

"Thank God he has gone," sighed MacKay.

"Aye. I don't think you have to worry," agreed the Dominie. "I'm certain that he believes the story about your nephew. Besides, there is no way he can check it, and he'll be too busy in the next few days nailing up his proclamations."

"I never want to go through anything like that again," declared Nora. In her soft Highland voice she recounted briefly what had happened before Murdoch and the Dominie arrived.

As he listened intently to grasp the meaning of the muted conversation, Duncan could hear the Dominie saying, "After what MacKay has told me, I think it's time we asked the lad to account for his presence."

The Dominie had barely finished when Duncan pushed aside the deerhide curtain and stood in the dim light, a strange and forlorn figure. Wearing the shirt that Nora had thrown over him when she burned his clothes, he paused in the portal for a moment, head erect, eyes wide open, chin thrust forward determinedly. The Dominie saw a young Highlander with red hair and strong limbs; the MacKays saw the ghost of another red-haired boy who had grown up in the cottage — the living replica of one who had come out of that portal many times and who now lay buried somewhere in a foreign land.

Nora smiled. "Don't be afraid, Duncan," she said quietly. "You're among friends."

The overwrought lad's breath caught in his throat and his eyes filled with tears as he rushed across the room and threw himself into Nora's arms. Nora's work-roughened hands gently stroked his head while he sobbed as if his heart would break.

"This is Angus Gunn, the Dominie. He will be your teacher," she said soothingly. "He would like you to tell us who you are, Duncan."

Duncan raised his head and rubbed his eyes with his fists.

He looked apprehensively from MacKay to the Dominie and then back to Nora.

"My name is Duncan Grant, ma'am," he stated slowly. "I've come from Drummossie Moor, near Culloden."

"From Culloden!" gasped MacKay and the Dominie in unison. They both leaned forward with renewed interest.

When Duncan had finished speaking a deep silence fell over the cottage. The fire was out and the candles were burned almost to the holders. Not a hostile silence, fearful and suspicious, as the earlier one had been, but a silence full of unity — a unity of resolve against inhumanity.

The Dominie was the first to speak.

"Hereafter, my lad, you'll be known as Mrs. MacKay's nephew from Tain. You'll still be called Duncan Grant since there's no point in changing your name. It's not important whether you are a Jacobite or a member of the Free Kirk like us. It's only important that you are one of us, kin of our kin. God willing, somewhere, sometime, the children of our tribe and their children's children will find peace and escape from the broadswords of England."

CHAPTER FOUR

The Black Act

"I went to the hall of shells, where the arms of his fathers hung. But the arms were gone, and aged Lamhor sat in tears."

DAR THULA

THE following week Duncan and Fiona attended school. Duncan was introduced by the Dominie as Fiona's cousin. The pupils were told that Duncan's father had been killed fighting for the King and on account of his mother being an invalid, Duncan had come to live at Blackwater.

Meanwhile, into every corner of the British Isles where the Jacobite spirit of disaffection had been known to exist, Cumberland's soldiers were carrying their depravities. The houses and estates of the wealthy followers of Prince Charles were confiscated or destroyed. The homes of all Jacobite sympathizers were burned to the ground, and places where Catholics worshipped were closed by the King's command. The red tunics Duncan saw in Rogart when he walked to Church with the MacKay family were the same as he had seen on Drummossie Moor.

When the minister announced from the pulpit that His Majesty's orders demanded the apprehension of all Jacobites and that his congregation should inform Mr. Roberts immediately they had knowledge of one or anyone harboring one, Duncan squirmed lower in his seat, not daring to raise his head.

He imagined fifty pairs of eyes bent accusingly upon him. He prayed for just anything to grasp hold of. Something firm and sure to support him. Then he felt a gentle movement on the hard fir bench as Fiona's little hand slipped quietly into his as if to say; "Duncan, you're with friends now. Forget you're a Jacobite. Learn to live our way."

It was difficult for the kindly Dominie not to look on Duncan as a favorite. More than any other of his class or of his age, his body and mind had been racked by suffering. Yet he was unfettered by deep, bitter scars and showed a love for learning and a cheerful spirit of helpfulness which endeared him to all his classmates and strengthened the old Dominie's regard for him. Along with the others, Duncan often earned corporal punishment with the broad leather strap which hung so suggestively on the wall by his teacher's right hand. He was a lad of spirit but also had a sincere regard for his friends and soon he became a leader among them.

Duncan was drawn easily into life at Blackwater. MacKay was strong and able, but he was not getting younger and young Duncan Grant quickly assumed his share of the field work. There were cabbages and turnips to hoe in the spring and when summer came, there was grain to be reaped. In autumn there was fruit to be gathered from the apple trees and berry bushes along the Brora. Always there were the animals to feed and the barn to clean. During the winter Duncan learned to make brogues and brew. He learned how to spear fish with uncanny skill and to repair the thatched roof when the winter wind wreaked its vengeance.

Fiona, meanwhile, grew up learning from her mother how to spin wool and flax, how to weave broadcloth, linen and tartan, how to knit and make her own bread. As the weeks and months passed, Duncan and Fiona became inseparable. When MacKay journeyed to the meal mill Duncan accompanied Fiona to the beach. She taught him the art of catching crabs and how to seek out the tastiest clams and mussels. There was much to do. So much, in fact, that the boy and girl were completely unaware of the drastic social and political changes going on about them.

But Murdoch MacKay and Nora were not blind to what was taking place. The day that John Bannerman died seemed to presage the doom of freedom in the valley. The hail of bullets that cut through the corn to take the simple life showed how precious the Highland freedom was to become. The raucous, ribald and derisive laughter of the Cumberland Dragoons, as they rode away, echoed up the Brora and over the divide into the valleys beyond. Soon it was to be heard in every Highland croft. There were to be many John Bannermans.

"He was suspected of being a Jacobite but you know as well as I do that John was no more Jacobite than the King is," said Murdoch. "I hear that Cumberland is in Fort Augustus and he's sworn to bring all the Highlanders to heel."

"Those bloody spectres I saw that night of the storm were real after all," Nora whispered.

"Aye, lass," agreed MacKay, placing his arm around her shoulder. "Things have changed in the Highlands since Culloden and I'm afraid there's more to come."

And so there was.

The next move from England was the proclamation of an Act of Parliament which decreed that no Episcopalian clergyman could officiate at any religious service without first having taken the oath of allegiance to the Crown. Each cleric was required to swear that he believed King George was the only rightful King; that James, the Pretender, was only the supposed heir to the throne and that Prince Charles was a bastard. At least once during each church service, the Episcopalian clergymen were compelled to offer prayers, asking the Almighty to grant good health to King George, his heirs and successors and to all members of the Royal Family. The penalty for failing to do so was specifically prescribed: for the first offence it was six months imprisonment; for the second, the culprit was to be transported as a bonded slave to the English plantations in the colonies. In event of the offender's unexcused return from banishment, he was to be hanged, drawn and quartered, his corpse burned in the public square and the ashes scattered to the four winds of heaven so that no trace of his evil presence would remain on earth.

In Sutherland County, where most people were loyal to the Earl of Sutherland and the King, the Presbyterian clergy were allowed to affirm their loyalty after each reading of the scriptures by simply pronouncing; "God save the King".

Then came the day when MacKay learned he would have to give up his beloved claymore. It was a family heirloom. It had been handed down from father to son through four generations. MacKay had expected to pass it on to Duncan in an uninterrupted line of succession.

So the traditional arms of the Highlander were to be banned! What else could be expected of a Government that declared the bagpipes an 'instrument of war' and, after Culloden, ordered forty unarmed Highland pipers to be executed in London for the dastardly crime of arming themselves with that deadly weapon!

The finely tempered steel which had spanned the centuries from the days of Rome and Tacitus was to rust in the dungeons of London. The respect and sentiment behind the *Claidheam-mor* — the terrible weapon which would bend but never break — was to fall from memory before the onslaught of the English cannon. And the pride, privilege and inspiration of youth who dreamed of bearing it fearlessly in the cause of right was to fall victim to the creeping pestilence of English sovereignty.

Only after being bared with honour could the blade be sheathed with honour and merit its traditional place in the Highland family.

As MacKay gazed forlornly at the silver-mounted scabbard and the blood-stained leather padding of the hilt, he cringed at the dishonour which would be his if the blade were now sheathed forever in the name of cowardice.

The Dominie had brought the news that evening, and as MacKay turned slowly back to his seat, leaving the claymore to hang over the mantelpiece in the dull glow of the fire, he felt sure that he was watching MacKay age before his eyes. Now they realized that Culloden was not just another skirmish. It marked the end of an era.

"I have more bad news," announced the Dominie.

MacKay's eyes widened.

"Cumberland has decreed that from now on we are forbidden to wear the kilt or plaid."

Gunn's words fell like a thunderclap on the simple crofter's ears. "Not wear the tartan!" he gasped in disbelief. "The tartan is as much a part of the Highlands as the oatmeal, the claymore and the pipes." He paused for breath. "What in heaven's name shall we wear?"

"I suppose they'll make us wear breeches," replied Angus Gunn. "English breeches!"

A nervous laugh rippled round the intent group. Now they knew for sure that the Dominie was not being serious. Whoever heard of a Highlander in English breeches! The laughter was of short duration, however. The Highlanders had suffered increasing ignominy. The returning seriousness of Gunn's eye told its own story.

"They'll never get me into breeches," growled Murdoch Mac-Kay.

He was not alone in his resentment. Duncan and Fiona were

aware of the outrage inherent in the government decree. The *breacan-feile*, or belted plaid of tartan, pleated from belt to knee, was the essential feature of the Highlander's garb.

"What do they mean by it?"

"I'm not sure," replied Angus blowing a mouthful of smoke thoughtfully toward the ceiling. "It would appear that the abolition of the claymore, the pipes, and the tartan is an attempt to eliminate our national unity. We are one through language, dress and custom and for as long as the English have known us we have worn tartan. To their way of thinking we appear to be a particularly rebellious race. They must feel that by wiping out our national dress and our way of life they'll be able to shatter our unity and so compel us to become loyal subjects of the Crown."

"But we're already loyal subjects of the Crown," protested MacKay.

"Of course we are! But don't you see that Cumberland is using the Jacobite uprising as an excuse to wreak his vengeance on all the Highlanders?"

"I'll not wear breeches," MacKay muttered.

"This is something I copied from the proclamation. It's an oath we're all required to take."

"An oath?"

The Dominie reached into his sporran and drew forth a folded sheet of grey-white paper. He opened it and bent towards the candle-light so that he could read the writing.

> I DO SWEAR, AS I SHALL ANSWER TO GOD AT THE GREAT DAY OF JUDGMENT, THAT I SHALL NOT RETAIN IN MY POSSESSION ANY GUN, SWORD OR PISTOL OR ANY OTHER OFFENSIVE ARMS WHATSOEVER. I DO FURTHER SWEAR NEVER AGAIN TO USE OR POSSESS ANY TARTAN, PLAID OR ANY PART OF THE TRADITIONAL HIGHLAND GARB.
>
> IF I DO BREAK MY SOLEMN OATH IN THIS RESPECT, MAY I BE CURSED IN ALL MY UNDERTAKING. MAY I NEVER AGAIN SEE MY WIFE, CHILDREN, FATHER, MOTHER, OR ANY OTHER OF MY RELATIONS, AND MAY I BE SLAIN AS A COWARD, AND LIE WITHOUT CHRISTIAN BURIAL IN A STRANGE LAND FAR FROM THE GRAVES OF MY FOREFATHERS AND KINDRED.

Angus Gunn straightened up but the paper fell with his hand

to his side and for a moment he gazed at the flickering candle with a sigh of resignation. "It's quite clear," he said.

"That cursed Cumberland!" exclaimed MacKay.

"Look at the wording of the oath. How does he expect us to swear an oath like that?"

"Cumberland," said Angus, "well knew the innate love of kith and kin bred so deep in the heart of the Highlander. He is aware of our strong Christian faith, and the dread of being buried on foreign ground that is so profoundly a part of our character. He must realize that this oath strikes deep at the heart of Highland tradition. If his soldiers can shoot a man down in the field for no reason at all, what would they do to a man who refused to take the oath?"

The cold, cruel logic of his words cut through the gloom of the cottage like the glint of steel — sharp and incisive. No one spoke.

Life went on as usual at Blackwater Croft, although MacKay was forced to turn his claymore over to a party of redcoats that clattered by, and the tartan was banished except for use in military service. The experience was galling but not too much of a hardship, they simply had to obey the law and wear the clothes Cumberland had prescribed.

But worse was still to come.

It was called *An Act for the Abolition of Hereditable Jurisdictions*. Like the other edicts, it was proclaimed by the Duke of Cumberland — "the Butcher" as he came to be known throughout the Highlands. The statute deprived all the Highland chiefs of their hereditary rights. It took away the source of the power which, for centuries, the chiefs had held over their people.

Under the system, the clansmen considered it their duty to support the chief. In return the chief guaranteed them the necessities of life and the right to maintain a fair share of the land that the chief held in trust for the clan.

Angus Gunn saw the Act as an end to all Highland freedom. "Cumberland knows that if the control of the chiefs can be eliminated, the power of the king's government will be strengthened," he told Murdoch. "The foundations of the chief's influence over the clan will be destroyed. He will now become a titled landlord with no responsibility to the clan. He will collect rent from the clansmen and pay a subsidy for this privilege to the English Crown."

"Then," interjected MacKay, "we're sure to have a raise in rent."

"That's exactly what will happen," agreed the Dominie.

Murdoch pondered this. He had a fairly good piece of land, probably as fertile as any in Sciberscross. He had worked it hard and to the limit. In the summer he fished and picked wild berries which Nora put away for winter. In the winter he hunted for venison and other meat that sustained them till spring. He had been accustomed to giving a poke of meal to the taxman twice a year, and he had given an occasional donation of his produce directly to Dunrobin Castle to relieve the less fortunate. If the rent went up he knew he would be unable to pay.

"Cheer up, Murdoch," Angus Gunn commented as he observed MacKay's doleful expression. "The king has commanded Cumberland not to disturb the friendly relationship that exists between the Crown and certain chiefs who have demonstrated their loyalty to the royal cause. This includes the Earl of Sutherland who allied himself with Cumberland's army at Culloden. You are getting a reprieve."

But time would tell.

CHAPTER FIVE

Engagement and Death

*"The trembling harps of joy were strung. Bards sung the
battle of heroes: They sung the heaving breast of love."*
FINGAL

THE years that followed were maturing years for Duncan Grant.
He was a strong youth and though he grew taller than MacKay
he still retained his stocky physique. Before his twelfth year he
could swing a sickle and flail with the best of the crofters. He had
helped MacKay build a quern to grind their meal and soon his
dexterity with the grinding stone became so well known that
neighbours for miles around brought their oats to Blackwater Croft
for him to grind into meal. In payment for his services he received
a portion of the oats.

Often, as Duncan worked, Fiona loitered around never taking
her eyes off his strong muscular body. One day she put her
thoughts into words. "Duncan, you're so big and strong!"

"Fiona, haven't you work to do?" he asked with a grin. "We'd
all starve if we dawdled about like you."

Suddenly Nora's voice came from the open doorway. "Come,
Fiona, come inside and take care of your weaving."

There was also time for play and Duncan and Fiona spent
many hours roaming the countryside picking berries, gathering
flowers and fishing the Brora.

They swam in a deep backwater of the river a short distance
from the croft, plunging into the clear blue depth naked like
animals of nature full of the joys of Highland freedom. Often

Duncan would dive into Loch Brora for freshwater oysters that occasionally contained pearls. He found several and they were hidden in the MacKay household in case of an emergency.

In general, life for the Highland crofters was difficult. Late springs and early falls ruined many crops in the fields. Summers were never really hot and winters seldom extremely cold, but snow fell in a deep blanket over the whole countryside. Duncan, however, when not occupied with routine chores, kept himself busy patching the roof, or chinking in the mud and stone walls of the cottage. Soon he became indifferent to hardship, hunger, and fatigue.

Much of his early life was spent in the company of the Dominie. Angus was an enthusiastic sportsman. He taught Duncan how to spear a fish in Blackwater pool and how to tie a fly from the plover's feather so that he could cast for the trout and salmon. Under Gunn's instructions Duncan also learned how to make and set snares for rabbits and how to handle a musket — one that the Dominie kept hidden in his shed behind the schoolhouse.

There was always venison on the MacKay table. In the wintertime Duncan would kill the deer by driving a sharpened spike into a tree and suspending a sheaf of oats overhead. The deer would stretch up for the oats and on its way down, the spike would pierce its throat. Or he would leave little bunches of hay from the deer run to the door of the barn where, inside the open door, a larger bunch of hay would await the hungry stag. Duncan would watch in the brilliant Highland moonlight and when the deer entered the barn he would pull the door closed with a rope stretched from the barn to the house. Next morning the stag would be skinned and quartered.

Winters were long in Sutherland. The surrounding hills gathered in the darkness early and held it late. But this did not prevent the people of the parish from trudging through the deep snow at least one night a week to meet in a neighbour's home.

They called these social gatherings *ceilidhs*. Sitting on rough, homemade stools and chairs, or sprawling on the deerskin covering the flagged floor, they would loll round the peat fire and entertain one another with story, song and dance.

Many a night Duncan sat entranced against a rough bench whilst the entertainment rolled on. Fiona was learning the traditional dances of the Highlands and over the years Duncan had watched while she grew from a halting, timid dancer into a graceful and beautiful woman who drew the eyes of all the men in the glen. But she danced only for Duncan and Duncan's eyes never left Fiona when the pipes skirled and her dainty feet flashed in time to the music.

At every *ceilidh* the minister was present. He would read and comment on the laws and prophets in the Old Testament and discourse at length upon the revelations and the good tidings in the New. The other leaders at the ceilidh were Murdoch Mac-Kay and Angus Gunn. Each had his specialty.

MacKay could recite endless stanzas of Ossianic poetry from memory and was often referred to as 'The Bard'. He had a way about him which commanded attention. He had a deep love and reverence for the Highland past and he knew that he had been handed down a tradition which formed the chief amusement of the *ceilidh* during the long winter nights.

Ossian was one of these traditions. A singer and story teller who told of the great deeds and loves of the Highland ancestors. A story teller who down through the ages had carried comfort to the lonely Highland hearth and inspiration to its youth. A singer who had spurred timeless echoes in the hills and in the hearts of the people of Sutherland.

MacKay remembered how his father used to travel into Strath-naver and Strath Oykell to hear the tales of other bards and to recite the new tales he himself carried. He realized, however, that this was a dying custom that few would follow and carry on. Murdoch loved nothing better than to tell his tales.

When the gathering clamoured for a story he would sit down on the rough flagstone on the edge of the flickering light of the peat fire, raise his hands to his shoulder as though in an attitude of supplication and wait for silence. Then in the quiet he would begin.

"In the hours after Drummossie the storm broke over Scibers-cross and it was on just such an occasion that Fingal, the father of Ossian, found Starno and his son Swaran consulting the spirit of Loda on the outcome of the battle."

Then he would begin his story in the old words of the Bard himself.

Fingal again advanced his steps, wide through the bosom of night to where the trees of Loda shook amid squally winds. Three stones with heads of moss are there; a stream with foaming course rolled around them, in the dreadful red cloud of Loda. High from its top looked forward a ghost, half formed of the shadowy smoke. He poured out his voice at times amidst the

39

*roaring stream. Near, bending beneath a blasted tree two heroes
received his words, Swaran, of lakes and Starno, foe of strangers.
On their dun shields they darkly leaned: their spears thrust forward through might.*

So great was Murdoch's power of story-telling that the stark
and lifeless scene lived for a moment around the fire and the
listeners were carried back to the night of the storm over Ben
Horn at Sciberscross. His eyes would sparkle as he continued
the tale, pausing as he went to dramatize the story and allow
the beauty of the Gaelic to sink into the romantic soul of his
listeners.

*They heard the tread of Fingal
The warriors rose in arms.
'Swaran, lay that wanderer low,' said Starno in his pride.
'Take the shield of thy Father. It is a rock in war!'
Swaran threw his gleaming spear. It stood fixed in Loda's tree.
Then came the foes forward with swords. They mixed their
    rattling steel,
Through the thongs of Swaran's shield rushed the blade of
    Fingal.
The shield fell rolling on earth. Cleft the helmet fell down.
Fingal stopt the lifted steel. Wrathful stood Swaran unarmed.
He rolled his silent eyes; he threw his sword on earth. Then
Slowly stalked over the stream whistling as he went.*

As he came to "The warriors rose in arms," Murdoch would
rise and reach for an imaginary claymore. His story then became
a living drama. He would stand tall and proud as the defeated
Swaran. He would roll his eyes in silence, throw his claymore
to the ground in contempt and then fade into the darkness of
the room whistling a lilting Gaelic air.

It was a great climax and always drew a laugh and a cheer
from his audience.

As the story-telling came to an end Murdoch would rise to
acknowledge the applause and Duncan loved the way his eyes
would gleam with pleasure.

Then he might describe the Countess of Sutherland. "She was
covered with the light of beauty but her heart was the house of
pride." Or in some tender moment he would recount the tale of
the love of the daughter of Lochlin for Ardven of Argyle.

    *She left the hall of her sweet sigh!
    She came in all her beauty,*

40

Like the moon from the cloud of the east,
Loveliness was around her like light,
Her steps were the music of song,
She saw the youth and loved him.
He was the stolen sigh of her song.
Her blue eyes rolled on him in secret.
She blessed the Chief of resounding Morven.

In these moments the bard was at his best and many a youth of Sciberscross was to serenade his love in the words of Ossian, just because he had seen them in the deep glow of Murdoch's eyes and heard them in the tender cadences of his Gaelic tongue.

The pathos which Murdoch built into his words wrung a tear from every eye and brought home to all the echoes of a bygone age as they still sounded down through the corridors of time. As he came to the last few words Murdoch's bold voice would fade away and his heavy head would bow in respect.

A long silence would follow as his listeners tried hard to turn away a tear with a wan smile.

The Dominie often spoke of Alexander, the bastard son of Earl, John of Sutherland.

"When the Earl died the estate naturally went to Adam, the oldest legitimate son. But Alexander resented this. When his claim to the title was rejected, he visited a witch for advice. The witch prophesied that his head would stand highest of all the Sutherlands. This inspired Alexander and he rushed off to raise an army in support of his claim. He fought Adam's men in a great battle on the coast near Brora, but he was beaten, taken prisoner and beheaded. The gory head of the bastard was carried to Dunrobin Castle and placed on top of the highest tower. Thus was the witch's prophecy truly fulfilled."

Then the tragedy of the night would be forgotten in the wild whirl of the dance. The old folk would sit in the corner and beat out a lively tune with their hands and feet as the young danced with abandon on the little space that had been left for them round the fire. Granny Bannerman sat like an old witch, sucking a piece of nettle root in her toothless gums. She loved every moment of the *ceilidh* — the laughs, stories, and the tears. As she turned, nodded and laughed a high-pitched cackle of approval to Maggie Grant at her side, Maggie would tighten her shawl around her shoulders and with her scrawny hand take her old clay cutty from between her brown-stained teeth.

41

These were the things that Duncan had grown to love. It was his life. This was the life of the glen. From these stories he had quickly realized that the history of the Highlands was a desperate and cruel story, a tale of pillage, murder, hardship, and horror. And it was, withal, a story of fantasy and the supernatural.

When Duncan was twenty-two he was taller than many of his companions, more muscular and sturdy. The Dominie had trained him to run, jump, and to use his strength and dexterity in competition against the athletes of the country. One such event occurred at Lairg village, in July of 1759, when men from all over Sutherland met to compete for the glory of their clan.

Duncan and Fiona went to the village with friends. Murdoch MacKay stayed at home because Nora was not well.

"You two must go," he said to Duncan and Fiona. "This is the big event of the year and I don't want you to miss it."

It was a gala occasion. Hundreds of people milled and thronged about the fair ground. Young athletes strutted and jostled their way through the crowds while waiting their turn for the events and the pretty young lassies giggled and laughed as they followed their men with admiring eyes. The older clansmen gathered in groups, talking and occasionally hailing far-away friends they hadn't seen since last year. Behind the men the older women gossiped about their children and their current afflictions. Over the field a holiday atmosphere prevailed and competition, while intense, was conducted in a free and easy manner.

Duncan had entered to throw the fifty-pound stone and toss the caber. When his turn came he out-threw the other contestants by such distance that the assembled spectators gasped. He then won the preliminary heat of the caber tossing.

When he strode to the sidelines to prepare himself for the finals, Fiona hovered admiringly by his side. She was thrilled with his earlier successes.

"You'll win, Duncan. I just know you will," she exclaimed encouragingly.

"Fiona, you're too sure about it," Duncan answered in a dour manner, but secretly he was pleased with Fiona's words of encouragement as he stripped off his shirt and removed his bonnet.

Fiona had often watched Duncan as he worked the quern, stripped to the waist, but never had she seen his muscles ripple as they did now when he bent over to pick up the massive caber. Other contestants had tossed and now stood on the sidelines watching.

42

Duncan lifted the heavy pole in the palms of his powerful hands. A hush fell over the gaping throng. For a moment he stood breathing deeply and marking the distance he must run before he started the toss. Fiona was breathless with anticipation. Suddenly Duncan was running and tossing. She watched as the heavy caber somersaulted through the air, landed on end, and fell perfectly. The crowd roared its applause. Duncan's mark bettered the best by a full five feet.

"Duncan's won! Duncan's won!" she shouted jubilantly. "He's won!"

Oblivious of the spectators she raced onto the field to congratulate her hero.

Duncan turned to see her racing to him, her face flushed and enraptured. His arms drew her to him and, momentarily, their lips met in sudden awareness of the depth of their love. It was a brief moment of passion that told them both what they had long suspected.

Dawn was breaking over the valley of Strath Brora on that fresh July morning as the two walked hand in hand back from Lairg. After the games rounds of eating, drinking and revelry had spanned the night and whenever the music struck up Duncan and Fiona had danced. Even now as they walked over the hills Fiona was humming the music of the last dance and she would break off to do a pirouette on the rough mountain track with her shawl flying in the early morning sunrise. Duncan was content to walk and listen and hold Fiona's hand. On the crest of a hill they stopped to look down into the glen. Fiona leaned gently toward him and he drew her close in a fond embrace.

"Oh, Duncan. I've never seen such a beautiful morning!"

"Nor I," he agreed. The rising sun turned the rocky slopes and face of Ben Horn to burnished gold. The mountain and the glen looked quiet and peaceful now as housewives prepared their fires of bogwood and black peat, and blue smoke rose lazily from the chimneys of the little thatched cottages which straggled through the valley.

"It's usually such a wild and windy country," Duncan remarked. "But it looks so wonderful and calm from here."

"Oh, Duncan, let's hope that it stays this way."

"There's no reason why it shouldn't, Fiona. Since I came here . . " His face grew solemn. "Since Culloden, we've been at peace. I see no reason for things to change."

"When we get married we'll have to get our own house."

"Aye. Our own croft!" agreed Duncan. "I know where there's a good one. It's Fuarach-Coille, just over the hill from home. I'll see about renting it right away."

"Look! The Dominie's up." Fiona pointed to his biggin where a wisp of smoke curled its way into the clear blue sky.

As Duncan eased Fiona into his arms and gazed blissfully into the depths of her blue eyes, he followed the perfect contour of her glowing cheeks and the whiteness of her well-formed bosom. His brow gently pressed her long auburn hair and Fiona surrendered her first passionate kiss.

"We'll go tell Angus," he suggested.

The passing of time since that first day when he met Duncan had gradually slowed the activities of the Dominie. Still he was strong and straight, only a little grey at the temples and somewhat slower in his walking.

"Glad to see you," he greeted the young couple. "Come in and share breakfast with me."

"We'll go home for our meal," replied Fiona, "but we'll stop long enough for a cup of tea."

As he ate, Angus Gunn listened quietly while Fiona spoke excitedly of how Duncan had won the shot-put and the caber toss. Her eyes shone and her hand clung to Duncan's till finally the Dominie said, "Something's happened between you two. What is it now?"

When they told him they had decided to get married he congratulated them and poured a bumper of home brew for Duncan and himself. "Here's to a long and happy life! I couldn't be happier for you both."

When Fiona and Duncan arrived home Nora was asleep.

"Father, how is Mother?" Fiona asked anxiously.

"Your mother had a bad night, Fiona. She was hot, delirious and coughing a lot. But she's quietened down now. How did the fair go?"

"We have more important news, father. Duncan and I wish to be married."

MacKay slowly raised his head. A happy smile creased his rugged features. "You have my blessing, children. I couldn't wish for a better husband for Fiona than you, Duncan. Your marriage would normally call for a celebration if Nora weren't so sick, but we'll have one when she's well again."

Despite MacKay's hopeful words, Nora did not completely recover. The attack of pneumonia left her weak and listless. She

44

got out of bed after a month and performed a few chores. Fiona took over the spinning and weaving and much of the arduous house work that had to be done.

With the coming of winter Nora developed a persistent cough and grew thin and haggard. When the snow fell the family missed many *ceilidh*s because they didn't want to leave her alone. Occasionally the neighbours gathered at Blackwater and as the dancers swirled around the tiny floor Nora's wan face brightened and her eyes gleamed. When the gathering was over and the people gone, she went listlessly back to bed.

With the coming of spring Duncan was determined to strike out on his own.

"Come, lad, you're like my own son," argued Murdoch.

"I know that," replied Duncan, "and I appreciate it. But I would like to get a croft — a good croft for myself and build up something for my sons."

"You've a right to be concerned about your future, Duncan. Crofts are growing smaller as they are divided among sons. But you're as welcome as my own boy would have been to a piece of this land."

"I feel it would be best for Fiona and me to have our own place."

Shortly thereafter Duncan rented Fuarach-Coille. This croft was within a mile of Blackwater. Fuarach-Coille, with its grassy slopes and fertile bottom land, offered excellent prospects for grazing sheep and for growing oats and barley. The existing cottage, however, was not habitable and the young couple immediately started to build a new one. All that spring and into the summer they spent their spare hours working on their new home.

One evening in July they were eating their supper outside the half-finished cottage. Duncan had the stone walls in place and the frame on the roof and he was intending to start work on the thatching next day.

As they ate they were watching a big stag rise from among the bracken, toss its proud antlered head, sniff suspiciously at the air before trotting leisurely down the glen. Duncan suddenly stopped chewing. He rose to his feet and stood in trembling silence. A strange feeling came over him.

"What's wrong, Duncan?" Fiona asked, scrambling to her feet.

"I don't know, Fiona, but I feel that something is wrong. The folks must be in trouble at home. We'd better hurry."

They gathered the remains of the meal and thrust it into the basket. In the dusk their former high spirits became depressed. As they hurried home the evening seemed to draw in quickly and ominously and when they entered the yard at Blackwater they found several neighbours standing around the door whispering quietly.

An uncomfortable hush descended as the Dominie hurried forward and took Fiona sympathetically by the arm and said with a catch in his throat, "Your mother is very ill. Both you and Duncan should go to her."

They entered the cottage and in the dimness beyond the smouldering fire they could hardly see Murdoch as he knelt in prayer beside the covering of blankets and skins which was to be the last resting place of Nora in life.

Silently they moved around to the bed. The wick in the oil lamp spluttered on the wall. Below in the shadows lay MacKay's dog. He seemed to be waiting patiently for the inevitable. His two front paws stretched out like sticks in the darkness and his long collie-like snout rested gently upon them as he gazed dolefully at Duncan and Fiona. He hadn't even a wag of welcome for them.

Fiona waited until her father had finished praying and rose to his feet. Nora lay white and haggard, gasping intermittently for breath. Her thin frail hands lay pale and twitching on her chest. Fiona bent and grasped them in the warmth of her own, as she burst into a flood of uncontrollable tears. "Oh, Mother, my mother," she cried. "Don't leave me!"

As he knelt by her side and put a comforting arm over her shoulder, Duncan recalled how well Nora had accepted him when he arrived, cold, frightened, and uncertain at Blackwater Croft so many years ago. It was she who had taken him in without reservation, fed him, clothed him and shielded him from the king's men. Death had been so much a part of him then and yet she had driven its fear away. Now death was hovering at her own bedside. Duncan wanted desperately to stay its hand, but by the time he had finished his silent prayer he knew that it was too late. The hand he touched was cold and the cheek he kissed was lifeless. Silently he turned away.

The funeral ceremony preceding Nora's burial was a blur of gloom to Duncan and Fiona. In accordance with Highland superstition the door and windows of the cottage were left wide open to give free passage to Nora's departed spirit. The simple pinewood box in which the dead woman lay was raised on two blocks at one end of the living room.

46

Murdoch solemnly greeted the guests with a silent handshake. Fiona invited them to partake of the spirits, cheese and burial bread, and dance in solemn respect around the coffin. The watch went on day and night till MacKay knew that all their friends and relations had taken part in Nora's wake. The local women wailed and lamented. The minister's voice rose and fell as he intoned selected passages from the Bible. Outside the cottage the dogs howled as they sensed the presence of death.

When the lamentation had ceased and the minister shut the Book for the last time, the women and the men who had been waiting in the yard moved inside for the final wine, whisky and cheese that was served round the coffin before the lifting. The pallbearers shouldered the plain pine box.

When all was in readiness, Hamish Sutherland, the innkeeper, marshalled the mourners into line and the procession moved slowly forward to the dirgeful lament of wailing bagpipes. It gradually attracted more and more crofters and their families until almost two hundred people walked with bowed heads in a long straggling line behind the bearers. It was not a silent procession; Nora's virtues were freely discussed and praised. The mourners recalled that she had always been ready to help a family in need; she had kept a clean croft, she had dressed Fiona well; and her husband, Murdoch MacKay, had never left her side during the days of her last illness.

A mile from Blackwater Croft the cortege reached the halfway point to the cemetery. Here the innkeeper called a halt and the coffin was transferred carefully to the shoulders of four fresh pallbearers for according to Highland custom the corpse had to be carried the whole way without allowing the mournful burden to rest on the ground.

When the procession reached the grave-yard it halted at the low, moss-covered walls of rough sandstone. Within the enclosure the ground was dank and wet and nettles stung the ankles. The uncut grass around the stones grew with peculiar richness and rankness from the nourishment provided by the dead for more than fifteen hundred years. Into this secluded sanctuary, while a joyless sun hung in the misty air like a half-obscured lamp, Nora was lowered into her grave.

Duncan had followed the coffin as in a trance. Only when the thud of the first lumps of earth on the lid penetrated his apathy did he rouse himself. Now that Nora was gone he felt that a vital part of his life had been taken away.

CHAPTER SIX

Return to Drummossie

"Deep is the sleep of the dead; low their pillow of dust."
CARRIC-THURA

NORA'S passing marked the fifteenth anniversary of Duncan's arrival at Blackwater Croft. In the course of the ensuing years the MacKay household and Angus Gunn had carefully guarded the secret of his coming.

As he grew into manhood Duncan had often mentioned to Nora that he would like to visit his home at Drummossie Moor. Just before her death he had renewed his plea.

"There will be a time, Duncan. But it's not safe now. Promise me you will wait." Duncan faithfully kept his word but now that Nora had departed he headed across the fields to seek the Dominie's advice.

"You'll never be satisfied until you have visited your old home and met again with your own people. The danger is still great, but may not be as risky now. If you must go back, it should be before you and Fiona are married. Go, by all means, and may God watch over you," were the Dominie's parting words.

Soon afterwards Duncan stood gazing on the field of Culloden as the declining sun cast its lengthening shadows into the darkening valley below. The meadow was corrugated with the narrow, earth-filled trenches in which the corpses of the vanquished Jacobite army had been hastily interred in 1746. Stretching away on all sides to the base of the low-lying hills was a vast tract of brown and purple heather. The scene was dotted with outcroppings of grey stone and moss-covered rock together with the occasional blackened gables of the long-since burned-out crofters' homes. On the ruins, clumps of yellow broom, spiney whin and verdant bracken now sprouted in gay profusion.

Before one of the large mounds of earth where a stone marker indicated that the MacDonalds were buried, Duncan stood with his cousin, Willie MacDonald. Now in his early forties and in stature a companion to the twenty-three year old Duncan, Willie was the grandson of the chief of the MacDonalds of Glencoe and the son of Captain John MacDonald who had died with Duncan's father on that bloody field of Culloden.

They knelt in silence on the hallowed ground beside the only stone bearing the MacDonald name. For them the site may as well have been nameless, for none could tell how many of the MacDonalds of Glencoe lay with other MacDonald clansmen beneath the mounded turf. Duncan recalled the pitiless slaughter he had witnessed that day on Drummossie Moor — time could never blot out that deeply-etched grief — he could never forget.

At last he broke the silence. "Willie, do you think you could find the place where I was born?"

"Yes, Duncan. I'm sure I could. I've visited the ruins many times. Come."

Turning westward, they walked slowly into the sun whose setting rays were edging the clouds with lavender. Ferns and bracken had done their best to hide old wounds. Fire-blackened walls and stubs of rafters of the old houses stood out against the bare heather, but to Duncan the scars were engraved in his youthful memory.

He wrestled with the past as he strode along. The battlefield had appeared smaller than he remembered and the hillside on which he had crouched to watch the conflict seemed lower than the giant mountain of his youth. Perhaps the heather had spread profusely and concealed its vastness.

When Willie stopped by a gnarled apple tree and a row of straggling currant bushes, that marked the spot where once a garden had approached the stream, Duncan knew where he was. There was the heather thicket from which he had watched the king's soldiers murder his mother and his aged grandparents. The stones of the cottage were scattered among the patches of oats and barley, still growing wild in the unattended field. The desolate and oppressive scene where his mother had burned alive lived again in Duncan's mind.

"Tell me what happened after the burning, Willie."

There in the quiet of the evening as the fir branches crackled and spat under the starlight and the lone curlew cried its last plaintive goodnight to the silent winged gull, Duncan settled down to hear the long awaited conclusion.

"Looking back I see how hopeless the situation was," said Willie, squatted on his haunches by the fire. "The Highland Army had been victorious on several occasions, but to win at Culloden was hoping against fearful odds. Money sent from France and Spain to Bonnie Prince Charlie was seized by the English. With no money to purchase food we were hungry and tired. We lived on cabbage leaves for days before the battle. It had been a long and miserable retreat from Derby to Drummossie.

"When the Duke of Cumberland started his attack, many of the Highlanders didn't have the strength to stand up and fight. We were completely outnumbered and the English cannon fire was devastating."

"What about the Prince?"

"He was watching the battle from behind a stone wall on the hillside — with his seven men of Moidart* and his man-servant, Sgt. Ronald MacKenzie." Willie poked at the fire and gazed thoughtfully at Duncan. "Before God he vowed he had come to save Scotland or die. He let us down. He sulked all the way from Derby to Drummossie. But when he saw that the battle was lost, he and his cronies were seen riding towards the Nairn River. Death didn't seem to be attractive when they were staring it in the face."

He shuddered as the memory of the dead of Drummossie Field flashed through his mind. "I was one of about two thousand who escaped with Lord George Murray to Ruthven Glen. Our retreat had been previously arranged. Lord George sent a messenger to tell the Prince that he had rallied the survivors and that we were waiting for him to join us. The messenger brought back word that the Prince was grateful for our loyalty but that he was endeavouring to return to France because success was impossible. He also told Lord George to do what he thought best for his safety and ours."

Duncan spat contemptuously. He was not given to profanity but this time it was justified. "The bastard." Then, as if shocked by his own vehemence, "The deceitful coward. So that was Bonnie

---

* The seven men who accompanied Prince Charles from France.

50

Prince Charlie, the Highland hero! You must have been thoroughly disgusted and disillusioned with him."

"Yes, Prince Charles' refusal to join us was a bitter blow to Lord George. He decided there was no use in continuing the struggle so we straggled out of the glen and went our own way to fend for ourselves."

Willie told how for years he hid by day and travelled by night — cowering in remote glens and hills — playing hide-and-seek with Cumberland's troops.

"What did happen to the craven prince?" Duncan enquired.

"He escaped to France but at the cost of one more life — that's the sad part of it. Do you remember Roland MacKenzie? No, you wouldn't — you were too young but your father would.

"Sergeant Roland MacKenzie was about the same size and age as the prince. Both were tall and slender. Their features and manners were alike in many ways and because of these similarities the prince realized that Roland MacKenzie, dressed in his uniform, could easily be mistaken for himself.

"To guard his cowardly deception, he made all present at Cortuleg, including Roland MacKenzie, swear on the Holy Book. The oath called upon all the curses in the scriptures to fall upon them and their children should they not prove loyal to Charles or if they should disclose the prince's deception to anyone.

"Then the prince sent Roland on the road to Fort Augustus where Cumberland was quartered. He was told that if he were caught by the redcoats to fight to the death and he made promise that with his dying gasp he would shout, 'You've killed your Prince!' — This was to confirm that he really was the prince.

"A few days later Roland found himself surrounded by Cumberland's soldiers in a rocky glen. He killed several of the king's men but soon fell mortally wounded. Before he died he made good his promise, shouting, 'You've killed your Prince!'

"The English soldiers thinking they had actually killed the Prince, cut off his head and wrapped it in the Prince's coat and carried it in triumph to Cumberland. All they wanted was a share of the £30,000 reward the 'Butcher' had offered.

"So closely did Roland resemble Charles that Cumberland was certain the grisly remains were those of the Prince. He wrapped the head in the Royal Stuart coat and placed it in a box which he personally carried to London to present to his father, the King. Upon closer examination by the King's couriers it was discovered that while the coat belonged to the Prince, the head did not."

Willie grinned wryly as though he was watching the discomfiture of Cumberland and the triumph of Roland. "The Highlanders had beaten him this time and his pride was hurt. Back he came to Fort Augustus, breathing fury and swearing revenge."

"That's why Cumberland called for the utter destruction of the Highlanders," Duncan remarked.

"Yes," continued Willie, "the Butcher had started at Culloden to execute his revenge and the Prince's deception added the flames of hatred to his plans."

"Did the Prince escape then?"

"Yes, Duncan. A Jacobite lady named Flora MacDonald helped him get aboard a ship for France and although many Highlanders could have betrayed him — no one claimed the £30,000 reward."

"I suppose that made Cumberland even more furious."

"That and other things," responded Willie. "Since childhood, Cumberland had been taught that the House of Stuart and the Jacobites who supported it were hateful and treacherous. He sincerely believed that when they invaded England, his father's Protestant throne might fall to them and his hatred and fear of the Catholics led him to kill every Jacobite he could lay his hands on."

There was a long silence between the two as they gazed at the spluttering logs oozing their hissing wetness around the licking tongues of yellow flame. Duncan had pulled a long strand of grass from the clump by his side and he sat, elbows on thighs, chewing the end — the seed pods bobbing up and down in the flickering firelight, whilst his strong hands clung together in silent thoughtfulness over the fire. It was a moment of recollection.

Willie had picked up a stick and it dangled from his strong fingers. His thoughts continued to remain with the horrors of Culloden. Roderick MacLean, his captain, had had both legs smashed by cannon fire. Willie had carried him from the field to a sheepshed just over the hill where forty wounded Highlanders lay helpless, in abject pain and misery. Then he had gone out to find them some food and water.

On his way back, Willie could see a tall spiral of smoke which looked insignificant in the vastness of the morning air. Closer, the shimmering heat and yellow flames of fire which were now so obviously coming from the hut tore the water-bucket and bread from his nerveless fingers and drew him in one headlong dash through the heather. As he struggled the last few panic-stricken yards to the crest of the hill he could hear the agonizing screams of his kinsmen and the derisive laughter of the Redcoats. The heavy thump of stone hammers as the doors were nailed shut, and the flash of bloody steel told the final story of horrible death. What had he done for his captain? Carrying him from the safety of the battlefield he had only ensured his death by the most awful of all the weapons of treachery!

Now as he sat once more in the dusk of Drummossie, the stick fell silently from his taut, nervous fingers. The firelight played on his face, turning its shadows into a grotesque caricature — Willie, too, had a great deal to forget.

The wind sighed gently in the heather and the dry broom pods on the bushes at the side of the burn rustled as they crackled on the branches. A little gust blew the acrid peat smoke into Willie's eyes and for a moment brought tears and left him gasping for breath.

"Will this thirst for revenge never stop?" Duncan asked thoughtfully. "Since Culloden there has been no war but every Jacobite in the Highlands has been killed, hunted down or shipped to the colonies."

"They didn't get us," replied Willie with a wry grin, "and remember, too, there's still hope wherever decent beings can be found. I heard a story from Malcolm MacBeath, a Corporal on the left flank, who was separated from his Regiment. He ended up fighting with the Frasers but he lost his left leg and lay practically unconscious through most of the battle. He had some stories to tell! One of them was about Chief of the clan Ian Fraser, who had been cut down. Fraser lay a few feet away from him, as Cumberland and a group of his officers walked by. When the Butcher passed, he raised himself on his elbow and spat contemptuously on Cumberland's boots. MacBeath heard him say something about 'My dying respects to you, Sire,' and heard Cumberland tell one of his officers to destroy the scum that had affronted him. But do you know, Duncan, the officer defied him! Malcolm MacBeath couldn't remember his exact words but he offered to relinquish his commission and added, 'James Wolfe can never consent to become the executioner of so brave an enemy.'* So long as you find men of character on the other side, Duncan, this thirst for revenge, as you call it, is bound to stop some time."

---

* This same James Wolfe later became a General and died on the Plains of Abraham.

"I don't want to live in fear the rest of my life. I want to get married and raise children."

"And so you can, Duncan. We all must live again. Go home, marry your girl, raise your children."

Duncan reflected on his cousin's words. Perhaps peace had come at last to the family from which he had descended. The massacre at Glencoe and the disaster at Culloden had all but destroyed the tree. But, at least, he had been spared and he had the capacity to continue the line in peace, at Fuarach-Coille.

"Perhaps you are right, Willie," he smiled. "Perhaps God, in His mysterious way, has protected the children of his tribe."

Without another word he picked up his plaid and stretched out on a couch of heather on the same battlefield from which he had fled in terror so many years before. Almost at once he fell into a peaceful sleep.

From a high point overlooking the Moray Firth a few days later, Duncan could see in the distance the outline of Dunrobin Castle. The turrets and battlements shone gleaming white in the afternoon sun. The castle seemed to be silent and empty. But the wind-stirred trees that grew around it and along the crest of the hill on which it sat, hid the fields where Duncan knew the serfs of the Earl were working. As Duncan paused, on his way back to Blackwater Croft, he was comforted by the certainty that he had nothing to fear as long as the Earl remained in Dunrobin Castle.

Duncan had been to the castle many times as a youth. Often, instead of gathering shellfish on the beach with Fiona, he had gone on to the mill and had helped Alexander Sutherland, the miller, grind the meal for Murdoch MacKay and other crofters. It was on these occasions that he visited the castle and it had seemed to him then that the castle was the most gigantic edifice on earth.

Once, when he stood at the base and gazed up at its turret, he could barely see the top and he wondered how any army could ever assail such an impregnable structure of rugged rock and stone. He had only been inside its massive halls once. That was the year when the crops had been poor. He had gone with Murdoch MacKay and other representatives from the parish of Rogart to petition the Earl's assistance. The inside was cold and indifferent and not at all the grand place it appeared to be from the outside.

Although the Earl of Sutherland believed, as did the other Earls before him, that in the House of God the vassal was peer to his master, this did not extend to the castle. The Earl would

54

often be seen in church with his people but the people would not be allowed to visit him in the castle except in times of emergency, war or difficulty. The crofters of Strath Brora and Sciberscross did not resent this line of demarkation. They continued as in generations past to accord the Earl their loyalty and devotion in return for a piece of barren land, food in times of famine, and the feeling of security that the massive castle gave them in their precarious existence.

Fiona and Duncan did not get married when Duncan returned from Culloden. Nora's death had thrown a heavy load on Fiona's shoulders. When she should have been helping Duncan with the work at Fuarach-Coille, there were responsibilities to be met at Blackwater. Murdoch MacKay grew noticeably older and lost his zest for life. Very often instead of looking after the hundred and one odd jobs about the croft he sat by the ingle-neuk smoking his old clay pipe and staring blankly into the peat fire.

So Duncan's plans to renovate Fuarach-Coille were very slow in getting under way. Winter passed and spring came and he got the roof thatched at Fuarach-Coille. During the early summer Murdoch MacKay worked a little in the fields but he was still listless and the young couple decided to wait until the following spring before leaving Blackwater.

One fateful day Fiona awoke to find the snow was driving against the gable of the cottage. She went into the bedroom to find that her father had died in his sleep. Once again Duncan and Fiona and the simple crofters of Rogart made their sorrowful trip to the graveyard.

Murdoch MacKay's death released Fiona from the obligation she felt for Blackwater. Plans went ahead rapidly for the transfer of furniture and personal effects to the croft at Fuarach-Coille. There was a period of mourning during which Fiona felt it would be improper to wed, despite the long wait that Duncan had endured.

Before the heavy snows of winter fell, however, they were married in the little church of Rogart, an event which almost everyone in the parish attended. The wedding was followed by a feast and dance at Duncan's new barn at Fuarach-Coille. Crofters' wives from miles around brought food and heaped the tables in the new cottage. All night long the pipes skirled and the fiddles scraped as the crofters of Sciberscross celebrated the joyful occasion. To Duncan, Fiona had never appeared lovelier and the Dominie thought he had never looked upon a happier or more handsome couple.

CHAPTER SEVEN

Gathering Clouds

"There she is seen, Malvina! but not like the daughters of the hill. Her robes are from the stranger's land; and she is still alone!

CARTHO

"She was covered with the light of beauty but her heart was the house of pride."

FINGAL

WHILE Duncan and Fiona were enjoying being alone together in their own home, the Countess of Sutherland, ten miles away, was giving birth to her second daughter, Elizabeth. The Countess' first child had been called Catherine.

The winter was bitterly cold that year. The snow piled high in the hollows and the icy wind blew in hurricane force across the open valleys. There was less moonlight than in other winters, more hardship, and greater famine in the remote areas of Sutherland-shire. Duncan and Fiona were oblivious to all this; they found contentment and fulfillment in at last being alone together with their larder stocked with produce from Blackwater Croft. Their life was complete and untouchable by conditions in the glen. Fuarach-Coille was warm and cosy, and for them, life was good.

But the icy winds piled up around the crofters' homes and blew fiercely against the castle walls. While a crofter's cottage could become snug with confined heating, it was impossible to keep the large halls and rooms of the castle comfortable. The Countess' new baby, Elizabeth, was kept warm through special attention, but somehow the oldest daughter, Catherine, was stricken with pneumonia and died.

Duncan and Fiona heard of the tragedy, but they were more concerned with their own good fortune — Fiona was pregnant and expecting her firstborn that summer.

But more tragedy was to strike. One event after another was to cast a shadow over the house of Sutherland and seal the fate of its clansmen.

When the snow was gone the grieving Earl and his wife left Dunrobin. With their baby daughter they journeyed to Bath, intending to take up residence where the weather was not as inclement as in the Highlands. The Earl took sick after his arrival and the Countess nursed him. Because of the worry and stress which this entailed she too became ill and died.

With the passing of the Earl and his Countess the baby, Elizabeth, was now heir to the Sutherland name and fortune. The estates were placed under the control of administrators, and they in turn made Elizabeth's maternal grandmother, Lady Alva, responsible for her upbringing. Thus was Elizabeth reared in Edinburgh and transferred to a life away from the Scottish Highlands and into a situation where she was never really aware of the people of her clan, nor had she the opportunity to acquire any true sympathy for them as her forefathers had done.

Dunrobin Castle, vacated by its rightful heir, evoked its own rumours from the surrounding area. Agents were imported from Moray-shire to handle the estate, but to the crofters it was not the same and it wasn't long before they discovered there was no friendly Earl with whom they could discuss their problems.

Uneasiness grew into suspicion until the day came when John Harral of Rogart arrived from Edinburgh with a fantastic story about Lady Alva.

Duncan and Fiona remembered hearing it from Harral's lips as their sons, Walter and Murdoch, were scampering around the cottage and their youngest, David, sat quietly on Fiona's lap.

On this occasion, John Harral had been out for a walk through the heather with his dog Bruce and had stopped at Fuarach-Coille.

"John," said Duncan. "I've heard that reports from Edinburgh are full of strange happenings."

"Aye," replied Harral, as he sat down on the grass with his

back to a log. He picked up and sifted the thin layers of dry peat through his long fingers. He then took a good pull of whisky and licked his lips with enjoyment after his walk through the knee-deep heather. John meditated for a moment on how much he should tell of his strange story. "Well," he began, "you already know that Elizabeth Sutherland — we all call her Betsy — lived with her grandmother, Lady Alva, at Leven Mansion in Edinburgh. She had for companionship her second cousin by the name of Betsy Weems. It's my understanding she was brought from England."

"Are they of the same age then?"

"Yes, and they are almost identical in appearance. But Betsy Sutherland is taller." John Harral cleared his throat. "I mean —was taller."

"Was?" asked Duncan and Fiona in unison.

"The Sutherland people in Edinburgh have been very mindful of the young heiress," John Harral continued, "and from here they have sent her produce, fowls, venison, butter and cheese to show their loyalty. During my trip to the city I became acquainted with both Elizabeth Sutherland and Betsy Weems. They would run out to meet me at the Manor gate when I rang the bell."

"But we heard Betsy Weems had been stricken by some strange sickness," interjected Duncan.

Harral nodded. "That was the news we had in Sutherland before I made my last trip. This time I took along some special gifts for the young ladies and letters of good-wishes from the gentlemen of the County. I rang the bell and Betsy Weems rushed into my arms. 'I'm so glad to see you back on your feet, Betsy,' I remarked. 'Where is Betsy Sutherland?'

'I'm Betsy Sutherland,' came the astonishing reply.

"I was so taken-aback that I didn't know whether to laugh or be angry. She seemed so serious. 'Oh, no,' I said chidingly, 'Do you think you can pull the wool over my eyes, like that, Betsy Weems?' At that moment Lady Alva stormed out, wheeled the girl about and steered her quickly out of my sight. That was the last I saw of her. I just left the basket in the hallway and hurried away. You can imagine how surprised I was to hear a few days later that Betsy Weems had died. First she was very sick, yet at the same time she danced down to the door to meet and embrace me. Next she claims not to be who she is. Then, suddenly she's dead and Lady Betsy is spirited away to a boarding school in England."

58

A baby, who had been taken from Dunrobin Castle, was never to return. A spurious intruder, reared in the manners and customs of upper-class Georgian England, was being groomed to take over the ownership of Dunrobin Castle and the Sutherland properties in the wild Highlands of Northern Scotland.

Since the deceased Earl of Sutherland had been eighth in line for the throne, much of Elizabeth's early social life had been among nobility. Together with her companions in the boarding school she studied English literature, French, drawing, needlework, dancing and music. As she matured, she began to mingle with young English aristocrats. In the tradition of the day she read the same books as they did, talked current politics on an equal footing and dressed in similar finery. Occasionally, her English peers teased her as being a descendant of Highland barbarians, but the teasing was light-hearted and short for the extensive Sutherland estates were highly regarded in England. Thus at balls and parties Elizabeth was courted by many young men of noble lineage. Among them was the wealthy Leveson-Gower.

From morning until late at night Elizabeth's only concern was to enjoy life and bask in the attentions of the young men. As a result when the administrators at Dunrobin Castle came to Edinburgh to consult with her on estate problems, she found less and less time to deal with them.

One afternoon, as she was preparing to join a party for a fox hunt, her maid appeared at her elbow.

"Begging your pardon, ma'am, your agent, Mr. Sellar, is here from Dunrobin Castle."

"Oh, bother! What is it this time?" snapped Elizabeth. "I'm ready to leave and have no time for him."

"He didn't say, except that it was important."

Elizabeth hesitated. "Damn the Highlanders. Estate agents always seem to arrive when I'm ready to go out. Show him into the drawing room quickly."

Sellar's problems were simply those of a neglected estate. As Elizabeth took over the ownership, more and more decisions had to be made and they accumulated while awaiting her pleasure. One of the pressing needs was the appointment of a new minister for the church at Rogart.

"When will you come north to meet with the elders to discuss the appointment?" Sellar asked.

"Meet with the elders? I haven't time to meet with them. Why should I?"

"Your father always did, ma'am."

"Well, times have changed. If the Rogart church needs a new minister, I'll appoint one. There's no need to have a dreary discussion with the elders. Whom can I appoint?"

Patrick Sellar was a young man with strong and enduring ambition. He had come to work at the castle when it was under management of Mr. Young, one of Lady Alva's appointees. Since that time he had applied himself vigorously to his job. Having come from Moray-shire, he had little sympathy for the Sutherland crofters and would apply any measure, no matter how stern it was. He had already filled some positions on the estate with his own relatives. Now he wondered if he could apply his influence with the Countess in the appointment of his cousin, Rev. John Pollard.

"Have you anyone in mind?" the Countess asked curtly. She was tapping her riding boot impatiently on the polished oak floor while outside in the sun, her companions waited restlessly on their horses.

"There's one highly regarded minister presently available. He is the Rev. John Pollard."

"Good. I appoint him. So that is settled."

Sellar bowed low to hide his surprise and pleasure.

"I want you to tell the elders that henceforth I shall make all such appointments without their advice. Perhaps I might close some of the useless churches. That would save me a lot of time. You are dismissed."

News of Pollard's appointment reached Rogart like a thunderclap. Duncan, who had been for many years an elder in the church, was dumbfounded. He had expected the Countess of Sutherland would at least have Sellar consult with the elders before appointing a new minister. To have an unknown cleric from Morayshire succeed Rev. MacKenzie, without consulting the congregation, was an insult to every God-fearing member of the Free Kirk.

Duncan was in a disturbed mood when he told Fiona, "I'm going to see the Dominie."

Walter, their oldest boy, now growing straight and strong wanted to go with his father, but Duncan hurried through the door and strode off alone. He was disgusted with the way the affairs at the castle were being run by the woman John Harral had claimed was an imposter.

On his way to the Dominie's, he had to pass the croft of the

60

war hero known as The Soldier. The Soldier, a one-legged veteran of foreign wars, was not at home but his wife, Maggie, and a neighboring crofter's wife were gossiping in the twilight.

"Good evening, Maggie. And to you, Mary," Duncan said.

Stepping from her doorway, Maggie approached and whispered in Duncan's ear. "There are more evil days coming upon us!"

Duncan stared at the dumpy Highland housewife. He had been so engrossed by the appointment of the new minister that it took time for the sudden announcement to register and to ask the natural question which followed.

"What do you mean?"

Before Maggie could answer Mary blurted out, "The Countess is going to be married!"

"And to a foreigner!" interjected Maggie.

At that moment the Soldier, who was still a brawny figure of a man with a straight back, limped over the rocky roadway to the cottage.

Maggie turned to him. "Tell him, Soldier. Tell Duncan what you heard at Golspie and what's about to happen to us. Tell him about the foreigner who is going to be our chief."

"What is this all about, Soldier?" asked Duncan apprehensively.

The Soldier, resting on his wooden crutch, glanced up and down the glen before he spoke. "I've just returned from Golspie, the people are in turmoil. Wait and I'll get you the notice." He went to his cottage and returned with a printed bulletin. "Here it is. Read the bad news for yourself, man. The announcements are written in Gaelic and English and posted all over the village."

Duncan identified the parchment as being official. It bore the coat of Arms of the House of Sutherland.

THE PEOPLE OF SUTHERLAND

BE IT KNOWN THAT ELIZABETH, COUNTESS OF SUTHERLAND, WOULD MARRY GEORGE GRAN-VILLE LEVESON-GOWER ON SEPTEMBER 4, 1785. FOLLOWING THE WEDDING CEREMONY YOUR COUNTESS WILL ARRIVE AT DUNROBIN CASTLE, AND IT IS EXPECTED THAT ALL THE ABLE-BODIED PEOPLE OF SUTHERLAND WILL GATHER AT THE CASTLE AND PAY HOMAGE TO THEIR BELOVED CHIEF.

Signed: Patrick Sellar,
Factor.

Duncan raised his eyes to those waiting his reaction.

"We'll give them our blessing with clean hands and unbiased hearts," he remarked.

"But this man is a foreigner, an Englishman!" the Soldier exclaimed.

"And Elizabeth may be a foreigner, too," chimed in Maggie. "You know the story John Harral tells."

"John could easily have been mistaken," Duncan replied. "Elizabeth is the Countess of Sutherland and for that reason we owe her our fealty." He turned to the Soldier. "I'm on my way to see the Dominie. He'll want to see this announcement. May I take it with me?"

"Aye, Duncan. Take it with you."

When Duncan reached the schoolhouse, the Dominie was sitting with his back to the rough stone wall of the cottage drinking in the last rays of the setting sun. At his feet lay his old collie, Prince, almost as shaggy as the man himself, but not as grey.

"It's a fine evening," greeted Duncan, sitting down on the bench.

"Aye," said the Dominie, noncommittally, as though loath to lose a moment's beauty of the fading day. There was a long silence as they watched the twilight draw in over the moors.

This was what inspired the Highlander to take up arms for freedom — something which could never be taken from their native scene — its interminable and indestructible beauty and enchantment.

The valley below and the gentle slopes beyond were a shimmering vision of purples, greens, browns and greys — purple where the last rays of the setting sun lingered for a moment on the heather-clad slope, grey in the lengthening shadows, and brown, green and dancing purple where the gentle up-valley breeze rippled in wide swaths over the hills. As it flitted through broom and bracken, leaf and stem turned upwards to feast on the dying day.

In all that vastness only a few pines, stalwart accidents of nature, clung daringly to the slope while down in the lowland the alder hugged the river's edge, its roots drinking deeply of the brackish waters from Assynt.

As the eerie bleat of the lapwing echoed over the valley, he shut his eyes for a moment as though to capture the whole scene in his memory and turned to Duncan.

"You've got something on your mind?"

"I've brought an announcement from the castle." He handed the Dominie the bulletin. "The old Soldier got it at Golspie."

While the Dominie squinted and tried to read in the fading

light, Duncan explained it to him. Duncan could see the old man's face blanch and his hands tremble.

Angus turned quickly to Duncan. "We'll have a foreigner for a chief. My prayer is that the Countess and her consort may be richly blessed for themselves and for the people of Sutherland."

"Amen," agreed Duncan. He decided this was not the best time to break the news of the new minister.

"A free wedding supper at Dunrobin Castle will be quite a treat. I'm getting tired of eating brose and porridge."

On the day of festivities, crofters from the far reaches of Sutherland rode to the sea on horse-back while those nearer the castle came in carts, small wagons, or walked. The women carried wedding gifts—a bedspread or shawl, a clay vase, or some other simple artifact—and fresh food from the croft—preserves, eggs or butter.

The Countess and Leveson-Gower had arrived a few days ahead of time. They were pleased with what they saw. Dunrobin was one of the oldest inhabited castles in Britain and had been under control of the same family longer than anyone could remember. It stood high and defiant above the Moray Firth, sheltered by Ben Bhraggie on the west and surrounded on three sides by forests and tilled fields. Everything had been cleaned and polished inside the castle — including the servants — under the keen direction of Patrick Sellar. The bridal couple had heard of the courageous acts the men of Sutherland had performed in battle and it was obvious from the gala gathering that they expected the castle grounds to be filled with a host of well-fed, gaily-dressed men, women and children. When the first of the tattered peasants straggled through the gate, the Countess and her husband and the many guests who had come from England and the lowlands, were utterly shocked.

The tartan had been temporarily revived by the Countess for the occasion but none of the Sutherlanders wore it. They had donned the woollen jackets and breeches of English design, since, in most cases, these were the only clothes they now possessed. A few, such as the Grant family, were clean and well scrubbed. Many had walked for miles through wet, knee-deep heather and across rivers. Like a forgotten people they gathered in cliques to talk in their own tongue about the harvest and the change of ownership.

Elizabeth moved freely among her English guests but it was obvious that contact with her unkempt and hard-working tenants was extremely distasteful.

The momentary acknowledgement and the kindly word of cheer ever due from the considerate master to his faithful servant was denied. This did not go unnoticed by the people from the glens and straths. The day was a failure! Times had changed in Dunrobin Castle. The occasion was never to be forgotten in Sutherland.

Leveson-Gower's resentment still rankled within him as he and Elizabeth reached the privacy of their nuptial apartment. "Damn it, Elizabeth, I was utterly ashamed of this afternoon's performance. I thought you could parade an army of brawny Highlanders from this empire of yours. Where the devil did you collect such a rabble?"

"Don't forget, Granville, this is my first visit to Sutherland. My agents have told me it was a wild country but I didn't expect so much barbarism and poverty."

"How can they be so poor? I understand they live upon the most fertile parts of the land and poach your fish and game."

"The old Earl pampered them and encouraged them to do pretty much as they pleased."

"Well, I'd bloody soon put a stop to it," Gower growled. "Why, I couldn't even understand the language they spoke."

The Countess gave an impulsive twist of her hips. "Some of them are quite virile looking," she smiled coquettishly. "It might be exciting to be accosted on a lonely road by that handsome man — what was his name? Grant? David Grant? From Strath Brora."

"My God! Elizabeth," he exclaimed. "One of those Highland hags must have cast a spell on you!"

"You know, of course, there really *are* witches in this part of the country?" she teased. "Lady Alva told me about them. She said some of these Highland women possess what they call the evil eye and that many of them believe in necromancy and witchcraft."

"Aren't you supposed to burn these witches at the stake?" Gower remarked as he extinguished the candles and began to undress. The Countess followed suit against the glow from the open fireplace.

"Oh yes, 'tis true. Some years ago our agents burnt a witch at Dornoch. Her last words were to utter a curse on the House of Sutherland. She prophesied that it would eventually reach the end of its line."

As the peat fire warmed the room, the Countess finished undressing and came to sit beside her husband. Leveson-Gower

64

reached over and took her in his arms. She quickly responded to his passionate embraces and much later, when the pair were quietly relaxed in the huge bed, Gower grinned to himself. "It wasn't much of a curse. After tonight the Sutherland line is sure to continue."

By day the young couple amused themselves with their guests. When they returned to the privacy of their quarters, they enjoyed the intimate pleasure of their honeymoon, far into the night forgetting the bleakness of the land — warm and secure within the Castle walls.

On pleasant days Gower and his wife led riding parties over Sutherland. Here they found a barren, dismal country with crofters' cottages hugging the few patches of fertile hill-side land.

"There's not even a deer in this God forsaken county," Gower grumbled one night as he and Elizabeth rested in their bed chamber after a long day's outing.

"There will be," smiled the Countess.

He raised his head. "How can there be when the land won't even support the peasants?"

"Why should it support peasants? Deer are more valuable — in some circumstances the squatters would be better off somewhere else. Perhaps we can help them on their way and then there will be plenty of room for the deer, the sheep and the cattle."

Elizabeth got to her feet and strolled about the bedroom. As she talked, Gower thought he had never seen a lovelier and more seductive woman and was amazed how such gentle beauty could harbour such cruel and savage thoughts.

"Under the provisions of the Hereditable Jurisdictions Act, the majority of Highland estates have already been forfeited to the Crown," Elizabeth continued. "But Sutherland has been unaffected by this legislation. At the time of Culloden, when my father was certain that the Jacobite cause was lost, two thousand men were mobilized under his direction and sent out to fight for the king. Naturally, this loyal gesture was fully appreciated by His Majesty. He was granted many favours at Court — including a long-term exemption from the terms of the Hereditable Jurisdictions Act. He was accorded authority to use his own discretion in applying it. Since I am now his sole heir, it is within my power to do what I think is best for Sutherland. I have already appointed several clergymen. I have increased the crofters' rents and now, my dear Granville, we shall conscript the youth of Sutherland for the king's army." She reached over to plant a gentle kiss on her husband's cheek. "You watch! Within a few years, by means of increased rents, religious restrictions, and the enforced enlistment of the Sutherland youth, we should be able to drive those still remaining off their holdings."

Her words were uttered with callous conviction for she believed her thoughts and deeds were divinely inspired.

"Where will they go?" asked Gower.

The Countess shrugged. "Who cares? Some may go to other counties. Some may go overseas. Some may go and live along the seacoast which is barren and doesn't produce anything. They're hardly making a living here and we'll be better off with them somewhere else."

"Our land should produce something."

"Yes, Granville, we'll produce deer and sheep. Our sheep-grazing lands will expand enormously and the returns from that alone will surpass the miserable rents that we're collecting from the crofters. In addition, the county will make an ideal hunting ground for our English friends."

Gower pulled his young bride down beside him. "If you weren't the Countess of Sutherland," he declared, "I'd wager there wasn't a drop of Highland blood in your pretty body."

CHAPTER EIGHT

Betrayal

"It was then, O daughter of Toscar! my son began first to be sad. He foresaw the fall of his race."
THE WAR OF CAROS

A S WINTER approached and their friends had taken their departure, the young Countess and her husband began to yearn for the theatre, gay parties, and fashionable soirees of the big city. It was, therefore, no surprise to the natives when Elizabeth and Granville returned to London to join in the whirl of English society.

The family of Leveson-Gower, in three generations, was raised from baronetcy to marquisate. He had not yet inherited the marquisate and was still known as Earl Gower. But he was industriously striving toward his dukedom. With this objective in mind, he became an MP for Stafford. Then he plunged into a surge of political activity that appointed him, five years after their marriage, British ambassador to France. It was at this time that the French Revolution was reaching its bloody climax.

Despite the uncertainty of the period, Earl Gower and the Countess established a home in Paris and made preparations to send for their children.

"We're living in comfortable quarters just as if we were in the piping times of peace. We're going to send for our family and brave the tempests of revolution," Gower told a friend who had come over to observe the growing political disorder in France.

On her arrival in Paris, the Countess was presented to Marie

Antoinette. Later she told her mother-in-law in a letter: "It was a very formidable ceremony, performed 'en pleine cour', rather worse than dancing at St. James' in a most uncomfortable dress. I was very charmed with the Queen. 'C'est en vérité une femme superbe'. Her Majesty's manner has so much grace and is so pleasing at the same time 'qu'elle est tout à fait séduisante'."

And so it happened that the problems of the Sutherland people were entirely forgotten as the Countess and her husband joined in a gay round of diplomatic receptions.

Gradually the temper of France changed; the mob grew more bloody and demanding and the rich became fearful for their lives and property. Many fled. Foreign diplomats earned their salaries by manoeuvring constantly to maintain good relations with a country on the edge of revolution.

"Life in Paris has grown very dull," the Countess complained. "Everything is reduced so entirely to a 'système politique'."

Soon after the mob had imprisoned Louis XVI and Marie Antoinette in the Temple, Earl Gower, his wife and children were safely back in England. Still they did not return to Sutherland or concern themselves with the crofters' problems.

Meanwhile, Earl Gower was appointed Lord Steward of the Royal Households and in 1799 he was named Postmaster General. It was not until his father died that he became the second Marquis of Stafford, successor to a large fortune, and proceeded lavishly to improve his own and his wife's estates.

Whilst the Countess and her husband were expanding their political connections and increasing their fortune, the croft at Fuarach-Coille had grown and prospered. Duncan was now slightly stooped. His hair was turning white like Fiona's, but he still toiled vigorously in the fields or at other tasks around the croft. Having grown into manhood, his sons became responsible for the croft and for the stock. In these peaceful and contented surroundings, Duncan Grant smoked his pipe by the peat fire, and, with his worries over, firmly believed that he and his people were safe at last and that he could forget the horrors of Culloden.

He attended the *ceilidhs* regularly with Fiona. While the young ones danced and sang, the older people listened to the music, gossiped about crops and animals, and wondered if there would ever again be an Earl of Sutherland.

One Saturday night, after a day of rounding up the sheep and lambs on a windy hillside, Murdoch, Walter and David were dressing for the regular dance in the parish hall. The ban on

68

the kilt was still in effect so the young crofters were donning homespun breeches and jackets for the occasion when they heard the voice of the Dominie at the open door.

"Hello, Duncan. Are you in there?"

"Yes, Angus," Fiona replied for her husband, who was busy eating. "Come right in. Draw up a chair and have a bite of supper."

Care-worn and bent, Angus entered the cottage, slowly and unsteadily. He carried a cane and tapped over the rough flagstone floor to the fire. His face was lined but bronzed, his hair flowed in a white mane around his head. He had grown older in an imposing manner and still remained the most respected personage in all of Sutherland.

"What's on your mind, Angus?" asked Duncan, rising to welcome his old friend.

The Dominie frowned. "I'm afraid my news isn't good, Duncan."

"Out with it, man. It can't be that bad."

The Dominie shook his head. "Recruiting officers from Dunrobin have been in Rogart for several days. They intend to enlist one thousand men for the king's army. Proclamations posted everywhere state that all able-bodied men must apply for service with the 93rd Sutherland Highlanders."

"Well, if it's purely voluntary, we've nothing to worry about!" retorted Duncan.

"It's not. The choice is being made by ballot."

The Grant brothers stopped whistling and stood anxiously waiting for the Dominie to continue.

"If what you say is true, our farming days are over," commented Murdoch.

David slapped him on the back. "Och, Murdoch, don't be seeing the black side of things." He strode nonchalantly toward the door and stopped. "War or no war," he declared, "and regardless of what the Countess has in mind, I'm off to see my Jeannie."

"You'll have little choice, David," warned the Dominie. "The ballot box will decide whether you go or stay. Those who pick the black ones, go. So far, no one has picked a white ball. They have already taken all three of Widow MacDonald's sons."

"David's right," said Walter jauntily.

"To be sad about trifles is trifling folly,
For the true end of life is to live and be jolly!"

"Oh, Walter," Fiona sighed, "how can you say that? Think

of poor Widow MacDonald. With all her sons gone, how will she ever look after the croft?"

Walter shrugged his shoulders. "Let's forget about Widow Mac-Donald. This is my night to dance. Come, the lassies await us," he coaxed as he took Murdoch's arm and escorted him into the night.

For some time the three brothers walked in silence along the pitch-black trail. The only light came from the distant stars, sharp and clear in the deep blue heavens. They had tramped the trail to the parish hall so often that it didn't really matter whether there was a moon or not.

In the eerie light, Walter took Murdoch's arm. "Come, brother, what's troubling you?" he asked.

"I was recalling Mother's stories about the prophecies of old Granny MacKay."

"You're too young to pay any attention to an old wife's tale," scoffed Walter. "You know as well as I do that for a pinch of snuff, a pipe of baccy or a jug of grog, Granny'd conjure up the Devil and make him dance the Heilan' Fling!"

"She had the second sight," Murdoch insisted. "She could sense what was about to happen, just as I do!"

Hamish Sutherland ran the 'Antler' tavern in the village of Rogart. Despite its crude rock and mud construction, it was a place of cheer and merriment in the bleak country. Three large rooms downstairs accommodated the drinkers and diners and a series of smaller quarters upstairs offered a bed to the few travellers passing through that part of the Highlands.

The inn was also the centre of social activity in the parish. In the course of an evening one could sit at a rough table in the sand-floored bar and hear all the local gossip from one end of the parish to the other.

The brothers were heading for the tavern. As they approached they were greeted by a young man, short in stature and dishevelled in appearance. He was known only as "The Gipsy," or "The Piping Gipsy," and no one in the parish knew his origin. One stormy night Hamish Sutherland had found the lad unconscious on his doorstep. From then on, the Gipsy piped for the guests and did odd jobs around the inn in exchange for scraps of food and a place to sleep in the loft over the barn.

His clothes were ragged, his right elbow showed through a rent in the ancient military coat he always wore and patches of dirty skin were visible through the holes in his woollen breeches.

70

He wore his tattered glengarry jauntily on the side of his head and he had a perpetual smile on his furrowed face. As he sidled up to the Grants he looked for all the world as if he would burst with excitement at the news he had to relate. "There are some real high-class strangers at the inn tonight," he whispered coarsely. "Come to the stableyard and let me show you their grand coach."

The Grant boys followed around the gable of the inn. They whistled softly as the Gipsy raised his flickering lantern for them to inspect an elaborate black and gold chaise with the coat of arms of the House of Sutherland embossed on the outside panels. A jaunting cart for four stood alongside.

The Gipsy hovered nearby studying the reaction. "They have been here for several days," he explained importantly. "Two toffs came in the fancy coach. One of them was dressed in the uniform of an officer. I heard his name was General Wemyss. The other man was Patrick Sellar. Four others came in the cart. Two of them were soldiers. Two were civilian gentry. The soldiers are gone most of the time, posting the enlistment notices throughout the district." He leaned toward Walter. "If you want to know what I think, there's trouble brewing."

"God's sake! Not you too!" snapped Walter. "I need a glass of whisky."

The Gipsy tugged at Walter's sleeve. "Will you buy me a dram if I come and play the pipes?"

"Yes. I'd buy you Dunrobin Castle if it would brighten up this day," Walter declared with a touch of bitterness.

At the bar Hamish Sutherland spoke quietly in Gaelic. "There are strangers among us. Better watch your tongues, lads."

He rolled his large blue eyes towards a smaller room where an officer in a red coat sat writing at a table. Beside the officer sat an obese, middle-aged man with a neatly trimmed black beard. Like the general, he was well-dressed and well-manicured, in startling contrast to the roughly clad crofters who sipped their whisky and watched warily.

Walter noted that the two visitors were obviously out of place in the unventilated drinking room with its homemade furniture and walls blackened by thousands of flickering peat fires.

When the Gipsy took up his pipes the crowd buzzed with anticipation.

"Come on, Gipsy. Give us a blow!" they chorused.

The Gipsy grinned. "First, a dram to warm my fingers."

Everyone waited impatiently as he gulped it down.

Then with a sly wink, "Another to clear the drones and put me in fettle for the evening."

David reached for a brimming glass and handed it to the piper. The Gipsy held it up to the candles. "It's our own Clynelish*," he laughed and emptied the glass in two quick gulps. Grinning exuberantly, he threw the drones over his shoulder and caressed the tattered tartan bag.

As the first plaintive notes filled the tavern, all conversation ceased. The crofters were stirred by the deep emotion bagpipe music brings to every Highland heart. Even the officer and his bearded companion stopped what they were doing to watch as the Gipsy marched up and down. Walter could hear the civilians' feet beating out the time and before the Gipsy had reached his second tune everyone in the tavern was stamping and clapping until the smoky rafters shook to the stirring marches and lively reels.

"Ah! that Gipsy!' exclaimed Walter appreciatively. "We'd follow him into the valley of death."

"Aye, and on through the gates of Hell," commented Hamish, as he stood transfixed at the bar.

"Come, Gipsy!" invited David. "I'm going to buy you a bigger drink, then you'll give us another tune!"

As the piper prepared to play, two red-coated soldiers stomped through the open door. Their officious entry stopped the piper's hand in mid air as it was raised to clear his drone. The soldiers marched across the bar-room to the table in the adjoining chamber as the loitering crofters watched them morosely — suspiciously — skeptically — silently.

The smaller of the two, a cocky bantam-like man with sergeant's stripes on his sleeve, carried a red box which he placed on the table. From his tunic pocket he produced a scroll and presented it to the officer.

"The results of today's balloting, sir," he reported, raising his hand in salute.

"More victims for the cannons of the Dutch," commented Murdoch.

His voice broke the spell and the inmates began speculating on whose sons had been trapped in the day's recruiting. The piper had finished. The joy of the evening was over. The red-

---

* Legal whisky made at the local distillery.

72

coated officer and his civilian companion rose from their table and approached the bar.

The officer spread his feet, locked his hands behind his back and appraised the bewildered crofters with his bold eyes. He bade them a good evening and expressed his pleasure at being among them. Since he spoke in English his words were not understood by most of the occupants. The Grant brothers, however, could understand. Angus Gunn had taken pains to teach them this foreign language just as he had taught their father before them.

The corpulent man stepped forward. He was going to act as an interpreter.

"Good evening, gentlemen," he said in fine Gaelic, "and to your piper, a special good evening," he bowed to the Gipsy as he glanced around to evaluate the effect of his cordial words. "This is General Wemyss of Wemyss. He has just complimented you lads on the fine evening's entertainment. We thoroughly enjoyed it. Many of you know I'm Patrick Sellar, agent for the Countess of Sutherland."

A ripple of subdued excitement coursed along David's spine. So this was Sellar, the most hated man in the glen. David had never seen the notorious man before but stories of his ruthlessness had spread widely through the broad land of Sutherland.

The crofters waited. The General began to speak. He paused every few sentences for Sellar to interpret for him.

"You lads all know why I am here. Sergeant Stokes has covered the parishes of Rogart and Clyne posting notices of our intent. The Countess has offered the king a battalion of men to be known as the 93rd Sutherland Highlanders. These troops are needed to help his most gracious Majesty defeat the Dutch in South Africa and secure our trade routes to the far East."

It was obvious that the General loved to hear himself speak. He gave a long-winded account of his military career. He spoke of how the family of Wemyss in 1779 raised seventeen hundred men for the Sutherland Fencibles, and repeated again in 1793 with a like number. He went on so long that when he paused David muttered in Gaelic, "He's as full of wind as Angus MacDonald's old mare."

Eventually, the General walked to his table and returned with the red ballot box. He held it up for all to see. "In this box there are equal numbers of black and white balls. The fortunate men who get the black balls will have the honor of being enrolled in His Majesty's army. Who among you brave lads will be the first to come forward?"

There was no response. The men shifted uneasily. Several drained their glasses in silence and left the room.

David Grant stepped forward.

Sellar handed him the box. It was the same one that would be presented to every young man of fighting age in Sutherland. As David placed his hand beneath the shutter, Sellar pressed a trigger that released a black ball. Black meant conscription; white meant release. Sellar controlled the flow of balls and, thereby, many of his relatives and friends escaped conscription.

David Grant grinned as the ball fell into his palm.

Sellar smiled. "You'll be told when to report for your uniform and musket! Next."

The men in the room followed David's example. The Gipsy and the one-legged veteran from another war drew white balls. Everyone else, including Walter and Murdoch Grant, drew the dreaded black one.

When Fiona heard of the balloting later that night, she burst into tears. Beside her Duncan Grant sat silent. Tyranny had again reached out to shatter his life.

Before the fatal Tuesday was over, one hundred men had been blackballed in the parish of Rogart. By the end of the campaign almost every able-bodied man in Sutherland had been recruited. The McLeods from Assynt, the MacKays from Strathnaver, the Gunns from the border of Caithness and the Sutherlands from the parish of Clyne, Rogart and Golspie — all left the glens and all displayed traditional obedience to their Chief although it was to mean insurmountable hardship for those left at home.

When the roster was completed, the men of the 93rd Sutherland Highlanders were outfitted with kilts, military jackets and muskets and marched to Dunrobin. Here they were addressed by the Marquis who had arrived in Sutherland County to inspect the progress on road and bridge construction.

"Men of Sutherland," he said from the steps of the Castle. "Your willing attendance here confirms your readiness to follow me wherever the fight for freedom takes us, and if necessary to sacrifice your lives in the cause of His Majesty and in defence of your homes."

The men of the 93rd shifted their feet uneasily and looked questioningly at one another. They were wondering how their homes could be threatened by Dutchmen on a continent five thousand miles away. The Marquis paused. He had expected some enthusiastic response to his words, but all he saw was a mob of silent, grim, unsmiling countenances.

"To show our appreciation for your loyal response the Countess has decided to cancel all debts and rent arrears for the families and relations of all the crofters in Sutherland."

Resentment had become so ingrained in Sutherland that only a half-hearted grunt of approval arose from the lips of the conscripts. The Marquis realized that he would have to call upon his cunning and imagination if he was to convince the Highlanders of his courage and sincerity. Striving for composure and to find the words to convey the plan he had in mind, he dabbed at his lips with a lace handkerchief. He continued, "As Colonel of the 93rd I am personally going to lead you into battle. To any of you who might not return, and to those who could be rendered incapable of supporting their families, I swear that their welfare will be the particular concern of the Countess and myself. In case I do not survive the campaign, I have drawn up the necessary documents to ensure that these solemn pledges are executed on my behalf by my heirs and successors. With this guarantee you'll not have to worry about those you have left behind."

The recruits, convinced that the Countess' husband was an honourable man, responded with a burst of applause.

"Maybe we won't have to worry about our parents' welfare after all," declared Walter. Many, however, were still hesitant. The shadow of the past hung ominously over the future. Murdoch shook his head. "I'm not so sure. This all sounds too promising to me."

"Old gloomy Murdoch again," laughed David as the Marquis continued.

"Finally men of Sutherland, your Countess guarantees that none of your dependents will suffer either hunger or want during your absence. The storehouses of food at Dunrobin Castle will be open freely to those in need."

When Duncan Grant and Fiona heard of the Marquis' promises Fiona wept in silent thankfulness. Duncan knew that promises had been guaranteed by chiefs in other wars. "But wars," he reasoned, "are uncertain affairs. This makes promises uncertain, too."

Jeannie Gunn, a silent little figure stood in the crowd, her eyes rivetted on the broad back of David. David was the tallest of Duncan's three sons and, like his father, he excelled at school and at sports. Duncan had taught his boys all the skills he knew and encouraged them to participate in public contests. David, to a greater extent than Walter or Murdoch, had brought glory to Fuarach-Coille. At the Brora games his good looks and wide, handsome smile won the hearts of all the girls. He enjoyed their attention and their company.

It was not customary for young folks to marry at an early age in Sutherland and David Grant was no exception. He was having too much fun and freedom to consider marriage until he met pretty Jeannie Gunn from Dach Hoille.

Jeannie was eighteen and very pretty. Her silky brown hair was braided in a thick mass over her temples and behind tiny ears. Enough remained to form a heavy knot behind her head where two bewildering little curls, that were the joy of David's eye, played around her white neck. Her eyes were large, very blue and expressive. A healthy bloom that came with the fresh mountain air, tinged her rounded cheeks. Her figure was firm and graceful and her breasts full and provocative.

During their years of growing up they had lived as neighbours and occasionally met at a *ceilidh* but their conversations had been brief. She was a shy retiring girl and did not join the other girls as they clustered around David. He was so involved with work at the croft or with hunting, fishing, or tests of strength that he had no desire to court anyone in particular. One day, he met Jeannie alone on a windy hillside. He had been chasing sheep through the heather when he came across her lonely figure sitting on a rock.

"Jeannie Gunn, what are you doing up here?" he chided.

Startled, Jeannie swung around and David suddenly realized he had never seen such warm blue eyes.

"I don't know if it's any business of yours, David Grant," she replied. "Up till now I was enjoying the summer sun and solitude."

David showed his even white teeth in an agreeable smile. "Now Jeannie, there's no need to be sharp."

"I have as much right to be here as you have," she pouted.

"Of course you have. It's just that I'm not used to seeing girls alone so far from home. Do you mind if I sit down?"

Jeannie shrugged. "You're free to sit if you want to."

David tossed his knap-sack on the heather and flung himself down beside her. "I've been looking for my sheep. They're up here somewhere. But it's time for a bite of food. Would you care to join me?"

76

Jeannie flushed at the invitation and hesitated. David thought he had never seen such a pretty face, or such lustrous, brown hair, now loose and cascading about her trim shoulders. Why had he not noticed it before?

He opened his pack and produced slices of chicken, and some oatmeal cakes that his mother had prepared for his tramp through the hills. For hours they sat and talked and David forgot about his sheep. When the afternoon shadows began to lengthen, he walked Jeannie to the stile at her father's croft.

He held her hand. "There's a dance at the hall on Saturday night. May I call for you?"

That was the way their courtship began. They attended the parish dances and the *ceilidhs,* and at every opportunity they met at their trysting place on the heather-covered hillside.

In the year that David and Jeannie planned to be married, Sellar's ballot box conscripted David into the 93rd Sutherland Highlanders and their blissful days came to an abrupt end.

Since Scotland's union with England in 1707 much had changed. During the revolts that followed, many Highland feudal lords substituted their own laws to govern the rights of property. As a result of this encroachment, only a vestige of the former rights enjoyed by the Highlanders remained at the time of Culloden.

In the olden days each Highland Chief had been a sovereign prince whose power and prestige was measured by the number of well-equipped fighting men he could muster. No Highlander who had felt the winds of the Assynt bathe his sweated brow and seen them flow in waves over the heather-clad hills, would fail to stand by his chief's side. He would not dare to desert in time of trouble. Under the old Earl, the County of Sutherland volunteered over two thousand armed warriors on more than one occasion; now Gower could conscript only five hundred for the original 93rd Regiment. Many who could have fought had melted away into the Highland hills, to brave the discomforts of the wild heath, rather than serve under a foreign chief.

When the day arrived for the 93rd Highlanders to leave their native glens in the king's service, it became evident that the Marquis had no intention of going with the Regiment. He, who had delivered such an inspiring address at the castle, stayed behind in the loving arms of his Countess — the same Countess that had already envisioned the Highlands being repopulated by a race of sheep and deer!

Following the departure of the 93rd, the Countess journeyed to London and intimated to His Majesty and his counsellors that she had found strong Jacobite support among the Sutherland crofters and she was belatedly enforcing the provisions of the Hereditable Jurisdiction. She stated that her activities would begin with a few scattered evictions from the lands of Sutherland.

The king still feared a Jacobite uprising, and assured her of the military aid she might require to suppress any rebellion. So it came about that just as the last ship was landing the 93rd in Capetown, South Africa, Countess Elizabeth was sitting down with quill and paper in her elegant London drawing room writing.

"Dear Sellar: My husband and I were very disappointed with the response to our request for troops for His Majesty's service. We had expected at least one thousand men to join the 93rd Regiment.

It would appear that the men of Sutherland no longer feel an obligation to help His Majesty in time of need. Because of this unhappy situation it is impossible for me to continue operating the estates without a full return on the properties.

Will you therefore advise all crofters that due and overdue rents must be paid immediately? It is also my desire that only those who can pay will be allowed to stay on the land."

Patrick Sellar was having dinner in Dunrobin Castle when the Countess' courier arrived. He wiped the stains of meat from his mouth and chin with a fine linen napkin and gulped another mouthful of wine before he took the letter and broke the seal. Sellar was amazed at the quick turn of events, for though he was a party to much of the planning, he never thought that he would be called upon personally to destroy what little remained of chiefly honor. But his duty was to obey; he was paid for obedience and efficiency. When he had again perused the contents he called his clerk.

"A notice to all the people of Rogart and Clyne," he ordered. "Tell them they must appear at the village hall in Rogart on Monday next to pay all rents due and past due."

The following day Duncan and Fiona were among the crofters reading the notice on the church door. The faces of all were aghast with disbelief.

78

CHAPTER NINE

The Rent Court

"My light burns in a light of its own. I stand without fear in the midst of thousands, though the valiant are distant far. Stranger! thy words are mighty, for Clessammor is alone. But my sword trembles by my side, and longs to glitter in my hand."

CARTHON

FIONA thought of their humble home and of the hours of toil and tears that had gone to winning a moment of quiet and peace each evening. Of worldly goods they had little but with faith, patience and courage they were well endowed.

Wrath boiled in the heart of Duncan as he glanced at the tear-stained face of his wife. They were now alone — not even a child on whom to depend. He reached out and tenderly held Fiona's toil-worn gentle hand.

"It's impossible! No descendant of the House of Sutherland would issue such a damnable decree," he mumbled, pulling his bonnet over his heavy grey brows.

Fiona had been slower to grasp the meaning of the notice, but she understood the promises she heard at the Castle when the Marquis harangued the men of Sutherland — with the boys away the prop was neatly struck from under them.

"If only the boys were home we wouldn't have to bear this alone. We could have paid the increased rent. We'll still be able to pay when the crop is harvested," Duncan continued. "I'm sure the Countess will agree to postpone collections until then."

But it was not to be.

On the day the rent court was held, Sellar, James Loch, the tax collector, and Chief Constable McLeod arrived at the village hall in the same grand coach that had borne General Wemyss and Sellar to the inn on the night he had recruited the sons of Duncan Grant.

The excitement was general. Eighty families, most of them aged, stood disconsolately outside. They were all that remained of a noble people who had been welded into a powerful race by ties of blood and misfortune. Now they hovered on the brink of extermination. When Sellar's coach drew up, a group of them approached with bonnet in hand and before this man of power and parchment, they bent heads that under ordinary circumstances would not have stooped at the whistle of a cannon-ball.

Sellar dismounted and with his officials marched directly into the hall. His face was grim and he looked neither to right nor to left. To most he was a tyrant and oppressor. He had taken the lead in the Countess' well-organized system for the expulsion of the Sutherlanders. He was a vehement advocate of substituting bare sheep-walks and useless game preserves for the glens once peopled by a brave and hardy race, who in the ranks of war gave place to none and who were by right of inheritance the true lords of the soil and architects of their own destiny.

"Sellar is not a man we can trust," Angus Gunn whispered into Duncan's ear. "We'll get little sympathy from him."

At a table at the far end of the hall the Countess' three agents were seated. Loch, thin and sallow, leaned forward with his elbows on the table at Sellar's right. His fingers formed a tent under his chin and his long hooked nose marked him a typical tax collector. A large book lay open before him. On the left of Sellar sat Chief Constable MacLeod who was a brawny, wide shouldered man with the physique of a blacksmith. Sellar, who presided, was dressed in elegant breeches, lace shirt and woollen jacket. In front of him lay open an ominous black satchel.

There were no chairs for the crofters. They stood, shuffling their feet uneasily, while waiting for the proceedings to begin.

Sellar rapped on the table to call the court to order.

"People of Rogart and Clyne," he announced. "I have come here to collect all present and past dues. The Countess of Sutherland has ordered that all current rents and arrears must be paid forthwith. When Mr. Loch calls your name you will come forward and pay up in cash or kind."

80

There was a general murmur of resentment from the crofters. "Silence!"

As the murmur died down under Sellar's stern warning, Duncan Grant spoke up. "What about the Marquis' promises? He assured our sons, now fighting in Africa, that all rents would be cancelled and our crofts rent-free until they returned."

Sellar fixed the speaker with a disapproving eye. "The Countess needs the money to supply the 93rd Regiment in the battle field," he retorted.

"But we can't pay with our boys away," Duncan protested.

"I didn't come here for an argument, Grant. I came to collect rents. Now let's get on with the business."

"Margaret MacDonald, come forward," Loch intoned.

Silence fell on the milling throng as an aged, frail woman shuffled across the floor. Her clothes were tattered and patched and her bare feet showed through the holes in her deerskin shoes. She clutched her ragged shawl more tightly around her thin shoulders as she stood before the three glassy-eyed officials.

"Poor soul," murmured Fiona. "Both her sons and her husband John were killed in battle. Now look what they're doing to her."

"Widow MacDonald," said Loch, "our records indicate that your rent arrears amount to eight pounds. Are you prepared to pay the money?"

"What would you be asking of me, Mr. Sellar? I cannot even pay the old rent. By the sweat of my brow and the toil of my children's tender hands, I have scarcely kept body and soul together. You are aware that my husband and sons were killed in Africa, aren't you, Mr. Sellar?"

Sellar ignored the heart-rending plea. Widow MacDonald continued, "The famine was sore last year; our fruit was poor and as you must know our little crop of oats was literally thrashed on the mountain by the wind. All that remained was devoured by the game of the Countess. Please, Mr. Sellar, listen to me. I've given everything I have to you. Please give us a little time, for myself and our four children as well as for my old, bedridden mother now in her ninetieth year who will be homeless with nothing but the heather for shelter!"

Sellar smirked and ordered Loch to make an entry in his fatal book. A low groan was the only response from Widow MacDonald for too well did she know what he meant.

One by one the crofters were called to the table. Some produced a little money which Sellar scooped up and dropped into the black satchel. Others could produce nothing. None could pay the total sum the Countess demanded.

When the Soldier's name was called, he hobbled slowly across the stone floor on his crutch. Six war medals jingled on his chest as he pulled himself erect in front of the table and saluted. He was one of the county's most respected soldiers. His service in the field had been daring and heroic. One day a cannon ball had torn through the ranks shearing away his leg. He knew no language other than Gaelic. "Falte na maiduin dubh (Hail good morning to you)," he said. Sellar inspected the veteran with a frosty stare.

"Your rent is in arrears. Can you pay?"

The Soldier loosened the strings on his small deerskin pouch and drew out four pounds — all he had saved over the years from his pension. He could produce no more. "The amount of my rent is exactly three times what I paid Earl John," he explained as the Dominie stepped forward to interpret for him.

"The Earl isn't running things now," snapped Sellar. He scooped the four pounds into the satchel and motioned to Loch to write a note in the receipt book.

Duncan was next. With bonnet in hand he stood quietly.

"Are you ready to pay, Grant?"

Duncan looked Sellar in the eye. "I can only pay part. I can't pay it all. My boys are with the 93rd. When they come home we'll be able to pay all the arrears."

"That won't be soon enough," Sellar growled.

Duncan tried again. "Your records will show, sir, that before my sons left we Grants paid our rent on the day it was due. Now that the lads are in the army we are having a difficult time. The crop hasn't been good this year and I'm not as young as I used to be." He suddenly grew irritated at the smirk on Sellar's face. "For God's sake, Mr. Sellar, be reasonable!" he cried. "Ask the Countess to give us a little more time. Look at these wretches. Look at Granny MacLean. She's a veteran's mother. How can she hope to pay these high rents? And Granny Gunn. Already word has come that her grandson, her only support, has been killed in battle."

Sellar was apparently unmoved by Duncan's pleading. "I'm ready to take your money, Mr. Grant," he stated impatiently tapping the table with his beefy fingers.

Duncan sighed and handed over the few shillings he had saved. "Give him a receipt, Mr. Loch."

82

Angus Gunn walked towards the collector's table, a dark cloud hovering on his brow and a dangerous spark gleaming in his eyes. They were the outward signs of the fire that smouldered in his heart — a fire fanned by the lamentation of his people.

Sellar, who knew the esteem in which the old Dominie was held, proffered his fat left hand as his right held a pen but Angus drew back saying proudly, "Thank you, but I would not take the left hand of a king."

He looked searchingly at Sellar, then at Loch and Constable McLeod. They dropped their eyes.

"Gentlemen, surely something can be done to save these people. Certainly their welfare and those of their sons who will soon return is worthy of your consideration. If you proceed with this disgraceful plan and carry out your obvious intentions to de-populate the glen, you will dishonour the solemn promises of the Countess and the Marquis."

Sellar smiled urbanely. "We've received our orders, Dominie. A debt is a debt. We can show no leniency or favouritism."

Angus went on as if he had not heard. "Both you and I were present when our lads enlisted. You heard the Marquis promise to cancel rents in arrears. You heard him promise rent-free houses until they came home. What about the Countess' pledge to feed the hungry? Is this what their hollow words meant — a sham, hypocrisy? Or have you made a mistake?"

"There's no mistake." said Sellar impatiently. "We know what we're doing. Don't you forget, Dominie, that your first loyalty and responsibility, as well as ours, is to the Countess." He thumped his heavy fist on the table and his voice became threatening. "We could take it as downright sedition for you to speak against the Countess on behalf of these penniless squatters."

The Dominie's voice became suddenly cold and icy. "Don't you dare to threaten me, Sir. I'm not speaking for any group of squatters, I'm speaking for the people who have shed blood for Sutherland, who rightfully own this land — my people. God was kind to our ancestors long before you and I were born. He gave us this land to live on. Today, all of them have shown their willingness to pay rent but for the time being they can't raise the money."

"Mr. Sellar," the Dominie continued. "Highlanders are not half-wits. We know what is going on in the minds of the Countess and her husband just as well as you do. There was a time when the sun shone on a race of happy people in this glen and the woods are still as green as they were many centuries ago. Yet you want them to starve where their fathers lived in plenty! Why is this?"

"Because they're a pack of lazy dogs," said Sellar, unable to contain himself.

"Not at all," retorted Angus fiercely. "The dun hills swarm with deer, the green woods are alive with game, the clear rivers team with fish and who among us dare use a rod, net or gun? For now the land with all that is in its waters, its woods and in the air belong to the stranger. Don't you dare say, Sellar, that our people are lazy! Robbed of their natural birth-right they are wringing a hard-won existence from a heartless soil — all to feed the belly of tyranny! You are the agent of that tyranny, Sellar!"

Sellar, Loch and MacLeod cringed in their seats at the vehemence of the old Dominie's attack. Only Sellar could stare back defiantly at his accuser as his face turned more livid with each word.

The room was hushed. The shuffling of feet had stopped. None could afford to miss a syllable. The Dominie's tall, lean frame had become the anchor for every Highland heart. His hand trembled as it clung to his lapel. His lips quivered with the sincerity of his plea. In this dingy hall he was carrying aloft the last bright torch of Highland freedom and his frail body towered over the ignominy of the moment.

"God gave us these things because he saw that the land itself was barren but you and your ilk have robbed us of them. You can never escape His judgment. One day He will call you to account before His throne . . . "

Sellar jumped angrily to his feet — "Don't you dare . . ."

"Sit down, Sir," said Angus in a measured, incisive tone that allowed for no refusal. "I will say what must be said."

Sellar wilted before the storm.

"Look at the records. In the days of kelp-making we made 20,000 tons a year here in the Highlands—an income of £200,000 which came to the pocket of the crofters. Along with his cow, his sheep and potatoes, this kept many a large family in happiness, health, and comfort. Rents were paid strictly and regularly in money or kind and arrears were never heard of. What you now represent has taken many steps towards the destruction of our people. The Parliament of England, influenced by the gold-hungry

84

manufacturers of England, took the duty off the Spanish Bacilla*
and the Highlands have suffered. Remember what Lord Binning
said at this — 'A hundred-thousand clansmen will starve'. Perhaps
you are interested only in what Robert Walpole, Chancellor of
the Exchequer replied, 'Let them starve, I care not!' May God
forgive your souls their sin!"

A murmur of approval rippled round the hall as Angus Gunn
leaned on the rough table and fixed Sellar with a stern eye.

"Since then arrears, misery, and famine have fallen upon the
Highlands. The castle of the Chief has become a foreign grouse-
lodge, and the hills have become a voiceless wilderness."

"Where on earth did you pick up all this nonsense?" laughed
Sellar with unfeigned surprise tinged with uncertainty. But the
Dominie never heard him.

He turned to the elated crofters, then continued, oblivious of
Sellar's presence. "I could tell you more, my friends. I could
tell you that you who are about to be thrown out have an
inalienable right to your land — an even greater right than that
claimed by any landlord. You are not feudal serfs like the low-
landers or like the English. You are Celts, Highlanders, free
men, bondsmen to no one, owning your land. Robert the Bruce,
on the memorable field of Bannockburn gave a Charter to the
lands of Sutherland, that made your position clear. 'You and your
offspring,' he said to Earl William, **'and they and their offspring**
will possess the lands of Sutherland while you and they continue
loyal subjects and attached to the Crown of Scotland. No piece
of land susceptible of cultivation must remain uncultivated or un-
occupied and the mountains, the rivers and the forests will be
free to all!'

"There is your birthright, men and women of Sutherland. Your
forefathers fought and won it at Bannockburn. The chief was
a thing of your breath whom you could make or unmake, but
the land with its mountains, woods and waters was your inalienable
right. It was your home, your dwelling place — your final resting
place."

He paused to let the significance of his words strike deep in
the heart of all. There was a long silence. The moment was
charged with emotion and Sellar knew that one wrong word
would unleash a storm of uncontrollable fury from the crofters.

* A product used in the manufacture of iodine and imported from Spain.
  This was used as a substitute for iodine then obtained from kelp, collected
  on tidal waters of the Highlands.

They hung on the Dominie's every word. He had given them back their pride, their independence, their faith, their manhood. Sellar was afraid.

Angus turned towards him. "God gave us these rights, but no doubt a lawyer like you will have more faith in charters, bonds and bank notes than in them. Surely to God, Sir, the pledge of the Countess was not a deliberate lie to entice our sons to war!" He stared accusingly. "Are the people of Sutherland not worth as much as a herd of sheep and deer?" He paused. "May God have mercy on you all if what you do this day is part of a plot to drive our people from their land."

As he spoke Angus gazed fixedly at Sellar, his piercing eyes penetrating into his very soul. He straightened his frail shoulders, then turned his back on him and proudly strode to the door. The room emptied in hushed silence.

Behind him Sellar, Loch and MacLeod stared in helpless impotence as they watched their authority spurned before their eyes. Their money-bag was empty. New courage had been born in Sutherland.

CHAPTER TEN

The End of Fuarach-Coille

"He poured death from his eyes, along the striving fields. His joy was in the fall of men. Blood to him was a summer stream, that brings joy to withered vales, from its own mossy rock.

CATH-LODA

A FEW months after the rent court a party of men passed out of the gates from Dunrobin Castle. In the lead coach, bearing the coat of arms of the house of Sutherland, sat Patrick Sellar dressed in a manner that indicated he was on *no* mission of mercy. Beside him sat Loch. His hands were twitching and there was a nervous smile on his face.

The coach that followed contained five men along with Chief Constable MacLeod. In the rear were two carts driven by lackeys and loaded with faggots, straw, cudgels and fire arms. As the wagons lurched back and forth over the rocky trail the occupants continued to enjoy hearty swigs of the potent grog that Sellar had provided.

Every man in the blood-thirsty undertaking knew that he was going to destroy the homes and lives of the crofters and wipe out a way of life that spanned many generations. Only through an over-abundant supply of whisky and ten pieces of silver could Sellar have recruited men to carry out his plan of wholesale destruction. Chief Constable MacLeod was a native of Golspie. He had little choice. For years he had been employed by the Countess. If he failed to carry out her orders his own family would be

evicted or shipped to some colonial outpost as slaves. The whisky
gave him courage.

The program decided upon by the Countess and her husband,
while enjoying their honeymoon at Dunrobin Castle, was now
being carried out. It was a wicked, unconstitutional scheme where-
by Gower, his Countess and their rich accomplices had license
from the king to seize the property of the crofter, burn down
their habitations, banish them from the land and add their few
acres to their own extensive game preserves.

It was a lamentable truth that the beautiful Countess Elizabeth
had issued an order converting Sutherland into a howling, solitary
wilderness from which joy and rejoicing was to be gutted out
and in which the stirring notes of the bagpipes would be no longer
heard — a rape of the land which even the Romans, Edward,
Cromwell and other formidable invaders had failed to achieve
at the highest peak of their power.

What chance did the people have when even their ministers
failed them?

The Sunday before Sellar left Dunrobin, the Rev. John Pollard
had maintained in his services that the evictions were a merciful
interference by Divine Providence to bring the crofters to repentance
rather than to hell as they so rightly deserved. The ground work
of tyranny had been well and truly laid. The poor Gaelic-speaking
people, fearful of the wrath of God, quailed under such over-
powering influence. Their sufferings were regarded as a just
retribution on their damned souls.

These false prophets were also employed to explain and interpret the orders and designs of the Countess, and as they exhorted
some people to quiet submission, they scared others into leaving
peacefully so that they could acquire land for their own use.
New manses and offices were provided and roads built specially
for their accommodation.

Prior to the coming of Elizabeth the glebes were mostly situated
on the low grounds and the clergy held their land in common
with the crofters. This state of affairs established by law and
usage could be altered by no proprietor and had the ministers
not failed the people, they would have placed an effective barrier
to the oppressive proceedings of the Countess. But greed made
them tools of tyranny.

Sitting silently in his coach Sellar dolefully recalled the scene
when he was ushered into the Countess' drawing room in London.
After he had accepted a glass of sherry, the Marquis went into

88

a long-winded description of the Countess's future plans for Sutherland.

"England requires more food," he had said. "Since she is locked out of foreign markets because of her many distant wars, the country's resources must be utilized to the limit and food production increased. I have promised the king additional supplies of beef from Sutherland. The Countess and I intend to run sheep and cattle on our estates. Sheep and cattle will fetch higher prices than the rents we now collect and at the same time they will help to alleviate England's problems."

Here the Countess had interrupted to explain that it was Sellar's job to get rid of these human incumbrances and replace them with animals for the English market. She issued specific instructions on how it was to be carried out; another sherry and she dismissed him with this curt warning. "Mr. Sellar, you know your duty!"

Now as he came out of his reverie, Sellar looked across at the thin face peering inquisitively at him. He slapped Loch's knee and grinned. "Are you ready?"

Loch looked uncomfortable. "I suppose so."

"We'll proceed as planned."

As he uttered the dreadful words the first of the doomed cottages came into view. It was a small dwelling with a thatched roof set against the hillside. On the right stood the little barn, and a chicken house.

When the marauders stopped at the door there was no one in the yard. Sellar and Loch dismounted. Sellar yanked open the door of the coach containing his drunken aides.

"It's time you got to work, you drunken sots," he bellowed.

While the half-inebriated men tumbled out he strode across the yard and pushed his way through the open door of the cottage.

A middle-aged woman sitting at a spinning wheel in the gloomy peat-reek jumped up in alarm. "What are you doing here?" she demanded.

"Are you Mary Sutherland?"

The woman lifted her head erect. "That I am, but you've no right to break in and question me in this manner."

"We're not interested in manners," retorted Sellar brusquely. "You're in arrears with your rent. Here is your eviction notice." He snapped his fingers at Loch who took a paper from his satchel and handed it to the bewildered woman.

"What does this mean?"

"It means we've come to burn you out," growled Sellar. "You have exactly ten minutes to get yourself and your kin out of here."

"Merciful heaven! You can't be serious."

A boy of about ten came from the dark bedroom and sidled up to his mother. She put a hand on his head as he clung to her waist.

Sellar strode outside. "All right, MacLeod. Get your torches ready. You there, bring some of those faggots inside and stack them under the table." Seeing that his orders were being carried out, Sellar returned to the room where the helpless woman stood in a state of shock.

"You've got ten minutes," he warned. "If you want to save anything from the fire you'd better move quickly!"

Mary Sutherland bent her head to the boy. "Hurry Tom," she whispered. "Run over to Angus Sutherland's place and tell your father to come home at once."

The boy dashed out the front door, scampered across the clearing and disappeared over the hill.

Mary Sutherland stood against her spinning wheel in a daze, as a drunken bailiff staggered in with an armful of faggots and dropped them on the floor. His companion began breaking up the rough furniture and placing it on the pile of faggots. He was upending the wooden table when Mary found her voice. "For the love of God, stop it," she shrieked. "Are you all insane? Stop it!"

"It's too late," laughed Sellar. "You should have paid your rent."

"You know we can't pay our rent," the frantic woman screamed. "But you can't do this. Get out." She was attempting to herd the drunken trio out of her house when Sellar viciously slapped her across the face.

"Keep your filthy paws off me," he warned.

Mary's hand flew to her cheek. She began to scream hysterically. Sellar slapped her again. "Stop that bawling and get out!"

"Loch, Loch!" he yelled from the door. But Loch had no stomach for this sort of thing and having slinked away from the cottage was now huddled inside the coach.

"You can't burn down our home," sobbed Mary Sutherland from the open doorway. "My old grandmother is in bed. She can't be moved. She's over ninety."

"The old hag has already lived too long," retorted Sellar.

There was a commotion in the yard and two excited crofters pushed their way into the house. One ran to Mary.

90

"What is it, Mary? Are you all right?"

After Mary had blurted out Sellar's warning, the man turned angrily on Sellar. "What is the meaning of this? Get out of here at once!"

Sellar grinned maliciously. "You're the one who'll get out. You were warned several weeks ago that your rent was in arrears. You were told you had to pay or be evicted. You've had plenty of time to make up your mind."

"But you can't burn our house over our heads."

Suddenly there was a crackling overhead. One of the crofters rushed outside and ran back in.

"My God, they've set fire to the roof!"

Sellar strolled casually outside but Sutherland followed and leaped at his throat. "You rotten bastard!" he screamed.

MacLeod knew what to do. Stepping forward he cracked the man over the head with a heavy stick. Sutherland's eyes went blank and with the blood streaming from his scalp he collapsed in the yard.

"If there's any more blood spilled," Sellar raged at the weeping woman and her child, "the blame will be entirely yours."

As he spoke the second crofter appeared at the smoking door with an old woman in his arms. Her long white hair and skeleton arms hung limply and she was too dazed to know what was taking place.

"Her blanket's on fire!" Mary screamed. She rushed forward and began flogging frantically at the thin blanket wrapped around her grandmother. Eventually the flames were extinguished and the crofter carried the aged woman to the barn where he laid her gently on the straw.

"Fire the barn," thundered Sellar.

A drunken constable immediately threw a burning faggot on the straw. Instantly the dry bed on which Granny lay burst into flame. Again the crofter picked her up. As he eased the frail bundle to a bed of heather the roof collapsed and death stole her from him. All his efforts were to no avail.

When the roof of the cottage had caved in, Sellar exulted. "That's the first on our list, MacLeod! Give your men a good dram to celebrate the occasion."

As Sellar and his killers continued their ride of death through the valley, Mary Sutherland collapsed in tears by the side of her husband — the children watched as if in a trance.

Throughout the hours that followed, the Countess' agents

moved methodically from cottage to cottage. Kept drunk by accumulated swigs of special brew, they cursed at the wailing, half-clad, terror-stricken women and children who scurried to save themselves and their belongings from their flaming dwellings. Some of the more fortunate managed to remove chairs, tables, kale-pots and spinning-wheels, but in most cases the Chief Constable's men, in an excess of zeal, threw the salvaged articles back into the flames. Trinkets and heirlooms of value, protected for generations with reverence and care, were confiscated by the looting brigands.

One pregnant woman, whose husband had died a few months before, attempted to pull down her house to preserve the timber. She fell through the roof and immediately went into premature labor. Neighbours carried her to the sward. The house was fired as the woman, exposed to the night air, bore her child.

As the brutal killers' rampage moved on, old men and women sat dazed as their homes were put to the torch. Some of the bed-ridden were carried to safety, others perished in the flames. A feeble old man crawled into a dilapidated pig shed and lay unable to move. Throughout the night his faithful collie snapped at the rats and kept them away from his master but the poor wretch had neither water nor food and he died before dawn.

Elsewhere five sick people who had been carried out of their homes were placed in a deserted mill. One wandered away in a daze, one fell over a nearby cliff to a bed of rocks. Most, however, were too concerned with the removal of their few sticks of furniture to offer any opposition. So Sellar and his men worked largely unmolested amid crying, hysterical women and children, the roaring of the frightened cattle, the barking of excited dogs and the crackling of the fire as it whipped through the dry thatch exposing pale faces upturned in the grim embrace of death.

When the sun set on the second day over one hundred and ten homes in the parish of Rogart and Clyne had been put to the torch. The holocaust could be seen for miles around adding terror in the distant parts of the parish where the crofters, struggling to save their livestock and belongings, were hoping that darkness would give them a chance to escape into Ross-shire.

At Fuarach-Coille, Duncan and Fiona climbed to a hilltop from where they could see the flames spiralling upward and the smoke drifting like a giant miasma over the country.

"God help us," gasped Fiona trembling as she spoke. She had been ill for many weeks and as she turned her tear-stained face toward her husband the eyes that had first expressed her love for him many years ago reflected the turmoil that now gripped her heart.

Duncan took her in his arms. "We'll manage somehow." But his arms were weak, his head spun and he suddenly felt tired and discouraged.

During the afternoon Fiona gathered up her most precious belongings and stacked them in the cart. Duncan herded his sheep and cow from the hills and placed them in the stockpen. They had done all that they could.

Just before sunset Sellar and company arrived at Fuarach-Coille.

"Duncan Grant," Sellar announced. "Your rent is in arrears and we've come to evict you."

The unfortunate crofter groaned deeply and stood defiantly barring the way to the front door.

"You have no right to enter my home unless you have legal authority!"

"Loch. Come here. Show this fool his notice."

Loch, pale and trembling, climbed down from the coach and rifled through his satchel. After extracting an official-looking document, he handed it to Sellar who thrust it into Duncan's hand.

"There's your legal notice."

Duncan glanced at the document but did not read it. He was too numbed even to think. It was like a nightmare. They had built this cottage with their own hands when they were young. When his three sons were small children he had packed extra clay into the joints between the rocks and piled extra thatch on the roof to keep it warmer. During the ensuing years they had loved and laughed, quarrelled, entertained, and prospered. They had grown old contentedly expecting to die in the house. All this flashed through his mind as the agent of the Countess was urging him to move out of the way so that the roof could be fired over his head to satisfy a few pounds of unpaid rent.

"Only a madman would burn down the homes of innocent people. Where are we to go? Where are we to live?" Duncan demanded.

"That's your problem. We've got orders. You've had your chance, stand aside and let's get on with the job."

Duncan resolutely stood his ground.

"Damn you," yelled Sellar. "I didn't come here for a *ceilidh*." He raised his heavy cane and clubbed Duncan across the neck.

93

Duncan's eyes dimmed, he heard Fiona scream and he tried desperately to fend off the darkness. Sellar had fired the house while Duncan was unconscious and Fuarach-Coille was now a mass of flames.

When Duncan's head cleared Fiona was kneeling by his side weeping silently. "This, then, is the end," he thought.

Meanwhile Sellar's men were roping the sheep and leading them from the stockpen. Eventually they would be hauled off to Dunrobin Castle.

As if in a nightmare Duncan saw Sellar stride across the yard, pick up a burning brand and throw it into the cart-load of furnishings. He struggled up on the cart in an attempt to beat out the fire but his foot slipped and he fell to the ground.

Sellar laughed drunkenly and vindictively. Turning to Fiona sitting in her rocking chair, he ordered, "Get up, you useless bitch, or we'll roast you where you sit." He moved forward and grabbed her by the arm. Duncan endeavoured to go to her aid but his arms were pinned by the Chief Constable and he could only watch Sellar throw Fiona roughly to the ground, then toss her favorite chair onto the flaming cart. The wind-whipped flames burned gaping holes in her rough woollen dress and scarred her arms and legs.

When they had left, Duncan took Fiona in his arms and wept.

CHAPTER ELEVEN

Towards the Sun

"O ye ghosts of heroes dead! Ye riders of the storm of Cromla! receive my falling people with joy, and bear them to your hills."

FINGAL

O N THE NIGHT Fuarach-Coille was destroyed David Grant, from South Africa, arrived within sight of the heavy pall of smoke hanging over the valley of Strath Brora and Sciberscross. His worst dread had been confirmed but as yet he did not know what had happened to his parents and Fuarach-Coille. He had been eight days on the trails from Leith where he had landed after the long voyage.

The first inkling of trouble in Sutherland reached him at Atholl while he rested at the junction of the Garry and the Bruar. This was a favorite rendezvous for the drovers who followed the well-worn trails through the hills to the cattle market in Crief — a break in the long monotony of the drive over the rocky trails. Here they relaxed, exchanged gossip and spent hours on trials of skill and strength before they moved on to Strath Tummel.

Alaster Stewart of Gask had driven his herd over the Grampians from Loch Ericht and had carried with him the first stories of the clearances. He had heard the news from Sandy Grant who had come up the Spey from Glenlivet to Ericht. At the news, fear added wings to David's feet and he pushed north into the hills.

Passing through the village of Golspie he sought word of the evictions only to receive stories of death, pillage and remorseless persecution. No one knew what was taking place so he headed into the night towards the relentless glow in the sky. Before he had reached the ford of the River Brora he realized that the Countess had broken faith with the 93rd.

He recalled the suffering and privations at Capetown. He would never forget the sickening ocean journey to a place he had never heard of until the Regiment put to sea in four of the most unseaworthy vessels afloat. For months the ships had been buffeted by strong gales and heavy seas.

Many soldiers had developed scurvy; others in the vast endlessness of the ocean had gone insane and leaped overboard. The majority had survived and eventually they sailed into calm waters and sunny skies that continued until they reached the Cape of Good Hope.

They waded ashore at Capetown. A week later a blast of Dutch cannon-fire decapitated Walter. David and Murdoch had been so enraged that they personally carried out night patrols against the enemy's position and with bayonet and dirk killed forty-two of them. After the 93rd had secured the first vantage point the brothers went back for a last quiet moment of prayer over Walter. They sat and talked about Fuarach-Coille, about Jeannie, and dreamed of the day they would be home once more.

Murdoch was not to see home again. Two weeks later a huge black Bantu hurled a spear that pierced his chest and he died before David could reach him. A month later David's shoulder was laid open by a sword and he remained conscious only long enough to hear the Corporal say, "Duncan Grant has lost two sons already. So we'd better put this one on the first ship for Leith."

As he hurried up the familiar glen toward Balnacoil his mind was in a turmoil. How could he face his parents with his sad news? How could he add new despair to their present suffering?

He raced along the rough trail until he reached a point in the glen where the river flowed between Sciberscross and Balnacoil. Fear was in his heart as he drew nearer to the scene of death. He let out a gasp of amazement — men, women and children were dashing towards the river. They plunged frenziedly into the rushing flood-stream. They screamed, they yelled, they fought the swift current. He watched as they staggered, fell and disappeared into the whirlpool.

David ran to save an old woman but to no avail. She disappeared. So many were falling down and being washed away that he didn't

96

know whom to save first. Some struggled ashore and he assisted them up the steep bank. The scene of unmitigated suffering was worse than he had ever seen in the battlefields of South Africa. He could do nothing about it. Two women lay moaning and sobbing on the riverbank. A little girl was screaming and tearing her hair. A half-naked boy ran off into the heather incoherently gibbering to himself.

Among the survivors David recognized Mary MacLeod.

"Mary," he called. "You, Mary MacLeod! It's David Grant. What in the name of God's happening?"

Mary stared at him blankly. "I've lost my mother. I saw her crossing the stream ahead of me but she's gone."

David hurried past her and grabbed a man who was wading out of the river. "Charlie. Charlie MacKay! I've just come back from the war. Tell me what's happened. Where's my mother and father?"

Charlie gaped as if he had seen a ghost. "David Grant, I thought you were fighting in Africa."

"I've come back, Charlie. For God's sake what's taking place?"

"It's Sellar. He's burned us all out." He grabbed David by the arm. "How's my Sammy? How's Sammy? Where is he?"

"He was all right the last time I saw him. Where are my parents?" David demanded.

"Everyone has been burned out, everyone has been evicted. Can't you see the smoke?" Charlie pointed a gnarled finger toward the rising black cloud. "We're all burned out. We've got to find shelter somehow, somewhere."

David ploughed his way across the river. As he hurried up the glen he scanned the faces of the ragged, frantic natives streaming past him into an unknown future. Where were Duncan and Fiona? Where was Jeannie? My God! Where were they?

He passed fire-blackened mud and stone walls and smouldering ruins as he raced toward Fuarach-Coille. Cottages were burning and outbuildings blazed and collapsed as he hurried on.

When he saw his home, rage and despair made him frantic. Like a madman he repeatedly called for his parents; the crackling of the gutted mud and stone walls echoed his empty plea. The remains of the cart smouldered in the yard; the heavy wooden wheels recognizable. He spotted forms moving around the camp: fires glowing in the darkness by the old battle cairn near the ancient graveyard. He ran toward them.

"Father! Mother! Jeannie! In God's name where are you?"

No one answered. He had never seen such a pitiful sight. His old friends and neighbours sat stunned beside formless shadows that lay rigid and still on the ground. A few moved silently among the living or wept quietly in the shadows. The happy peaceful crofters he had left so long ago were in singed rags, their faces blackened by fire and stained by tears. Over by the cemetery wall he at last found his father kneeling in silence.

"Father! Oh father!" he exclaimed.

At the sound of the familiar voice, Duncan turned.

What David saw stopped him short, in disbelief. His father had become an old man in his short absence, the once proud spirit now dull and lifeless. His mother lay motionless on the ground. Moving forward, he knelt and knew that she was dead.

Father and son remained kneeling until darkness settled and the chill of evening crept over the hills. Together they bore their silent grief while the fire cast its shadows over Fiona's peaceful face. For Duncan Grant that chapter of the story which had opened on the stormy sea coast many years before had closed.

"What in the name of God has happened?"

Duncan raised his head. "Mother was seated in her rocking chair when they burned our home. I told Sellar she was too ill to stand. I told him she needed her rocking chair but he paid no attention. He threw her on the ground and then tossed her chair into the flames."

"Oh, God!"

"When I lifted Mother from the flames her clothes were burning. I carried her to the heather where she died in my arms."

"I can't believe it," moaned David. "I can't believe it. I'll kill that bastard Sellar."

"Killing won't do any good, my boy. There's been too much of it already."

Father and son rose to their feet. A grim shadow crossed the old man's face. Apprehensively he looked around before he turned to David and asked, "Didn't Walter and Murdoch come home with you?"

David felt numb all over. How could he tell his father that his elder sons would not be coming back.

"Didn't they come back with you?" probed Duncan.

David took his parent in his arms. The hot tears trickling down the wrinkles on the old man's face told their own story.

For a moment Duncan turned away. When he again faced David his pale complexion had changed — it now burned with an expression that is difficult to describe — no trace of the sacrifice he had made showed in his bearing. Calmly with a voice full and steady he said: "We'll bury your mother in the morning." After throwing the tartan shawl he had salvaged from the flames over the body of his dead Fiona he lay down at her side.

For a long time David stood staring at the smoke-laden sky. He moved over to the nearest fire and spoke to the old Soldier and Betsy. They looked up but did not greet him.

David broke the silence. "Surely, Soldier, the Countess didn't order this dastardly crime?"

"Yes, David, The warrants for eviction were issued with the Countess' authority and were enforced by Sellar, his Chief Constable, and his gang of thugs."

In the light of the smouldering fire David became aware of another form lying in the shadows covered by a tattered robe. "Who is that?" he enquired.

The Soldier glanced at the plaid-covered body. "It's the Dominie."

"Surely not the Dominie?"

"Yes, he stood up to Sellar in the rent court. Yesterday one of his men crushed Angus' head with a cudgel!"

David dropped to his knee by his old friend's side. Tears welled up in his eyes. A last tear for a lonely man who was everyone's friend. "God bless you Dominie," he whispered.

Next morning they buried Fiona and the Dominie at the old cemetery. In this place of solemn memories among the remains of their ancestors they knew that Fiona and the Dominie would be safe. The haunted precinct was so steeped in mystery and folklore that it was avoided by all.

After the burial, father and son turned their steps toward Dach-Hoille. Past blackened embers of cottages and sheds they strode. At the site of Jeannie's smouldering home there was no evidence of life.

"Perhaps they've found shelter in one of the caves," said Duncan. He pointed to a ridge of limestone about a mile away. Here the wind and rain had eroded wide crevices and the superstitious crofters believed that banshees, brownies, bogies and other spirits had made their homes there. As a boy, Duncan and his friends had explored the haunted chasms, but they had never found anything to scare them. Now he strode boldly on shouting Jeannie's name. Reaching the entrance he wormed his way in, calling, "Jeannie, Jeannie where are you?"

As hope waned, David heard a voice in the distance and a moment later he was holding his trembling, sobbing sweetheart in his arms.

"What happened to you, Jeannie?"

"I know not — I know not at all," she mumbled. "So many horrible things have happened that I know not — I know not at all." She clung to him and refused to let go. "Oh, David, I don't know what's happened to us. I was so afraid I'd never see you again."

David enfolded her in his arms. "There's nothing to fear now, Jeannie."

The girl pointed to one of the caves. "Mother is there but I fear she's near death."

At sunset Jeannie's mother died. Sunrise the following morning found David and Duncan carrying the body of Mary Gunn to the graveyard.

After the burial David heard his father's voice calling. "Oh, God. Oh God, do not forsake the children of our tribe." His shaggy grey head was tilted upward, his eyes fixed on the cloudless sky. David trembled. For a fleeting instant he knew that he had experienced some supernatural phenomenon. The tough, forthright David who had laughed at Walter's visions now recognized voices he knew were sent to guide him. "Grieve not, David, Mother is still with you."

The silence of the morning was broken only by the cheerful song of the skylark and the raucous scream of the seagulls as they flew inland from the stormy sea. "Are we alone, David?" asked Duncan.

"No, father! Not alone! We're never alone. Come let us build a new life together — the three of us."

All day they walked east towards the coast. David did not know how they would live when they arrived, for there was no shelter and he knew that the fisherfolk, settled along the beach had little hospitality to offer. Fortunately it was midsummer and the refugees could sleep in the heather; had it been any other season they surely would have perished.

At the end of the first day's journey the sun was shedding its fading rays across the marshy countryside when the trio approached the barren boglands known as Badnellan. On this low-lying meadow hidden from the sea David decided to stop for the night.

There was no sign of habitation. Someone had piled peat near-by and it was in this peat stack that Duncan, David and Jeannie,

100

ate the last scraps of scones and pieces of rabbit that they had brought with them. When darkness fell David wrapped Jeannie in his military coat to protect her from the bank of cold, foggy clouds which rolled in from the distant sea. With his father he lay down in the two singed blankets — the only covering they possessed.

At first light David left the crude shelter to scrounge the meadows for food. A short distance away he came to a stretch of bog. The land looked solid beyond the boggy soil so he waded through the black sludge until he reached firm ground. From the tough purple-flowered reeds he flushed a flock of mallards and the air was filled with their frightened squawks. Quickly he plundered each nest in turn. He deposited his collection beside a rock and hurried to the top of a nearby hillock. From the height he saw a succession of lush grassy hills, the kind he knew were the natural habitat of rabbits, pheasants, grouse and deer.

Here was an isolated, fertile area that could well be cultivated. To the south he saw the valley through which the Brora River coursed to the sea and beyond were wide stretches of meadowland fringing the shores of the Moray Firth.

About a hundred yards away, a stag with the largest antlers he had ever seen, trotted into view. It stopped on a rocky promontory, its stately figure silhouetted against the rising sun. David watched breathlessly as the graceful animal raised its head high and sniffed suspiciously at the downwind. Satisfied that no danger threatened, it whistled shrilly and as if in obedience to the master's command a herd of sleek does bounded up. David watched the animals mill around uncertainly before the stag pranced off down hill with the herd in pursuit.

"This is good land," David thought to himself. "This is where we'll start a new life. With God's blessing Jeannie and I will raise a family and cultivate the land."

On the way back he killed a rabbit with a stone and when he reached the peat-stack he found Jeannie and Duncan awake and refreshed.

Jeannie had rearranged her hair with a comb that Duncan had fashioned from the bleached antlers. The combination of some bogwater and a face cloth torn from a petticoat had restored some natural rosiness to her cheeks.

"Hurry, father," called Duncan. "Gather some dry grass and heather. Jeannie, you coat the eggs in mud and I'll light the fire."

They laid the eggs on the hot embers and soon the cracking

of the mud told them that breakfast was ready and they sat down to enjoy their meagre meal.

Scarcely had they finished when other refugees straggled up, among them John MacKay, the old Soldier, hobbling slowly on his crutch. In a gunnysack Betsy carried his bagpipes. The Gipsy had lost his pipes when Sellar's men fired the inn in Rogart.

From them David got the first coherent news of how the Countess and her husband betrayed the promise made to the men of the 93rd.

"Why don't you all stop here with us and we'll build a new settlement," remarked David. "We'll call it Cavaick."

The Soldier shook his head. "No, David, we want to get as far away from Sellar as we can. The sea is just beyond the hill and across the valley. This land belongs to you if Sellar will leave you alone.'

CHAPTER TWELVE

Cavaick

"The feast is spread. The harp is heard; and joy is in the hall, But it was joy covering a sigh, that darkly dwelt in every breast."

CROMA

THE DEVELOPING of 'Cavaick' from a few patches of barren land into a productive croft was not something that just happened because Duncan, David and Jeannie wished for it, any more than the digging of drains to dispose of the bog-water and the removal of brush, rocks, stumps and stones, simply came to pass. It required strength, forbearance, dogged courage and the determination to accept a laborious, gruelling life.

In the beginning it seemed that they had returned to the Stone Age. Their tools, crude knives, spades, and axes had to be carved out of stone and flint. The fat from the stag, with a twisted piece of rag, produced their candlelight.

With these crude tools Duncan, David and Jeannie worked the daylight hours through. It was a timely piece of good-fortune when David returned to the burnt-out glen and brought back a few farm tools, cart wheels, furniture and other charred necessities he had salvaged from Fuarach-Coille. On his return trip a collie dog, which Jeannie named Rock, followed him home.

The drudgery, however, didn't end with the day. There was plenty to occupy their toil-worn hands far into the night. Additional furniture was required in order to augment the pieces David had salvaged. Skins had to be tanned, shoes and clothing had to be made.

Gradually the croft became more productive, but it was not done without a price. Duncan was growing old and the long hours in the field were particularly tiring to him now, but throughout his waking moments he lived with the memory of the flames licking at Fuarach-Coille and Sellar mistreating his Fiona. These pain-filled memories drove him to constant activity; every night he fell into bed utterly exhausted. His whole world centered now in the croft.

David foraged far and wide to provide meat for his family. The collie kept the croft stocked with rabbits but the deer, which provided them with food, cloth, shoes and fat, were scarce. Sellar and his associates from the castle had been scouring the crofts and the glens in pursuit of game.

The Countess lived in London, but the Marquis visited the castle occasionally to inspect his road-building and bridge construction. Over these roads and bridges he hoped to drive herds of sheep and cattle to market. Indeed, he had noticeably increased the flocks of sheep after the first evictions and the animals roamed ceaselessly through the former farmlands of the evicted crofters. During his hunting forays for deer in the autumn, David often passed by the ruined town of Rogart and the burned-out cottages of Sciberscross, now overgrown by weeds and heather.

Occasionally, some of the crofters who had settled close to the limestone quarries at Badnellan, among them 'Big' Tom Sutherland, came to Cavaick; David provided them with whatever surplus food they had on hand. It was on one of these occasions that Big Tom mentioned having visited the refugees on the Brora beaches.

"How are they faring?" asked David.

"Just a miserable existence. The poor hillfolk will never get accustomed to the sea and even if they did they are not accepted by the fisherfolk who refuse to give any assistance, because they have a hard time catching enough fish to fill their own needs."

This constant rivalry was characteristic of the village-dwellers, the fishers, and the hill-folk. The village-dwellers looked down upon the fishers who in turn accused the hillfolk of stealing their fowl and plundering their gardens. "Of course," continued Tom, "this is creating problems for our people and making it more difficult for them."

On a Sunday afternoon three months later when the sun was

104

caressing the wild Sutherland hills Jeannie wandered to a hillock overlooking the Brora River valley. In this solitude she attempted to ease the tumult in her breast. She had concealed her fears until this morning when she heard Duncan remark to David, "Jeannie seems to be walking in a daze."

Far away on the horizon she could see where the green hills melted into the sea. She was all alone in the world, it seemed, as she stretched out on the warm grass under a covering of broom and heather. She thought wistfully of the first time she and David had come there to be alone and laid her hand gently on her abdomen where she felt the stirrings of new life. Then she fell asleep.

A touch of David's hand wakened her.

"Are you feeling all right, Jeannie?"

Jeannie reached up her arms and pulled David down beside her. "Oh, David, I feel wonderful! Look! The sun is sinking. I must have slept for hours."

"I was worried about you. You've been gone a long time." They kissed and David caressed her hair.

"David," she whispered, "I'm so happy yet I'm afraid . . ."

David looked down into her smiling face. "What's the matter, Jeannie?"

She raised her eyes to his. "I'm with bairn."

David's heart filled with tenderness. He wrapped Jeannie in his arms.

"Oh, David, I'm so happy. I'm sure it's God's way of blessing our dismal existence and giving us promise of a better future. If only we could be married."

She felt David's arm tighten around her.

"Damn the Countess."

These words of revolt told of the strength of David's new resolve. His arms tightened around Jeannie. "I'd rather our bodies rest in the bottom of Blackwater pool than have our child christened bastard. Our only hope is the Reverend Donald Sage of Kildonan; he alone has refused to carry out the Countess' orders."

The Countess knew that she must get control over the ministers in Sutherland if her plans were to succeed. She was aware that the Sutherlanders were of the Free Kirk and since they were devoted to their beliefs they continued to reject the sham and hypocrisy of those she had appointed to minister to their moral welfare.

She therefore deprived the people from entry to their places of worship and ministers like Donald Sage were forced to conduct clandestine services in the open fields, on heather-covered mountainsides, or in the alder groves along the river bank. In support of Sage, the people turned their elders into lay preachers and maintained their determination to adhere to the gospel of their forefathers.

Seeing her authority spurned Elizabeth retaliated by decreeing that anyone participating in rites performed by the Free Kirk would be arrested and transported to England's possessions beyond the seas. This decree forbade legal marriage.

David knew that Mary and the Braggart had taken passage on a lime-ship to Caithness and were married at Wick. He was about to discuss the matter but quickly put the thought from his mind as the sun was now setting beyond the hills and early darkness was fast approaching.

"It's time you had something to nourish our little one." He raised Jeannie to her feet. Together they walked slowly down the hill toward Cavaick.

Duncan was waiting in the doorway. "What about supper, Jeannie," he asked with a bashful grin. "I'm hungry!"

"We have news! Jeannie is going to have a baby," David beamed with true happiness.

Duncan held Jeannie at arm's length. He had wondered what was going to happen between his son and the girl. They had lived in the same house for over a year. How long would their sense of morality and their faith hold them apart? Now that the moment had arrived he felt relieved.

"Secretly, I've been hoping for such an event. Don't worry. How in God's name could it be otherwise when men and women are forbidden the Holy rights of matrimony? Yours is a common, everyday happening and a natural one."

"I intend to marry Jeannie legally, father. Tomorrow I'm going to Kildonan. Perhaps the Reverend Sage will help me."

The Reverend was sympathetic to David's plea but offered no encouragement. "It's the Countess' orders, David, so there can be no legal marriages in Sutherland," said the clergyman walking the floor of his study.

"You must marry us, Reverend. Jeannie is going to have a baby. It must carry my name."

Sage, a large ruddy man still strong and hearty, shook his silver grey head. "I know your problem, my boy, but there's nothing I can do to solve it!"

"You must solve it! I must marry Jeannie! And at Cavaick.

You'll have to perform the ceremony. You have God's authority, that's all the authority you need."

Sage had known David's father for many years and had held him in great respect. The tyrannical Countess' order had shocked this man of God and David's plight demanded a decision.

"All right, son. There may be trouble but when did our Shepherd turn his back on the needs of His flock?" — The battle between God and Mammon was not to be surrendered by the servant of God.

David hurried home with the news. But Duncan cautioned his son to keep it quiet.

"We will not keep it quiet, father. I want all our friends to know that Jeannie and I are getting married."

The following week Duncan posted notices throughout the parishes of Clyne, Rogart and Golspie. The wedding ceremony was to take place on the hillside near Cavaick, where David and Jeannie had conceived their child. It was a glorious day, the kind that often comes to the mountains overlooking the North Sea in early fall.

The Soldier and Betsy were first to arrive. After a happy exchange of greetings, there was a quick round of whiskey that Duncan had specially brewed for the occasion. Before noon the assembly stood poised, enjoying the panorama of valley and sea that stretched off into the distance as far as the Ord of Caithness.

The Soldier put down the gunnysack he was carrying and drew out his bagpipes, which had once been silver-mounted, but were now nothing but a spider of charred wood tied together with rough hemp grass. He remembered how, after his leg had been shattered by cannon-fire, he had sat within range of the enemy's guns and played on and on until the enemy was driven from the field. His companions carried him from the battleground to the casualty clearing station. Seeing him comfortably settled they left, taking his old bagpipes with them. When his amputated leg had healed and he could walk with the aid of his crutch, Soldier was invited to attend a party at the Regimental head-quarters. There they wined and dined him, and a Sergeant who had helped carry him from the battlefield presented him with silver-mounted bagpipes styled with the finest MacKenzie trim-mings — a grateful gift from the men of the 78th Regiment.

The much-honoured pipes were now a fire-blackened memorial. Pieces of sack-cloth had replaced the MacKenzie tartan ribbons. The air-bag had been repaired with patches of many colors. Only the weather-bleached ribbon attached to his ancient military coat showed the honours MacKay had won. He fondled his pipes as a child would its first toy; he looked up at David and smiled. "I'll admit they aren't as beautiful as they were the day I played for the old Earl's wedding, but they'll still sound off music as you've never heard before."

"Come on, Soldier! Let's have a reel," chanted his friends.

When the Soldier began to play the enraptured spirit of the throng knew no bounds. Old and young were dancing on the hilltop and down its heather-covered sides; lusty Highland voices echoed and re-echoed among the hills from every pinnacle all unaware that a troop of horsemen were at that moment fording the river on their way from Dunrobin.

Suddenly thundering horses crashed into view.

A woman screamed. "It's Sellar. It's killer Sellar."

The Soldier's bagpipes wheezed to a stop. The gaiety of the gathering changed to confused resentment, anger and apprehension. Silence like death followed.

Sellar, Loch and the Chief Constable rode at the head of the cavalcade. Behind them followed a fully-armed company of the Irish Dragoons, their swords and pipe-clayed breast bands shining in the brilliant sun.

Disdainfully Sellar reined his horse to a halt and rose in his stirrups.

"David Grant," he announced, "you are well aware that the marriage you propose is unlawful. I order you to disperse. If you persist in carrying out this illegal ceremony you and your seditious friends will be liable to imprisonment and deportation."

"That would be preferable to the miserable existence our people have been driven into," retorted David. "You've murdered our kinfolk and turned many out to die. Do you think you can frighten us with anything worse?"

"For the last time I order you all to disperse and return to your homes," Sellar thundered.

"What homes, for God's sake?" the Soldier roared. "Would you call my miserable hovel a home?"

The Chief Constable and Loch looked anxiously around. The people were regrouping and pressing in from all sides. Sellar was afraid. He had not expected any resistance.

The Gipsy sensed the change in the crowd's mood. Quickly he moved toward the Soldier and took the pipes from his hand saying; "Take a rest, my friend, I'll do the piping."

108

Immediately the air was filled with the rallying call of the Sutherland clan. The emboldened Highlanders responded with a surge of courage. As they pressed in on Sellar he put spurs to his horse and galloped furiously toward the Irish cavalry who had halted a short distance away.

"Chief Constable," ordered Sellar, "step forward and read the Riot Act to those bloody rebels."

The reading of the Riot Act could hardly be heard over the angry din and lusty singing.

When the clamour died down, the powerful voice of Reverend Donald Sage cut through the silence.

"In the name of God, Mr. Sellar! Is it possible that such a damnable incident could happen in a Christian land? Don't you realize the devilish crime you are committing against these innocent people?"

Sellar dismounted. He beckoned to the captain of the Irish company and accompanied by the Chief Constable they approached the bridal couple and guests. The presence of the military frightened many of the crofters and they gradually made room for them to pass.

"Who among you Highland scum would question an order from Dunrobin Castle?" demanded Sellar.

"I would," replied Rev. Sage. Before fixing his penetrating gaze on Sellar's angry face he bowed his head in momentary meditation. "I am the Reverend Donald Sage of Kildonan. I dare to question any unholy mandate from whatever source it comes."

The minister's bold words lifted the flagging spirits of the people and before Sellar could answer, the throng was cheering the courageous preacher.

Sellar seethed with rage. Cords were swelling in his neck and his face had turned purple. Stepping forward with his riding crop gripped so tightly that his knuckles turned white, Sellar stopped within striking distance of the man of God. "Damn your rotten soul," he said vindictively as he raised the crop above his head.

Before he could carry out his murderous intentions the Captain grabbed the uplifted arm. "Hold it. If you strike this holy man you'll have to fight not only the Highlanders but my Dragoons as well."

The blunt warning brought Sellar to his senses. He lowered the crop. His face surly with wrath, he turned on Sage. "You're committing treason by inciting these people to disobey the orders of the House of Sutherland."

109

The clergyman smiled. "No incitement is intended. I simply announced my name and expressed my feelings on the question!"

"You are aware that Countess Elizabeth has prohibited marriage in the County of Sutherland?"

"The House of God is universal," Sage replied urbanely.

Sellar was in a quandary. His vicious plans had been flouted by the courageous words of the gentle clergyman. Quickly he measured the danger of the situation if he tried to carry out his original intention. He was a frustrated and frightened man as he walked to where the Chief Constable and Loch were standing; but fear of the Countess' reaction, if he failed, was the most important consideration for him.

"What should we do?" asked Loch.

"We'll slaughter the rebellious bastards," Sellar vowed. "Captain O'Mally, tell your men to unsheath their sabres and get ready to charge. The feel of cold steel is the only way to disperse these Jacobite dogs!"

Captain O'Mally cast a careful eye over the ragged Sutherlanders. None of them had weapons. To order the charge would be outright murder.

"Mr. Sellar, my instructions are to preserve the peace, not to commit murder."

Sellar glowered. "Are you disobeying my orders, Captain?"

"My orders do not come from you, Sir. I have the authority to use my own judgment in matters of this kind. This is not a situation that calls for action by my men."

"I'll have you courtmartialed," Sellar snarled.

"I would advise you to withdraw," the Captain suggested, glancing back at the irate Highlanders. "These people don't want you here. They'll . . . !"

Loch interrupted the Captain. "Patrick, let's be sensible. Let these stupid crofters do whatever they want to. Let's leave with the soldiers before we are mobbed!"

Sellar focussed icy eyes on his henchman. "Don't you realize the Countess has outlawed marriage?" he asked curtly. "If we let these people continue we'll be condoning an illegal act."

"I know, I know," Loch agreed quickly. "But the marriage ceremony is without legal meaning in Sutherland anyway. Let's not get our heads broken over such a senseless issue."

"I certainly agree," the Captain declared. "This crowd is getting restless and forming ranks. I don't want my Dragoons to get involved in bloodshed. I suggest we leave immediately."

110

Sellar stared angrily at the defiant Captain. "So be it, but you'll rue disobeying my orders," he growled.

As Loch and the Chief Constable followed Sellar, across the intervening space Captain O'Malley's eyes met David's and a smile of understanding passed between them.

The Irish Dragoons headed back across the ford, and the Reverend Donald Sage stood before David and Jeannie and quickly pronounced them man and wife.

So life at Cavaick took on a new meaning and direction and the hard work of home-building continued.

Some months later while Duncan, David and Jeannie were resting on the heath, the conversation drifted to the people on the beaches.

"David," remarked his father, "your recent forays have provided us with an abundance of food. Some of it would be a god-send to our starving kin."

"Yes, Father. They've been much in my thoughts recently. Let's both make the trip. You'll enjoy seeing the Gow boys, the Soldier and many other old cronies. I'm sure Jeannie . . . "

"No, David!" interjected Duncan. "I don't feel well enough and seeing the desperate plight of my old friends wouldn't help my ailing spirit. Go with my blessing."

Early next morning, David Grant loaded the rough cart he had built on the two fire-blackened wheels salvaged from Sciberscross with bags of oatmeal, venison, rabbits, grouse and pheasants. The night before, he had borrowed Big Tom's horse and having yoked it to the wagon, all was in readiness for the trip.

As he travelled, the heart-rendering conditions at the miserable allotments filled David with despair. Huts, cabins, dugouts and deplorable hovels of all kinds were strung along the stormy shoreline. The rude structures were of every conceivable shape and size. The walls were built of boulders, mud and driftwood. The roofs were of bent, a stiff, wiry grass that is found on the shoreline.

As he drove through the settlement, a group of scrawny children in filthy rags stared curiously from behind rocks at his wagon. When he reined his horse to a halt, they scurried away like frightened rabbits.

The hillfolk who came to gather around presented a dark mass of humanity which the growing shadow of the damned had already embraced — the rocking of the head, swaying of the body, and flailing of the arms showed how easily they had lost physical control; while the crushed spirit, the dirty shawl, the tattered

111

clothing tied with twine, and the slipshod slovenliness of bare feet, or at best, worn out deerskin shoes stuffed with grass, told its own story of their new-found desperation.

David recognized many old friends — George and Alex Gow, Hamish Gunn (nicknamed The Mole) and others from the glen.

He recalled the pride that shone from their eyes as they looked out on their crofts at Rogart, the joy that had followed a lifetime of toil in the earth from which they had earned a hard-won existence. In those days they had something to live for — something to hope for. Now all were gaunt and emaciated and the light had gone from their eyes. They were without hope.

A wave crashed in on the shore splattering the cart with salt spray. David shivered as the blanket of brine gripped at his flesh. The squatters paid no heed to the icy wash — it had become a part of their daily life.

David reached into the cart and hoisted the carcass of a stag to the ground. "I've brought you some food," he said, as the famished crofters gazed in amazement. With Hamish Gunn's help, he carried the carcass to a large flat boulder. "My God," remarked the Mole, "where did it all come from?"

No one answered. The men and women were too busy scurrying around gathering wood for a fire and rocks to sharpen their knives. As the bustle increased more and more of the ragged and hungry left their hovels and hurried toward the cart.

"Where did you find clay to cake in the walls when all I can see is sand?" he asked Geordie Gow.

"Our women carried the clay from a pit more than a mile away," replied Gow.

"Where can I find Angus MacKay?"

"Angus isn't around any more. One day he put out to sea and never came back." Gow spat on the sand. "None of us like the sea but that's where the fish are and we must eat!"

"Why, Geordie, there are many places where they could find a piece of land, the Doll, West Clyne, East Clyne and around Kintradwell."

"I understand, David, you and your family have done well but what guarantee have you that you'll be allowed to stay on the land? Nothing is certain. John Ross, the grocer, brought news that Sellar is at this very moment making arrangements to collect rent from those who settled on the uplands. This will continue until every inch of arable land is in the Countess' hands. No, David, we'll wait to see how successful you're going to be."

112

David bid them all good-bye and urged his horse toward the Soldier's biggin, a quarter of a mile along the coast.

He was greeted by the Soldier, Betsy and the Gipsy. They were dirty, dishevelled and tired. Their eyes were red-rimmed and bloodshot from the acrid peat smoke that permeated their confined living quarters.

David unloaded the food. "This should keep you going for a while." He tried to be cheerful. "We don't want the Gipsy to get so weak he can't play the pipes."

"God bless you, David," cried Betsy. "This will be a real treat! For the past two days we didn't have a fish to eat, it's been so stormy. You're a good man, David Grant. If there's any hope for the Sutherland people it will depend on lads like you."

Little did David realize that while he was saying good-bye to the Soldier a mounted horseman was entering the yard at Cavaick.

113

CHAPTER THIRTEEN

Shades of Angus Gunn

"This is no time to fill the shell. The battle darkens near us; death hovers over the land. Some ghost has fore-warned us of the foe."

CARTHON

RETURNING from a long day's work on the acres of struggling crops, old Duncan found a stranger at Cavaick.

"Are you David Grant?"

"No, David is my son. He is visiting some friends. I'm Duncan Grant."

The man dismounted and tied his horse to a whin bush. "My name is Gordon White. I'm from Dunrobin Castle and I've brought a lease for your signature." He extracted a document from his pocket and handed it to Duncan.

Duncan tried to read the parchment, but his frail eyes weren't good enough. "What does it say?" he asked.

"It's a lease agreement that the owner of this croft will have to sign. The Countess has officially designated this place as Cavaick Croft. The rent is fixed at ten sacks of oatmeal a year."

"That's robbery," Duncan declared. "Surely the land the Countess confiscated from us should satisfy her ambitions and let human decency make amends for the havoc she has already wrought!'

"You still live in Sutherland county and you must rent the land. If the owner doesn't sign the lease in forty-eight hours we'll have to take over your croft in the name of the Countess. Tell your son to report to me at Dunrobin Castle immediately upon his return."

On his way to the Castle, David was convinced of the truthfulness of Gow's statement — maybe the struggle to cultivate Cavaick had been for naught. He recalled Gow's words — "Even if you can pay the first rent the second one will be that much more difficult."

"What else is left?" he asked himself. "I couldn't take Jeannie, the baby and my father to live on the Brora beaches."

Upon presenting himself at the castle David was admitted to the office of Sellar's new assistant, Gordon White.

He placed the document and a leadstick before David, pointing to an imprint which indicated the contract was with the House of Sutherland. "Sign here. The first rent is due one year from today. Just remember ten sacks of oatmeal must be delivered to Dunrobin. Good day, Mr. Grant."

When David returned to Cavaick his father was sorely troubled; he was pale and he trembled as though his doom had already been sealed. "You didn't sign, did you?" he asked.

"Yes, father, I signed. There was no alternative!"

"It won't save us. As a boy I tried to find peace at Fuarach-Coille but we were evicted." He paused in deep distress while a pang of pain convulsed his tired features. "You defied Sellar at the time of your marriage. The lease is simply a blind for things that are to c . . . " Before the sentence was completed the old man slumped forward and would have fallen had not David sprung to his aid.

"Come inside and lie down. You need rest."

He guided his father toward the door. Hardly had Duncan reached the sill when he collapsed and before David could give him support had fallen forward on the stone floor. David gathered the old man in his arms.

"He must have fainted," exclaimed Jeannie.

David put his ear to his father's chest and chafed his hands but it was of no avail. The limp fingers quickly grew stiff and cold.

With tear-filled eyes, David and Jeannie knelt by the cot and prayed until it grew dark. When the crying of the hungry baby could no longer be disregarded Jeannie whispered, "Father's at rest now. I'm sure he's found peace."

David got to his feet, a tumult of fierce emotion raging within him.

Jeannie placed her comforting arms around him; planting a gentle kiss on his lips she remarked, "Come, David, there's no place for anger in the presence of the dead!"

On the second day every exile in the parish of Clyne who had the strength to travel was at the funeral. During the night David dug a deep grave on the hillside overlooking Broughrobbie. As the sun dipped to the western horizon bathing the valley in shadows, Duncan was lowered into the grave. Jeannie, David, and many of the people from the beach community wept silently as the Soldier recited the 23rd Psalm.

Duncan Grant's passing wasn't just the death of one man. As a boy he had witnessed the Highlands being conquered and ravaged on the field of Culloden in 1746. He knew that what he saw on that fateful day wasn't merely the defeat of the Highland army but the revelation of the larger truth that Scotland had forfeited her proud position among the peoples of the world and had ceased forever to be honoured as a nation.

Duncan Grant had witnessed the coming of the 'Black Act' which deprived the Highlander of his traditional garb and his claymore. Later in the County of Sutherland, he had seen his religion and the right to marriage become pawns in the grand design of Elizabeth.

The life of Duncan Grant was a symbol of man's struggle to exist through one of the most vicious land-grabbing and soul-destroying periods ever known, a period that overthrew the fundamental patriarchial laws of property in Scotland.

Duncan Grant had sent his three sons to protect this right by fighting in a strange land ten thousand miles away. The day on which two of them lay dead on that foreign field he had been evicted from his home — evicted by the same Countess who had vowed protection for those who were unable to go to war.

In total, the death of Duncan Grant was but another act in the diabolical drama that was to heap degradation upon degradation while the Countess of Sutherland was asserting her claim to the whole creation of God in Sutherland for her private use. What did it matter that all the rest of God's creatures forfeited their right to life in the process?

Duncan Grant's death was one more contribution towards the success of Cumberland's plan for the complete annihilation of the Gaelic-speaking people.

When the earth had closed the grave and the mourners withdrew to Cavaick for refreshments and to drink a toast to the spiritual journey of their departed clansman, Jeannie and Betsy remained to erect a little fence of whins, broom and heather to protect the burial ground. They gathered clumps of wild primroses, buttercups and bluebells and carefully planted them over the fresh mound of earth.

"Peace to your soul, Duncan Grant," said Betsy MacKay. "Of all the land that is rightfully yours, only this mound can you call your own."

When the two women walked down the hillside, they found the men sitting in front of the cottage discussing the question foremost in everyone's mind — the evictions.

The Braggart raised his powerful voice. "Gossip from the castle says that the parishes of Kildonan and Strathnaver will be evicted before the May term!"

"Yes," the Soldier agreed bitterly. "If those glens are evicted the Countess with her final fiery sweep will have destroyed the homes of twenty-five thousand innocent souls and a great tradition will have perished from the earth. Ten tons of gold," he continued, "couldn't pay for the poor wretches' suffering." He looked around the circle and his voice broke. "God alone knows what's to become of them."

Jeannie called the men to supper. David held up a warning hand. "I'd rather we didn't continue our talks. This day has already seen much sorrow."

But it was useless to ignore the uncertain future. The women were thinking and talking. "There's trouble brewing with the fisherfolk," the Soldier announced. "We're being looked upon as poachers. For some reason the shoals of herring aren't running past the beach any more and the fishers insist that we have brought them bad luck. They think someone among us with an evil eye has scared the fish away."

"Oh, Soldier, you're talking like a drunken dotard," chided David. "The fishers aren't stupid enough to put the blame on us for the missing herring."

"Maybe I'm drunk. But don't forget that in the old days when the fisherwives peddled their wares in the glen, they wouldn't enter our homes. You remember how they would stop a good distance away and shout:

'Herring, fresh herring, two a penny,
If you don't be quick, you won't get any'."

The Soldier put a friendly hand on the Gipsy's shoulder. "They have decided that this lad is the one with the evil eye. They claim his music has scared the herring away. If the fish don't soon return, they say they'll sacrifice the Gipsy to the sea gods."

David wrinkled his brow. Endeavouring to understand the link between the missing herring and his friend, he determined to go to Kildonan and visit with Wemyss Sutherland. Wemyss was well-read and he could know of some specific reason for the disappearance of the herring.

David's first meeting with Wemyss had taken place under rather strange circumstances. On that memorable occasion, intent on pursuit of a stag, he had wandered into Kildonan. Darkness was closing in and snow was falling. Realizing the danger, he was searching for a place to shelter when he saw a shaft of light guttering dimly through the darkness. Weary and tired, he staggered up to the door and rapped on the panel completely unaware that the house was owned by Wemyss Sutherland, the taxman for the Countess in Kildonan.

The white-haired Wemyss and his wife made him welcome; they handed him a brimming cup of Highland whisky, served bowls of mutton broth and finished with prime slices of venison and baked potatoes.

Later, as David and his host sat chatting in the glow of the peat-fire the conversation drifted to the evictions. "I'm opposed to Sellar's ruthless actions!" the taxman stated. "I'm sure the Countess is unaware of what is taking place."

"You're a very loyal man, Mr. Taxman."

"I ought to be. My father, my grandfather and my great-grandfather were honoured by the House of Sutherland. There was evidence of irritation in his voice as he continued. "I feel that until events prove otherwise I'll remain loyal!" He paused. "If I had any proof that a threat was contemplated against the people of Kildonan and Strathnaver I would resign. I have repeatedly urged Sellar to release the grain and other provisions from the Castle, and feed the poor creatures who are living like animals on the Brora beaches. So far he has refused."

For a moment both men had sat gazing into the smouldering fire.

David broke the silence. "Rumour has it that something big is taking place at Dunrobin!"

"Something big? What do you mean?" demanded Sutherland with a withering frown.

"Sellar is preparing to evict the people from Kildonan and Strathnaver!"

118

"Where did you hear such rubbish?"

Noting the taxman's indignation, David dropped the matter. He knew how far apart they were in their thinking; and time alone could prove the seriousness of the situation.

During the months that followed, David made occasional trips to Kildonan. He enjoyed visiting Sutherland and his wife. Their home, Corrie-Loskin, was a substantial dwelling set on a a large, park-like estate. Stretching to the west, the north and to the south were fifty acres of fertile land surrounded by a border of stately Lombardy poplars. To the east, extensive farm and grazing lands were protected by a range of rolling hills that separated the farm from the sea.

Wemyss' seventy years in the parish had taught him not to meddle in the personal and spiritual affairs of the crofters. At the time of the evictions he had made no effort to conceal from those at Dunrobin his anger at the treatment of the crofters in Rogart and Clyne. Following David's earlier visit, he went to Dunrobin Castle to determine the Countess' intentions respecting Kildonan and Strathnaver. Sellar and Loch assured him that the people in these glens would never be molested. Wemyss, in turn, relayed this information to his people and assured them that they had nothing to fear.

After Duncan's funeral, David Grant visited Corrie-Loskin intending to discuss the herring shortage with Wemyss. He was greeted at the gate by Donald MacLeod, a thick-set muscular man who was the chief mason at Dunrobin Castle. Together they proceeded up the path.

"Well! This is a doubly pleasant surprise," exclaimed Wemyss as he opened the door. "Two friends calling at one time. Come in. Come in." After directing the men to a couch by the fire, he poured three glasses of grog.

As he handed the brimming glass to MacLeod, Wemyss sensed that something was wrong.

"Anything troubling you, Donald?"

"I've been discharged, Wemyss!"

"For heaven's sake. Why were you discharged? I thought you were the master mason — probably the only one there."

MacLeod nodded.

"I accused Sellar of plotting to evict the people of Kildonan and Strathnaver."

Sutherland stepped back in amazement. "You must be mad, MacLeod."

119

"Careful, Wemyss," David cautioned. "I told you about the rumour."

"It's no rumour," MacLeod interjected. "I came to warn you, Wemyss, that active preparations are under way."

Wemyss leaned forward and looked earnestly at his friend. "Forgive my rudeness, Donald, but it can't be. Only a fortnight ago I had assurance from Sellar and Loch that our people would not be evicted. I couldn't believe what you are telling me!"

MacLeod drained his jug. "If you weren't blinded by loyalty to the Countess, you'd see what's taking place under your nose. Strangers from the south have constantly visited Dunrobin and what they've been discussing hasn't gone unheard. Servants have big ears!

"Were you aware that over £300,000 have been subscribed by the overseas colonies to aid the distressed Highlands? Lord Trevelyan in England is responsible for its distribution. Tons of meal, and potatoes purchased in England by these funds, have been lying in the castle dungeons for months. Yesterday precious quantities were fed to the swine and poultry. The food had become so rancid in the damp cellers that the pigs refused to eat. I understand Sellar gave instructions to dump it in the Firth. All this, while the true owners of the soil are living on shell-fish, fish heads and sea-weed, their ministers answer their supplications and famished cries by telling them that 'the Lord had a controversy with the land for the people's wickedness and in His Providence and in His Mercy, he has sent this scourge to bring them to repentance.' How could I hold my tongue, Wemyss, in face of such damnable blasphemy? There is a time when blind loyalty can no longer be allowed to destroy the soul's freedom."

"I heard about the food," said Wemyss. He gazed thoughtfully at MacLeod. "A lot of it came from America, didn't it?"

"Aye, and it's a pity they don't know how it's being used."

Donald eased forward and looked intently at his two companions. "More than that, David — I heard this morning that the Gunns are in revolt. They haven't forgotten how Angus was treated in Sciberscross. They have had their fill of the Countess and today they routed a Lincolnshire sheepfarmer by the name of Reid who has been scouting sheep lands. When he wouldn't get off their property, Angus' brother Hugh, with the help of four crofters, drove him from the glen. The Gunns are riled and determined to fight for their land.

"When news of the Gunn's actions reached Dunrobin, Sellar

120

swore in over a hundred constables and expressed a message to the 21st Foot at Fort George. There is blood to be spilt in Kildonan, Wemyss, and I don't like it. The natives have been pushed to the brink — they're in an ugly mood."

David felt the blood course through his veins. He wanted to rise and cheer, then to burst out of the house and marshall the men on the coast to march with the Gunns. Hatred of the House of Sutherland welled up within him. Again he saw the vision of Angus Gunn at the rent court which his father had conjured before him so often. His thoughts were interrupted by MacLeod.

"Wemyss, my friend, I've known you better than any man in the parish. You're symbolic of all that's straight-forward, honest and loyal. These are valuable attributes if you are dealing with honorable people, but Sellar and Loch are not honorable. Your own trusting nature has blinded you to their treachery."

Wemyss' white-thatched head dropped dejectedly to his chest, he was unable to answer.

"There are few days left, Wemyss. One of the gillies at the castle told me that he overheard Sellar boast he was going to seize the best part of the glen for his own use."

"I've seen strangers in the parish with Sellar and Loch!" Sutherland mused. "I understand they were examining the site for a new road." He licked his dry lips. "I just can't believe it."

MacLeod rose from his chair shaking his head slowly. "I'm sorry, my friend. I only hope your eyes will be opened before it's too late." He glanced at David. "Good-bye, Grant. I'm going to keep close to what's taking place. I hope the rest of Sutherland can escape the suffering of the people from Rogart and Clyne." Turning to Wemyss he concluded, "Perhaps the words of the Brahan Seer will enlighten you." He held out his hand. David took it and gathered strength from the firmness of his friend's grip. Wemyss took Donald's hand, with his left he gripped him firmly by the shoulder and led him across the room to the open door.

"Thank you, Donald, and good luck." He stood for a moment watching his friend disappear slowly along the footpath in the evening twilight. As he turned back into the room, his precarious position between loyalty to the House of Sutherland and his bonds of kinship with the people was painfully borne in upon him.

David learned from Wemyss that the disappearance of the herring was nothing new.

"About fifty years ago," said Wemyss, "when I was a lad courting my wife, we often climbed to the top of the Robbers' Roost. On a summer's evening we would watch the shoals of herring skipping across the surface of the North Sea like millions of sparkling diamonds. Then suddenly there were no more herring — they just disappeared. My father remembered a similar experience."

"Why would the fishers want to blame the Gipsy?" asked David.

"That is not ususual, David. The fisherfolk have a different way of life from the crofters. They depend on the sea — on the fish, the tides and the winds. They know the sea and must never offend the spirits of the great realm which brings them their livelihood. Some people in the world believe that they can't die except when the tide's out and they can't be properly born till high tide. Those who get their living from the sea believe that something or someone has offended the spirits of the sea so much that they have driven away the herring. They think the Gipsy with his strange music is most likely to have been the one who did it.

"This is something like the second sight of the Brahan Seer. We'll go to the library and check on what Donald said about the prophecies!"

After supper they moved into the den that served as Sutherland's office and library.

"I've heard of the Brahan Seer, but I've never read any of his prophecies," David remarked. "How did he receive the gift?"

From his bookshelf Wemyss selected *"The Prophecies of Coinneach Odhar,"* written in Gaelic and subtitled, *"The Brahan Seer."* "There's an explanation in the book of prophecies," he replied, as he sat down in a nearby chair. "Let me read it to you."

Coinneach Odhar, otherwise, Kenneth MacKenzie, was born at Baile-ne-Cille on the Island of Lewis about two hundred years ago. When he was a little boy, Kenneth received a magical stone under very supernatural circumstances. One summer night in Uig, Kenneth's mother was tending her cattle in a shealing on the side of a ridge called Cnoceothail. The shealing overlooks the burying-ground of Baile-ne-Cille. As she watched, all the graves in the churchyard opened. Then she observed a vast multitude of ghost-like people of all ages, from the newborn to the grey-haired sage, rising from their tomb and flitting in every direction. After about an hour of the weird vigil,

122

the spirits began to return. When all were apparently back in their graves, and the earth closed upon them as before, Kenneth's mother, on scanning the burying-place more closely, noticed one grave still open. Being a courageous woman, she determined to ascertain the cause of this singular circumstance. Hastening to the grave she placed her 'cudgel' athwart its mouth (for she had heard it said that no spirit could enter the grave while interference was upon it) and sat down to await the result of her experiment. In a few minutes she noticed the spectre of a fair lady coming in from the north. Upon arrival, the fair one addressed herself to Mrs. MacKenzie. 'Lift thy distaff from off my grave and let me enter my dwelling of the dead,' she pleaded.

'I shall do so,' answered Mrs. MacKenzie, 'when you explain what detained you so long after your neighbours.'

'That you shall hear,' the ghost replied. 'My journey was much longer than the others — I had to go all the way to Norway, the land of my birth. I am the daughter of a long dead King of Norway. Drowned while bathing in that country, my body drifted to sea, the tides brought it to this shore and the seafolk interred me in this grave. If you'll be good enough to remove your distaff, as a small reward for your intrepidity and courage, I shall give you a valuable secret.'

Mrs. MacKenzie removed her distaff; but before the spirit disappeared into the black earth, she instructed, 'Go and find in yonder lake a small round blue stone. Give it to your son, Kenneth, who by its magic shall be able to predict many future events.'

The woman did as requested, found the stone and gave it to her son. Immediately he received the talisman gift of divination, Kenneth began to make remarkable auguries and soon his reputation had spread the country round. Many of his prophecies have already been fulfilled.

"He predicted the Battle of Drummossie Moor, didn't he?" said David.

"Yes," agreed Wemyss. "It appears that the Seer at one time visited Drummossie Moor and, while passing over that part now known as the Battlefield of Culloden, he told his associates of the slaughter that would take place." Sutherland paused as he turned over the pages. "Here it is."

Oh, Drummossie! Before many more generations have passed thy bleak moor shall be stained with the best blood of the North; scores of Highland heads will be scattered like turnips among the gory heather. Fortunate are we who will not live to see that terrible day, for it will be followed by an orgy of burning, death and destruction that will annihilate many of the relatives and descendants of the Highland clans.

Sutherland fell silent but he continued to peruse page after page of the seer's prophesies. David watched the old man read silently on. The cozy glow from the open fireplace was so comforting that at times David dozed, but underlying all his physical comfort was a sense of dejection and despair. Donald MacLeod's news had troubled him greatly. He recalled his own unfortunate encounter with Sellar and he knew that the man was capable of any type of treachery.

Wemyss glanced at David. "This may be the prophecy MacLeod mentioned." He rose and slowly paced the floor as he read.

The day will come to Sutherland when the natives of the soil will be forced by their chief to submit their whole land to foreign proprietors. Under the strangers, the whole of Sutherland will become a huge game and sheep preserve. During this time, all the native settlements in Sutherland will become de-populated and so utterly destroyed that the crow of a cock or the cackle of a hen will not be heard in the County. The natives who survive the treachery of their chief and the scourge of the foreigners will be forced to emigrate to lands in a New World, now unknown, but which shall later be discovered beyond the Western Ocean. After many generations have passed, sheep will disappear from Sutherland and their existence will be so thoroughly forgotten that a man finding the jawbone of a sheep will be unable to tell to what animal it had belonged. When that day comes the progeny of the native people will again return to the glens to take undisturbed possession of the land of their ancestors.

David's mind had fixed on the part of the prophecy dealing with the emigration to lands in the Western Ocean.

"Surely life in those lands couldn't be more difficult than the beach where the poor crofters are striving to survive," he declared.

Wemyss stopped pacing and shelved the book. He smacked his palms together. "I've got to go to Dunrobin Castle. I must have a showdown with Sellar and Loch. If they mean to proceed with this wickedness I must warn the people of Kildonan and Strathnaver."

124

CHAPTER FOURTEEN

Kildonan Evictions

"Arise, winds of autumn, arise; blow along the heath!
streams of the mountains roar! roar, tempests, in the
groves of my oaks! walk through broken clouds, O moon!
show thy pale face, at intervals! bring to my mind the
night, when all my children fell."

THE SONGS OF SELMA

THE NEXT day was one of activity in all parts of Sutherland. At the Castle, Sellar made preparations for the threatened attack by the Gunns on Dunrobin. The Gunns were gathering in Strathnaver. David Grant was on his way to the coast to discuss the turn of events with his friends from Sciberscross and Strath Brora. Wemyss Sutherland had saddled his horse and was off to Dunrobin to learn for himself what Sellar's intentions were.

Sellar, fearful of coming events, was waiting anxiously as the courier from Fort George clattered into the Castle courtyard and headed straight for his office.

He and Loch were sitting at a huge table before a crackling open fire when the dusty rider entered. Snatching the dispatch from the courier's hand, Sellar waved him from his office. "Good!" he remarked with a smile, "the 21st will be here tomorrow afternoon. Along with our armed constables, that should be enough to fix the Gunns. We'll head north to meet them as soon as the military arrive."

Meanwhile David Grant was at the coast. He gathered together the men from Rogart and Clyne to determine what action they were prepared to take to support the Gunns. No one accepted the challenge and David discovered how far had fallen the pride of his people, how abject was their misery and mental lethargy. The youth who would have supported the Gunns had died on the battlefield of South Africa. Those who could summon the energy had long since left for neighbouring Caithness or the lowlands to serve as cattle drovers, labourers, or in the army. The few who remained had no desire to fight. Insurmountable odds, and the hypocrisy of those who praised God and treachery in the same breath, left them confused, frightened and without hope.

David returned to Cavaick to consider his own position. How did he stand with the Gunns? How far was he prepared to sacrifice the safety of Jeannie and little Fiona through a rash act on his own part? The chances were too slim for the success of the Gunns' foolish challenge to Sellar's authority. He was saved from making his decision when into the yard drove Wemyss Sutherland and, half an hour later, Donald MacLeod. Donald had seen Wemyss drive off the main road ahead of him and had assumed he was heading up the Brora for Cavaick.

The news was grim. Sellar was preparing to murder the Gunns. They hadn't a chance against him. Sellar would use revolt as an excuse for their extermination with police and military might. MacLeod reported that a messenger had been sent to Kildonan to warn the Gunns and that he was heading home to make ready for the immediate removal of his family from Kildonan.

"It's a blessing the warning came in time," remarked Wemyss. "Had we resisted, Sellar would have rejoiced in our complete destruction."

"A bootless boast," said MacLeod gloomily. "What does it matter? Evil has come to us like snow upon the mountains, unsought and unsent for. A chial! A Highland soldier's mother is of less value than a grouse or plover, a sheep or a cow, for they cannot be shot for pleasure like the former, nor fattened to feed the southern market like the latter. It's for the Government that treats us thus our soldiers fight and die! Is Samhach An Obair Dol A Dholaidh!"

"Alas yes! Silent is the progress of ruin," Wemyss remarked, repeating the proverb. "But had Rogart and Clyne been in Tipperary, at what premium would the lives of Sellar and Loch be insured?"

Next day the 21st Foot with artillery and fresh reinforcement of constables marched to Kildonan. There was no bloodshed;

126

the Gunns, realizing their position as hopeless, had removed their stock and personal effects to a place of safety, and declined to engage or even provoke the military.

Meanwhile, at the Castle, Sellar was studying a rough map of Kildonan and Strathnaver indicating cottages and outbuildings.

"We're going to have trouble," he remarked. "They've taken the law into their own hands. That's all the excuse we need to make them remember the day they ran afoul of Patrick Sellar. Have the cannon on the battlements primed and get the constables ready for action."

A manservant entered the room. "Wemyss Sutherland awaits your pleasure," he announced.

Sellar looked quizzically at Loch.

"Show our friend from Kildonan in."

When Wemyss stepped through the door, his usually florid face was pale. Loch and Sellar affected an air of cordiality. "Welcome to Dunrobin, Wemyss."

Sutherland ignored the greeting. He came right to the point. "It's reported you're preparing to evict Kildonan and Strathnaver."

Sellar pursed his lips between his thumb and forefinger and walked to the fireplace before he asked, "Did MacLeod visit you?"

"Yes. He was on his way to Strathnaver. He told me he had been dismissed."

"The Reverend Sage is also a friend of yours."

"MacLeod, Sage and I went to school together," came the bold reply. "We've been close friends ever since."

A fierce curse exploded from Sellar's lips. "You're a damn fool to associate with such subversive scoundrels!"

Wemyss was startled by the venom in the voice. He gazed unflinchingly as the Countess' agent raged on.

"You are aware, Sutherland, that Donald MacLeod is a Jacobite, that his house is used as a shelter for dissenters and outlaws. As for Donald Sage, he's nothing but a fraudulent rogue who has no right to wear the garb of a clergyman."

"You are speaking of my friends," Sutherland said coldly. "Please remember that."

"Your fellow traitors, Mr. Sutherland?" Loch interjected.

Sellar laughed loudly.

For a moment Wemyss stood in helpless dismay. He saw all the loyalty which his family had given to the Earl's service over three generations dead at his feet. 'You misbegotten young reprobate. You don't know what loyalty is. Your service is to the devil.

127

You have disowned Almighty God and the human race,' Wemyss thought to himself, his knuckles white against the oaken table as he strove to stay under control. His mind was in turmoil, he was searching for words to describe the repugnance he felt for these men. His frame shook as he exerted his willpower to keep from dashing forward and dealing a blow at the supercilious smile which lingered on Sellar's face.

Forcing composure Wemyss spoke calmly, "I came to learn at first hand your intentions regarding Kildonan and Strathnaver, but, let me make it known that nothing justifies your foul accusations against Donald MacLeod for I know it's a damnable lie! As for the Reverend Sage, he cares not what you think of him. He's always had the love and respect of the people of the glen and all others who believe more in honesty and decency than the questionable virtues of wealth and power. I would be careful of repeating your foul comtempt in the glen."

"You disloyal ingrate," Sellar thundered. "Are you threatening me?"

Wemyss shook his head. His voice was steely cold. He was under perfect control. "I only speak the truth. During my long years in the Earl's and the Countess' service, I have carried out their orders faithfully and well and at the same time maintained my self respect. I would be a blind fool if I couldn't visualize what you have in mind."

"What do you mean?"

"I didn't believe Donald when he said you and Loch were land-grabbing pirates. I came here to find out for myself. Now I am beginning to understand why the Countess and her Marquis live in London; it's much easier to employ depraved creatures like you to steal the inheritance of my people — no other men could be more fittingly employed to carry out their despicable instructions."

"Watch your mouth," Sellar snarled. He stood up to Wemyss. "Does this mean that you intend to oppose us?"

Alone and helpless, Sutherland faced the brutal man whose whisky-laden breath irritated his nostrils.

"Aye, I'll oppose you. I'll stand with the people of Kildonan and Strathnaver. I know that you have decided to evict them. I also know that any appeal I might make for justice would have no effect." The old Highlander threw his plaid proudly across his chest. "For two years you have cunningly awaited public reaction to the evictions in Rogart and Clyne and the murder of many

128

unfortunate Highland souls. The Countess should hang her head in shame for recruiting our young men for Africa so that she could strike the aged and infirm."

In calm and scathing indignation, Wemyss recounted the horrors that resulted from the first evictions and the pitiful existence that the Sutherlanders were leading on the cold beach. He denounced his listeners as miserable scum not fit to associate with honorable men. He drew his resignation from his pocket, threw it at Sellars' feet and strode from the room. Wemyss Sutherland had cast his vote for loyalty to humanity.

He knew what to expect. The notices told the crofters that arrears would no longer be forgiven, that all rents owing over the past five years must be paid to date. The penalty for non-payment — eviction.

Sutherland quietly prepared for the worst. He wrapped his precious books in a heavy cloth. With other personal effects he placed them in a small shed in the woods with a few sacks of meal, warm blankets, pots, pans and other valuable necessities.

One afternoon in mid-June, a group of mounted men and carts were seen approaching Corrie-Loskin. In front rode Sellar, Loch, Atkinson, Marshall and the Chief Constable.

Sutherland watched their approach from the door of his house and placed a protecting arm around his wife's shoulder.

At the garden gate the constables detached themselves from the train and formed a semi-circle behind their leaders. In the distance, a company of Irish Fusiliers approached at a trot.

Wemyss' wife stood nervously holding her husband's hand. They had lived in dread of this moment.

Sellar scanned the old couple with an indifferent smile. Often he had exchanged pleasantries with each of them at this very gate. But that was when Wemyss was loyal and useful. Today there was no exchange of greetings. The warrant ordering the eviction was read and Sellar's henchmen stormed into the house and set it on fire. Then they walked away to watch Corrie-Loskin being gutted. A light breeze fanned the flames from whose bowels a multitude of sparks swirled upward to drift through the smoky air. Wemyss approached Sellar. His long grey hair was matted with perspiration and clung in knots about his temples, his eyes were red and wild, his whole stance proclaimed the fierce pride and love that he had for the land.

129

"You, Patrick Sellar. Only God can judge you and to your dying moment you'll live in the fear of what that judgment will be."

"You and those howling squatters better be gone in twenty-four hours or we'll start shooting," snapped Sellar.

Arm in arm the aged couple joined the burnt-out crofters who had come to Corrie-Loskin in the hope that the taxman could be of assistance. "We must leave this glen," Wemyss told his countrymen. "Gather up what food and tools you can carry; to-morrow at dawn we will take our departure."

He paused, knowing he should say more. "I know the hate in your hearts. I have never felt it before, but it's with me today. Nurse it well and never let it die until this terrible wrong is righted and we come home again."

And so it happened that the evicted natives of Kildonan and Strathnaver were driven to the shores of the North Sea to take up a new way of life on narrow rocky strips, promontories, cliffs, and deep crevices. One man joked that his plot of land was so small that he could pick it up in a creel and carry it away if there was any dispute over its boundaries. In many places the land was so steep that while the parents were hoeing, the children held the soil together with their bodies or it would have blown into the sea. Often it did, and every spring the patient Sutherlanders travelled to the fertile side of a ravine, dug fresh soil and carried it on their backs to their wretched holdings.

The cows and goats they had brought with them wandered back inland and were impounded by the shepherds now working the land for Sellar, Marshall and Atkinson. On other occasions the animals wandered by night and fell over the cliffs to be drowned and washed away.

In the face of these difficulties the people of Kildonan and Strathnaver built their dwellings and grimly accepted their new environment. Around them, heather and broom grew apologetically among the rocks and boulders and a stream flowed over the precipice to drop a cascade of white foam into the rolling breakers far below.

At Cavaick, David Grant again loaded his cart with all the food he could spare and drove down the rocky road along the sea cliff until he reached the new settlement built of mud, drift-wood and rocks, matted over with divots to keep off the rain. It amazed him to see children tied to boulders by lengths of heather rope. Along the way he saw an old man laboring wearily in a patch of rocky ground.

130

"Why are these little ones tethered like animals?" he demanded.

"It's because of the angry blast! My little granddaughter, Jessie, was blown from the cliff and dashed into the sea. It also happened to the Elder's lassie."

Beside a miserable shack David found Wemyss building a heather and whin fence around a garden plot twelve feet square. He was so engrossed in his task that he failed to hear the cart approach. When he turned, David noticed that Sutherland was no longer a proud, erect Highlander. He was an old man with a worn and wasted face and frame and listless eyes. He extended a shrivelled hand.

"David," he said, "so you've come."

"Yes, only recently I heard of your plight. News travels slow in this part of the country."

"You've brought us some food."

"Yes, Wemyss. I know it's not enough. Come, help me unload."

When the food had been distributed Wemyss remarked, "I feel responsible for bringing them here. Yet, what could I have done? I've written the Countess many letters, pleading with her for relief."

"Did you ever get a reply?"

"Yes, she advised that any complaints should be taken up with Patrick Sellar, that he had her complete confidence."

"Look at these biggins," the old man continued. "Everyone toiled like slaves to get them built. The young and the old, the well and the sick, even those heavy with child. The women collected soil in their aprons and carried it from the banks of the stream to make their garden plots. While the older people laboured, the children got water from the stream to wet the earth and keep the soil from blowing away."

At that moment Wemyss hailed a tall lean Highlander. "Did you get any food, Tom?"

"Nothing! The storekeeper informed us that free food required written authority from an approved minister. Though the Reverend Sage explained that he was an ordained minister his name is not listed on the Countess' special list as a minister who has authority to approve relief."

"We also learned that restrictions have been placed on the mussel beds at the Mound."

"What do you mean?" David demanded. "How could anyone put restrictions on the mussel shoals? They're in tidal waters? No one has a claim on them."

"The Countess thinks she has," replied Tom. "No trespassing signs are posted along the beach. Guards armed with guns and dogs patrol the area. Poor Kate Urquhart and Bessie MacRae couldn't understand because the signs were in English. They had creels loaded with mussels when the bailiffs stopped them. Quick as a wink they slit the shoulder straps and the poor women fell forward on the rocks. *Kate was heavy with child.*"

"My God, what brutality," declared Wemyss.

"What happened next then?" asked David.

"They were dragged off to Golspie jail. On the third day Kate gave birth to a stillborn child on the stone floor of the prison. Eventually they were summoned to Dunrobin and told they had two days to get themselves and their kin out of Sutherland County."

In the fall Patrick Sellar rode his coach-and-four over the new bridges and highways Gower and his Countess had built. He was on his way to make his semi-annual report to the Countess. He enjoyed these trips. His expenses were all cared for and he stayed at the most fashionable hotels in central London. With the extra money the Marquis usually placed in his hand, he had his pick of the most desirable wenches in town.

"My Lord and Lady," he began, after they were all seated in the ornate private library, "according to your instructions all the crofters have now been evicted from the glens and straths of Sutherland and fences enclose the lands. The hills, forests, bottom lands, and mussel beds are being protected by guards with dogs and guns twenty-four hours a day."

He handed the Countess his report and after glancing quickly at it she passed it to the Marquis and continued her interrogation.

"What about the sheep farmers, are they making progress?"

"They're doing very well, your Ladyship. Thousands of sheep are grazing on the hills of Rogart and Strath Brora. Thousands more are on their way from the south." He referred to his report. "You'll note, Countess, for the first time receipts from rentals are greater than the expense of operating the estate. Your Ladyship will be interested to know that those who have leased the land presented me with your personal letters of approval.

"The first to arrive were Marshall and Atkinson — two North-cumberland sheep farmers. They brought several thousand Cheviots. You are aware of course that they will occupy over one hundred and twenty miles of grazing land. Starting at Loch Naver, they come east by Loch Shin, Sciberscross and other smaller settlements. We evicted over five hundred crofters to make room for their sheep.

"James Hall of Roxburgh also arrived. In keeping with your instructions this gentleman has grazing rights, starting at Blackwater Falls through the valley of the Brora, to the Ford bridge, including both sides of the river and loch. Thirty townships were evicted to feed Mr. Hall's sheep."

The Countess and her husband gazed lovingly at each other and smiled.

Suddenly an angry cloud changed the Countess' features. "What about the evicted squatters?" she demanded. "I understand they still clutter up our beaches."

"Yes, your Ladyship. We tried to starve them out. Many died during the winter, but others are clinging to the rocks like barnacles. They're . . ."

"Seriously, Sellar, I expected better things from you."

Sellar's heart sank as the Countess rose to her feet and paced the polished parquet floor. She spoke sharply to the Marquis. "Granville, it's imperative that we act before these gipsies deplete our fish and game." Her icy blue eyes glared. "Well, Sellar, do you think you can handle these instructions a little more efficiently than you did my orders banning the marriage of the Sutherlanders?"

Sellar flushed. "Damn that David Grant", he thought. "I was too easy on him. First I let him settle away from the coast, then he defied me and got married. I should have run him into the sea."

"We can't stop people taking a personal oath of attachment," he protested. "We can keep them out of the churches, except for those who attend the church your Ladyship demanded they adopt, but we . . ."

Sellar was rescued from his dilemma by Gower.

"Never mind, Patrick. You've done a good job getting the crofters out of the glen. We can't expect you to work miracles." Sellar was relieved at the Marquis' encouraging words. "There's too much adverse publicity wafting into the newspapers about what's taking place in Sutherland, Elizabeth. It would be wise to tread more carefully for a little while. I spoke with the Earl of Selkirk a few days ago. He has some grand colonization plans for the New World — for Canada. We'll work with him."

CHAPTER FIFTEEN

We Shall Return No More

"Farewell, ye rocks of Ardven! Ye deer! and ye streams of the hills!
We shall return no more. Our tombs are distant far."
CARRIC-THURA

ONE HUNDRED and forty years before the Sutherland evictions, two adventurous Frenchmen, Chouart Sieur des Grosailliers and Pierre Esprit Radisson, first unlocked the secrets of the vast land lying to the west of Hudson's Bay. They returned to Quebec with a fabulous fortune in furs, but ran afoul of the French Governor when they refused to give him half their profit. As a result of this unhappy experience and to obtain money to develop their fur trade, the two traders returned to France. Here they also failed. However, their fantastic stories of the limitless quantity of furs to be collected in the Hudson's Bay region reached the ears of the English ambassador at the Court of Louis XIV and the two coureurs des bois were quickly whisked to the court of Charles II. There, darkened and bronzed by sun and wind, dressed in furs and wearing buckskin mocassins they told their story to Prince Rupert. An interview with the king followed; and it was in such conditions that there came into being the Governor and Company of Adventurers of England Trading to Hudson's Bay, where Henry Hudson, the English navigator and explorer, had been deserted by his crew and left to perish in 1611.

King Charles II's dear and entirely beloved cousin Prince Rupert, together with other Noblemen, Knights and Squires, could hardly have been given greater concessions or more dictatorial power. In addition to the sole control to trade in the vast territory, the company was awarded rights to all the minerals and animal life in the land, to all the birds in the air and to all the fish in the rivers and lakes. The company was given power to build forts and ships and to man and arm them, to make laws for the management of its affairs, to establish courts, levy fines and to send prisoners back to England for trial or punishment. Prince Rupert became the first governor of the new company and the English were firmly established in the Canadian fur industry.

Establishing the new company was not without problems. The French, unwilling to relinquish their stake in the rich resources of the North, sent their fur traders and trappers into the Hudson's Bay territory, with instructions to destroy the English forts and disrupt their fur trading activities. Even when the territory was ceded to Britain by France through the Treaty of Utrecht, French-Canadian traders from Quebec moved farther and farther north plundering the English company's rich fur lands. There was also opposition from the North-West Company, formed by a group of independent Scottish traders in Montreal. This company petitioned the Crown for a perpetual monopoly of the trade in the remote west beyond the boundaries of the land granted to the Gentlemen Adventurers. The refusal of this petition signalled a clash between the North-West Company and the Hudson's Bay Company and the ensuing conflict set in motion an adventure that plucked many of the evicted Sutherlanders from the Brora beaches.

It took one more event to bring the picture into clear focus, however.

The Earl of Selkirk's son, Thomas, of the Red River Valley fame, was a boy of six at the time Captain Paul Jones raided his father's estate on St. Mary's Isle in the River Dee. Paul Jones had been born and bred in Kirkcudbright, only a short distance from St. Mary's Isle and was convinced that he himself was the natural son of the Scottish nobleman. His real intention was to threaten to carry the young Selkirk away as a hostage and so compel the Earl to acknowledge him as his true son. Unfortunately, the Earl was not in residence. The Captain did, however, take possession of the household plate and carried it on board the *Ranger*.

So Thomas was the only surviving son, and when his father passed away on May 24, 1799, he was left the ancestral estates and became the fifth Earl of Selkirk and a very worthwhile stockholder in the Hudson's Bay Company.

135

In his father's library, he discovered a most inspiring book — Alexander MacKenzie's exciting story of his journeys to the Arctic and Pacific. This book described a tremendous country and the fascinating deeds that transpired there. Enthralled by the story the adventurous young Earl journeyed to Canada, and spent the winter of 1803-4 in Montreal.

His cordial personality, suave tongue and aristocratic demeanour made him many friends. He had little difficulty convincing the wealthy merchants and Highland stockholders in the North-West Company that he was interested only in establishing a colony in Nova Scotia or Prince Edward Island where the Sutherland evictees could find a haven.

In Montreal Selkirk made the acquaintance of Colin Robertson, a keen-minded, energetic Highlander who had spent many years in Manitoba as an agent for the North-West Company. Robertson's enthusiasm convinced Selkirk that the vast prairie could be changed into farm land that would support thousands of colonists. The following day he invited Colin to the Dillon Hotel. "Colin," he said, "if you had your choice of all the land in that prairie, where would you plant a colony?"

"At the fork of the Red and Assiniboine Rivers, your lordship." Robertson swept his arm in a semi-circle as if he was trying to encompass a limitless expanse of territory. "It's virgin land. It's fertile and it's easily cleared. It's at the crossroads from east to west and from north to south. Some day a great city will be there."

Selkirk grasped Colin by the shoulder. "How would you like to take a leading part in the building of an empire?"

"Just what do you have in mind?"

Selkirk paced the plank floor as he spoke. "A few years ago I was in the County of Sutherland and there I observed hundreds of people living under intolerable conditions. They had been evicted from their crofts and driven to the sea coast."

"I heard rumours. How did it happen?"

"The Countess found it more profitable to raise sheep, cattle and deer on the land and she has fenced in large tracts of the Highlands which used to offer the crofters a lean but adequate existence. If I can persuade the Hudson's Bay Company to sell me the land in the Red River area you mention, I can offer new life and hope to these evicted Sutherlanders. At the same time we'll be developing an enterprise that will return untold dividends in furs and agricultural produce. From what you've told me it

136

would appear that neither the Hudson's Bay Company nor the North-West Company is interested in the Red River Valley. Everything, therefore, seems ideal for such a project!" He stopped pacing and fixed his eyes on Robertson. "What's your opinion, Colin?"

"It's a dream I've lived with for years. If you can bring this about you'll have my support."

A deep silence followed before Selkirk turned to an oblong table where the decanters stood. He poured a glass of brandy for himself and a whisky for Robertson. "Here's to the future," he toasted with a smile.

Next day Selkirk and Robertson discussed plans to colonize the Red River Valley. They planned how they would provide comfortable quarters, farm equipment and stock for the hardy Highlanders.

"It isn't going to be as easy as you imagine, sir" said Robertson. "The North-West Company is not going to welcome colonists in the Red River. You see, sir, their trappers have to cross the valley to service forts and trap lines and they depend on the buffalo herds there for pemmican to keep them provisioned over the long journey. If the valley is settled, the buffalo will move away and the trappers will lose their pemmican. Even with luck it will be a dangerous undertaking, your lordship."

"The Northwesters have no rights to the valley," Selkirk declared. "Under the existing charter the land belongs to the Hudson's Bay Company. I can get the English company to sell me the entire area." He clapped Colin confidently on the shoulder. "There's nothing to worry about, Colin. I'll see that the settlers have ample protection. The title to the land will be in my name and I'll protect my property with arms if need be."

Anxiously awaiting Selkirk's homecoming was his fiancée, the beautiful heiress, Jean Colvile. Shortly after his arrival they were married. Jean's father, James Colvile, was a major stockholder and influential director in the Hudson's Bay Company, and there is little doubt that the position of his father-in-law in the company had much to do with determining the Earl's intentions. By this time the company stock had dropped from £250 to £50. Taking advantage of the low value and the plans the Earl had proposed, Selkirk, his father-in-law, and their friends bought all the company's shares which could be obtained and in a short time they had effective control. In due course the Company voted to sell Selkirk 116,000 square miles in the Red River Valley for the magnificent sum of ten shillings.

"It's the only way we can survive," Selkirk told the directors. "The North-West Company are murdering our agents, poaching our trap lines and stealing our furs. To put an end to this we must recruit a strong staff of reliable employees to man our forts and protect our interests. My intentions are to colonize the valley with hardy Highlanders, in particular the men and women from Sutherland. Only in this way can we hope to retrieve control of the Canadian fur trade."

The meeting with the Directors of the company had scarcely been accomplished when the Earl entertained the Countess of Sutherland and her Marquis at his island residence on St. Mary's Isle. Here he enthralled them with stories of Canada, astounded them with descriptions of its vastness, and spoke glowingly of the great future that the Canadian West had to offer.

The Countess rejoiced in every word Selkirk spoke. Finally she interrupted, "Thomas, the last time we met you implied that our Sutherland crofters would make good colonists for your Red River empire!"

"Yes, Elizabeth. My colleagues are thoroughly convinced that these Highlanders of yours are ideally fitted to withstand the rigorous Canadian climate."

"Have your colleagues been to the Red River area?"

"Oh, yes, I've hired Colin Robertson, who was with the North-West Company, and Captain Miles MacDonell who has lived for many years in Upper Canada. These two Gaelic speaking lads will have no difficulty in persuading your people to leave your barren beaches for a life in a new land."

"They are a hardy race, and Granville and I will assist you in every way possible," concluded the Countess.

Selkirk cringed inwardly. He had seen the Brora beaches and he was amazed how a beautiful woman, enjoying high respect socially and politically, could be so despicable and heartless.

Five months later David Grant was repairing his cart in the yard when an unknown horseman clattered up to Cavaick. It was a chilly day but the rider seemed not to notice the raw weather as he dismounted and walked casually over. He wore a type of jacket that David had never seen before. It was obviously made of soft leather, fringed at the collar and cuffs, and curious designs of dyed porcupine quills were sewn on the front of the coat. The man, bronzed from wind and sun, wore a fur hat, deerskin shoes and soft hide pants.

"Hello," he greeted in Gaelic, "I'm Colin Robertson."

138

David introduced himself.

"I'm surprised to find a croft away out here," Colin commented as he looked over the tilled land.

David smiled. "Are you one of the Countess' agents?"

"No! I'm here recruiting colonists for a fine new settlement in Canada to be created by Lord Selkirk. I was on my way back to the Brora beaches when I came across your croft."

"You'll find plenty of recruits down there! Anything would be better than what they have now."

"What I have to offer is better than any of you could imagine in your wildest dreams. May I stop and talk to you about Selkirk's plan?"

David put down his hammer and invited Robertson into his cottage. He introduced Jeannie, Fiona, who was now seven, and Joseph, his young son. During the introduction Colin spoke pleasantly and easily to the children while David poured two bumpers of grog.

"Tell me about Canada," David said as he sipped at his brew.

"The part of Canada that Selkirk has purchased is like nothing you've ever seen," Robertson began. "The country is wide and flat with a river greater than you ever dreamed of flowing through the Red River Valley. It is virgin land, rich and easy to clear. A man can have a hundred acres — a thousand even!"

David and Jeannie eyed the speaker in amazement.

"The seasons are similar to those in the Highlands only more extreme, the summers are hotter and the winters colder. But the air is drier and there is an endless supply of timber to build warm houses and provide fuel for fires."

"Is there any game?" asked David.

"Game?" Colin grinned and took a long sip at his whisky. "Game! You couldn't imagine anything like it! The valley is teeming with buffalo, moose, wild fowl and other animals. I have seen so many buffalo that the prairies have been black with them. Indians talk of herds taking days to pass. The rivers and lakes abound with fish."

"Yes, but I'll wager the king would stop us from fishing and hunting," interrupted David.

"Not at all. The settlers are going to be free to take all the fish and game they need without licence or restriction. In fact, there's no restriction on personal liberties of any kind. All the Highlanders who take up land will be allowed to carry arms and wear their kilts or any other type of Highland dress they wish."

"What about religion?" enquired David.

Robertson warmed to the occasion. "Those who emigrate to the new colony will select their own minister and attend any church they choose. There are no churches now, but we'll build them."

"Oh, David, it sounds wonderful," exclaimed Jeannie.

David's head was beginning to whirl. While he had a good croft and had worked hard he was eking out a mere existence. Tax time was at hand and he knew that if he couldn't deliver ten bags of meal to the Castle he'd be driven to the beaches.

"Tell us more, Sir."

Throughout the afternoon David listened while Robertson described Lord Selkirk's plan. He spoke of how the Earl was prepared to supply farm equipment, guns, ammunition, seed and prize breeding stock free of charge to the first hundred males who signed the application forms.

David recalled the prediction of the Brahan Seer that his people would migrate to lands in the western ocean and he felt strangely thrilled.

"Would you be interested in coming with us?" Robertson asked.

David hesitated. "It would require some thought — what are the others doing?"

"Many have already signed. We need men like you for leadership; I can assure you that Canada is a paradise compared with this. There a man is free and the land is his own. The first brigade of Selkirk settlers will make the Red River Valley a Sutherland community.

"Why David, it sounds wonderful," exulted Jeannie. "We'll be with all our friends: the Braggart, Mary, the Soldier and the Gipsy."

"That's right," said Robertson, producing a scroll from his pocket, "some of them have already signed."

"Come back and see me," said David.

"I will that," replied Robertson in the Gaelic as he rose to leave. "You're the kind of self-reliant settler we want."

Selkirk's recruiting team, having received instructions from the Countess, was working day and night encouraging the Sutherlanders to leave the beaches. Robertson himself had been leery of any scheme in which the Countess of Sutherland, or her husband, was involved and only became reconciled to his role when Selkirk assured him that his sole objective was to improve the condition of the evicted Sutherlanders and that Sellar would have nothing to do with the recruiting scheme.

140

Many of the people, too old or too feeble to leave, proclaimed Selkirk the Messiah that God had sent to deliver His people to the new land. They encouraged their sons and daughters by repeating the predictions of the Brahan Seer, and in a short time Robertson's quota for the settlement was reached.

Their passage was not free. Each emigrant had to make a token payment, but since these people had escaped Sellar's torch with practically nothing and had been unable to earn anything on the barren land to which they had been condemned, even this was a great hardship. Now payment for the passage meant the parting with humble but precious heirlooms — prized rings, snuff boxes, dirks, broaches, even the pearls culled from the River Brora were sold.

During the recruiting period David came upon the old Soldier sitting near the beach with the tip of his wooden leg stuck deep in the sand.

"Aren't you going with us?"

"No. The Gipsy's going. The lad deserves a chance in the New World. He has no ties with this land. So I've sold my bagpipes to Hector MacKay and with the few shillings the pipes brought, he can start a new life. Betsy and I are near the end of the road and we've decided to stay here," the old warrior replied.

At Cavaick Jeannie was furiously spinning wool to make warm coats and pants for David, herself and the children. She had paid special attention to Colin Robertson when he talked about the cold Canadian winters and she was going to be prepared. Apart from the warm clothes and extra food tucked in a box there would be nothing else required for hadn't Selkirk promised to provide all the homes, implements and tools they needed to colonize the Valley?

Before leaving, David visited the old battle cairn at Sciberscross to pay his last respects at the grave of his mother and the Dominie. Upon his return with Jeannie and their children, they stood in silence beside Duncan's last resting place.

At last the family was ready to join the emigrant ship. Although they looked forward eagerly to the voyage because of their confidence in Robertson, many of the settlers became less and less enthusiastic when the Reverend Donald Sage insisted that Selkirk's motives for colonization were purely selfish. He moved up and down the beach telling the people that Selkirk's only purpose was to use the Sutherlanders to establish a Canadian empire for himself. "The newspapers in Edinburgh," he declared, "are re-

141

ferring to his lordship as a mountebank who, with his beguiling promises, is capitalizing on the ignorance of the destitute people."

"You think we've been betrayed again?" an old crone asked.

"You can draw your own conclusions," Sage replied. "It's my opinion Selkirk and the Countess are using the Red River colonization plan to serve their own selfish ends. The Countess sees the colony as an excellent means of getting rid of us. Selkirk, on the other hand, as a large shareholder in the Hudson's Bay Company, hopes to use the Red River settlement to provide furs and other products that will make him richer."

Robertson agreed with Sage. "The opportunity is there," he declared. "It's a blessing for both the Countess and Selkirk; but you will also have the chance to make good. Canada offers unlimited opportunity for a happy and prosperous life. Perhaps Selkirk will enrich himself through the land settlement scheme. But you and your children will become equally enriched as part of the general plan!"

Notwithstanding Colin's optimism many who had signed contracts disappeared and never did reach Canada. Under terms of their agreement, the Marquis sent his dogs and his bailiffs to enforce the contracts. The men and women who had escaped were found in caves, in dense growths of heather, in old outhouses and in abandoned cottages. They were arrested and herded into the hold of the "Prince of Wales."

In addition to the bitter attack on Selkirk by Reverend Sage, the directors of the North-West Company in London sent agents into Sutherland in an endeavour to discourage Selkirk's recruiting drive. Articles were inserted in Scottish newspapers declaring that his lordship's motives were most mercenary. The news vividly portrayed the dangers and hardships of pioneer life in remote Rupert's land.

At last the day of departure arrived and as David, Jeannie and their children descended into the confusion at the pier, they could see their friends milling around nervously. Red-eyed women and sober-faced men paced aimlessly up and down or stood stiffly and awkwardly in one place striving to conceal their emotions. Among those on the jetty was a group of old women whose sons and daughters were about to sail. Suddenly they gave vent to their grief in a chorused dirge similar to the lamentation they had voiced countless times at Highland funerals. When the old women began to moan and sob, the children cried and the mothers attempted to soothe them with quiet Gaelic phrases. Other mothers

142

clung possessively to the little ones they were about to take on this frightening journey.

The sound of Chief Constable MacLeod's whistle hushed the assembly. "Start loading. Clear the pier of all those not entitled to board," he bellowed.

In spite of MacLeod's curt command, many failed to respond. "Come on, move!" he repeated. But his urging was in vain.

During the period of indecision Colin Robertson, accompanied by a distinguished looking gentleman moved up to David Grant.

"David, this is the Earl of Selkirk."

David, a poor Highland crofter, and Selkirk, the nobleman, boldly appraised one another.

Selkirk held out his hand. "I'm happy to hear that you're joining our venture."

"Thank you, sir."

"David," said Colin, "what can we do to get these people aboard? They're scared stiff."

David took a long look at his friends and countrymen. "God help you all," he said to himself with a proud, fierce emotion of defiance against Selkirk's scheme swelling within him. His anger, however, was of short duration. He couldn't turn back now. He had disposed of Cavaick — he had signed a contract with Selkirk — he must abide by it.

"What a melancholy sight," he thought. The apprehensive look of the men, the short, quick, broken step, their impulsive running around to say farewell, all told of the deep agonizing feeling they were striving in vain to overcome. The grief of the women continued loud and openly. Clinging to the relations they were parting from, they poured forth in almost unintelligible ejaculations their agony at leaving the land where they were born and where they had hoped to die. Mingled in the same breath were their blessings and prayers for those dear friends they would never forget. Children, stupefied and bewildered at the scene, clung to their mothers. Others made a brave effort to throw some appearance of heartiness and good spirit into the last moment they were ever to spend on their native heath. David watched hands being wrung and wrung again and bumpers of whisky tossed off wildly.

His searching eyes found the Gipsy. He was leaning against an old capstan — like a thing apart from the assemblage — and paying no attention to what was going on around him. David noticed that dangling like a tattered sheep-skin from the Gipsy's

143

arm, were the Soldier's prized bagpipes. "I wonder how he got possession of the pipes," he asked himself as he hurried across the dock. When he stopped before the Gipsy he was shocked by the man's haggard countenance; his eyes stared around fearfully and his chalk white face had all the appearance of some miserable creature striving to die.

David placed a gentle hand on his old friend's shoulder.

"What is the matter, Gipsy?" he asked in the Gaelic.

Something like a bitter grin twisted the haggard face. "I'm scared to death, David," he muttered, tears rolling down his cheeks.

"But why, Gipsy — why?"

"It's the pipes, David. The Soldier sold them to Hector to obtain my passage money. Hector made a gift of them to me this morning. I'm . . ."

David grasped the opportunity and quickly stopped whatever the Gipsy was going to say. "Hector made you a present of the pipes because he wanted our people to enjoy your music before leaving, during the voyage and in the country beyond. What better time than now to show your appreciation?"

"I can't play, I'm scared!" came the sobbing reply.

"So was the Soldier," barked David, "when he played the Highlanders to victory with one leg blasted away by cannon fire! Come, my friend, you're going to play as you never played before —more inspiringly than you played that night in the tavern— the very same tavern where you lost your own pipes, and General Wemyss was blackballing us into the 93rd. That night we'd have followed you through the gates of Hell. You've got to play now because fear like Hell is not only in your heart, but it's raging in mine and in the heart of every soul on the dock."

The Gipsy shouldered the drones and was about to tune up his pipes when Hector MacKay, a flagon in his hand, staggered to a stop beside them.

"Hold the music, we're going to have a good dram — this is special Clynelish I snatched from the Castle — and after that you're going to play 'Cock of the North'. That's an order, Mr. Gipsy."

After a few healthy swigs of the local nectar, the Gipsy stepped out with his pipes skirling; he staggered a little but there was no bungling chord to the rousing air.

As he marched across the pier all eyes turned on him. The men smiled, the women stopped crying, and feet began to tap

144

and stamp as a path widened through the crowd. Before he had reached the boarding plank the Sutherlanders had begun to cheer. Under the influence of the stirring music, hearts began to beat faster, fears were dissipated, and the first steps on the way to a strange adventure became less frightening. The emigrants, almost in unison, picked up their belongings and followed the Gipsy along the jetty to the ship.

Cheers were loud and long, bonnets were thrown into the air. Women were forced almost fainting onto the boat while the poor, forsaken dogs stretched their heads after their masters and howled piteously.

Lines and moorings were cast off, the sails unfurled and the ship moved away whilst high above the din the wild notes of the Gipsy's pipes continued to be heard pouring forth: "Cha Til Sinn Tullie" — "We Shall Return No More".

David Grant put his arms around his wife and children. Together they watched as the shores gradually receded. Jeannie tightly held her most precious possession; a small ball of turf which clung around the roots of heather she had dug from the soil at Cavaick. When she reached the Red River Valley she would plant this bit of earth and heather as a permanent link with her homeland.

CHAPTER SIXTEEN

Three Thousand Miles
of Hell

*They lifted up the sounding sail; the wind whistled through
the thongs of their masts. Waves lashed the oozy rocks:
the strength of ocean roars.*

THE WAR OF INIS-THONA

COLIN ROBERTSON was apprehensive as he watched the
Sutherlanders shuffle up the gang plank. What was to be
their fate? How could they, whose quiet way of life before the
evictions had seldom been broken by more than the yelp of a
dog or the scream of the stag, suffer the wind howling like an
angry demon as every wave crashed against the ship's side
demanding instant surrender?

How could they know the awful terror that faced them? How
could they forsee the long, hungry hours that lay ahead in the
untamed wilderness? And how could they supply the courage
and endurance which would be required in the face of death,
disease and the deadly dangers of the wild? If they knew what
lay ahead would they still be prepared to give up the security
of their present existence for a dream which could offer little
or nothing to themselves and which was of questionable value
to their children or their children's children? Above all he could
see them crouching in the ship's hold, a dark, dismal place where
a glimmer of light was seldom seen.

But he had a job to do. The seventy-six who now crowded
around the cheerless deck were only the first of many for whom
he was going to be responsible. From bitter experience, he knew

that if half of them reached the Red River it would be a miracle. In a way he felt like a shepherd of death. He could guarantee nothing, except the things he couldn't tell them about. That was his job; however odious the task, he had to do it.

Colin could see the fear in their hearts reflected on their sombre faces; they were without hope. Each carried a bundle of worn rags, and in their pockets some scraps of food donated by a friendly fisherwife. Their appearance and belongings testified to the hunger, misery, sorrow and nakedness the Countess had imposed upon them. He knew that two years before they had been driven from their comfortable crofts, left to shiver and starve on the moors and the storm-lashed beach until someone who had endured as much misery as they, themselves, invited them in. There they crouched in the damp, fireless hovels, thankful that despite their hunger, they had not to endure the pitiless pelting of the outer storm. But was their present misery any excuse for inflicting on them greater trials, disappointments and even utter destruction?

He was awakened from his reverie by the voice of David Grant. "I have been watching them from below, Colin. Sympathy is of little worth to a people who exchange sighs for sighs and mingle tears with tears. Nothing but Hope," he continued, "with her 'golden hair' streaming out, will herald the way to a land beyond the rim of the horizon far over the sea and bid them remember that God is also there. There we can build our homes in peace and comfort. From our cottages the blue smoke will ascend through the pine trees and then mount in circling shadows over our golden harvest fields."

"David, you're a sanctimonious old fool," jested Colin as he strode away thoughtfully toward Selkirk who was pacing the poop deck. "You have no idea what the future holds."

David caught the last words and he suddenly realized that the glitter and excitement of preparations for sailing were wearing thin. The boat which heaved under his feet was hard reality. The fond goodbyes and the feverish packing seemed a little more hollow now that the moment had arrived, and as he watched Colin's back disappear up the ladder and along the poop deck he knew that many of his companions faced a harsh awakening.

Selkirk beamed a wide smile at Robertson. He was quite pleased with the initial success of his venture. With these sturdy emigrants safely on board, he began to realize that his dream of a great empire in Canada was about to come true.

"May I have a word with you, my lord?" said Colin striving

to regain his composure. From his experience with Selkirk he knew that he was the supreme optimist, a man of keen, analytical mind who had long since struck the word failure from his vocabulary. Selkirk thought and acted positively. He liked people around him to operate in the same way. Colin respected him.

"Your lordship, I understand we are leaving the ship at Stromness."

"Right, Colin. Miles will join us there. He will be responsible for delivering the colonists to the Red River. You'll return to Sutherland and recruit settlers for the next ship."

Colin cleared his throat. "The Sutherlanders are asking questions that are difficult for me to answer. Can we discuss their problems?"

"Problems, Colin? There are no problems! Not unless we create them ourselves, in our own minds, and we can't do that if we know the answer and plan the campaign. Come, let's adjourn to the Captain's cabin." He sniffed the breeze, glanced over his head at the yard arms as the free sails billowed out, then led the way aft.

In the comfortable sterncastle, he motioned Colin to a chair and poured two glasses of brandy.

Selkirk spread the tails of his coat and settled himself in the Captain's chair. "Here's to the success of our venture," he toasted, rolling the brandy around on his tongue while he waited for Colin to continue.

"Your lordship, the Sutherlanders expected the Reverend Donald Sage to accompany them. I knew he wasn't coming but is it possible the gossip I've heard is true?"

"What gossip?"

"Rumour has it that your lordship tried to enlist Donald Sage as minister for the colony. Sage has told the people that he was suspicious about your motives and when he asked for an honest explanation you refused to give it."

Selkirk shrugged his silk-clad shoulders. "I've explained many times our prime intention is to help the evicted Sutherlanders rehabilitate themselves in the Red River Valley. You picked the site for me."

Robertson smiled. "That is true. It is a fine place for a settlement. But the Sutherlanders have been told that your prime motive is to take possession of the North-West Company's routes through the Red River Valley."

"Not at all," Selkirk retorted tartly. "I offered the Reverend

148

Sage a stipend of fifty pounds a year and other privileges if he would accompany the first brigade. He rejected my proposal saying that he was too old for such a long journey. I've now made arrangements with the Church of Scotland to have James Sutherland take his place. Sutherland is a respected elder of the Free Church and is fully authorized to administer to the religious needs of the people. He has agreed to follow on the next ship."

"The story about Reverend Sage will satisfy some," admitted Colin. "But many believe they are to be used as gun fodder in a conflict between the Nor'Westers and the Hudson's Bay Company. Unless we can provide a better explanation, there could be trouble on board."

Colin was nervous. Selkirk's stern countenance disturbed him and for a moment he wondered how his next words would be received by the great nobleman.

"Your lordship, of all the men I've known, you come first in my respect. I admire your boldness, your vision and energy. Your determination to colonize the primitive Red River Valley does me a great honour because I feel that I have aided your endeavours. You are well aware of my loyalty but I speak bluntly, my lord, because I can't figure you out. I can't make up my mind whether you are a saint or a scoundrel." He paused for a moment to see how his words were being received but seeing a gentle smile flit quickly over Selkirk's lean countenance, he continued, "We both know the Red River Valley. We both know that the Nor'Westers will fight. McGillivray, MacKenzie and Cameron will never give up their hold whether it's your land or not. It's their life — their very existence depends on free passage across the valley. Tell me, why did you purchase the Valley? Have you for one moment considered the chance of survival for the Sutherlanders once the Nor'Westers find that they have come to farm and occupy the Valley? Who is there to protect them? Not a single friendly gun. You are throwing them to the wolves!"

Selkirk did not answer directly. Calmly and deliberately, he rose from his chair and refilled the goblets. Handing one to Colin, he remarked. "Having reached this conclusion you probably have already eliminated the word 'saint'. Anyway, Colin, here's to you." With these words he picked up his coat tails and sat down. "Have a seat, Colin, there are things I would like to say to you. The Sutherland crofters will win through. There are none more staunch or loyal, none more hard working or imaginative. Don't worry about them. They have always made the finest

149

soldiers and settlers. They will handle themselves well in the Valley. Would you rather have them sail with hope or die in hopeless despair on the beaches of Brora?"

"Sail to life, sir, but not to death," said Colin with the feeling he was not getting the answers he sought.

"What do they have to lose? They no longer enjoy the peace and comfort of their native heath. For over two years they have existed through a living hell — markers in the cemetery on the hillside testify to the swiftness of their passing. Colin, they are doomed and my being a saint or scoundrel will in no way add to their misery."

He stood up and pointed his finger. "Answer me one question. If you happened to be one of these lingering objects we left on the Brora beaches — suspended somewhere in the vagueness between life and death — and I came along and offered you a slim chance to survive and build a new life for yourself, what would be your decision?"

"I've always been a gambling man, my lord, I'd take your bet."

"Thank you, Colin. Hope is what you have been given — hope is what we must give them. For those who survive the sea journey, brighter and broader landscapes will spread before them in the New World. But that is no safeguard against the wrath of the Nor'Westers. Nevertheless, it's a new opportunity—freedom from the paralysis of slavery. When the Christmas bell tolls out on the Brora beaches they will simply see that nights are growing longer, fuel and food growing more scarce."

As Colin turned to go, he realized the strength that was in this man's convictions but he still couldn't make up his mind what was the most fitting epithet. Did Selkirk avoid answering him directly or was he himself reading into the story something that didn't really exist? Somehow he felt glad that he was leaving the ship at Stromness.

David Grant had also listened to the grumblings of the Mole and others; but he knew that of all who set sail on the *Prince of Wales,* he, himself, was probably the one who had given up most. He had surely burnt his boats when he sold out to Joseph Sutherland at Cavaick. Before doing so he had considered the prospects in detail and long chats with Colin Robertson had convinced him of the merits of the undertaking. He knew it was a dangerous adventure and many problems would arise, but having reached a decision there was no turning back. He had decided to challenge the future, and Jeannie was with him all the way.

150

Following his greeting with Colin he accompanied his family down to the hold which was fitted with berths of raw boards, resembling large hen-coops piled one on top of another. It made his heart sicken to picture what it would be like at sea with the hatches secured and the vessel driving into the teeth of a gale.

Glancing around, his eyes fell upon his old friend John Bannerman, whose countenance would have caught the imagination of any artist. He sat on a bundle of baggage in a dark corner of the hold with the family Bible upon his knee. It was the Bible that John had turned to for strength. Around him little children played hide and seek among the bales and casks; all were full of heart and hope.

Others sat chatting or humming Gaelic songs to while away the weary hours. Many slept listlessly as the ship heaved and tossed on the gentle swell along the Caithness coast. The Gipsy whittled wood and carved handsome deer heads and toy claymores which he passed on to the children for their amusement. The women sewed, but the long hours of freedom gave much time for expressions of fears, criticism, and gossip which formed factions and set group against group, man against man.

David's unfailing cheerfulness and helpfulness cut across this division. He and Jeannie found that their strength increased from the teachings of their fathers, from the Holy Book and from the hours they spent in helping others.

Aboard to take charge of the settlers when the ship left Stromness was Captain Miles MacDonell. The Captain was born in the Highlands, but the family had emigrated to the United States and there he had passed his youth. During the American war of Independence he had fought on the British side as a Captain in the Queen's Rangers. When the war was over Miles didn't find the country a congenial place for loyalists and he returned to his native land. He married there and a few years later came out to settle in Upper Canada. Captain MacDonell was cast from the same mould as Selkirk; he was a man of wide experience in pioneering, in people, and in the new land for which they were heading. He was direct, positive and confident.

On the first day at sea, he called the Sutherlanders together and in an authoritative voice told them who he was and what he expected of them during the journey.

"I am Miles MacDonell. It is my responsibility to see that you arrive in the Red River Valley sound in mind and limb. The ocean voyage will have many ups and downs, and being huddled together like herring in a barrel isn't going to help conditions. At any rate, the adventure was voluntary and if you will accept it as such and give me your wholehearted support, I'll see you through."

MacDonell's introduction was greeted with silence, and uneasiness spread through the huddled group.

"David Grant, I want you to be my second in command." He looked at David sternly, and respect for his directness and his leadership welled up in David's soul. Almost unwittingly, he found himself murmuring, "I'm at your service, sir."

"Every family will have its own designated area as far as possible. Living quarters will be ready for inspection at eight bells each morning. Children must be kept clean at all times and regular washings will be carried out in sea water. An area in the fore-castle has been set aside as a common eating room. Meals will be served in relays at specific times during the day. Organized play times are being designated for children. At six bells each morning all passengers will assemble for instruction in ship safety. At six bells in the afternoon, men over sixteen will parade on the poop deck for rifle drill.

"In the evenings I will do my best to tell you what to expect in the Canadian North-West, and teach you some of the things you'll have to do to survive in its barren lands."

There was an uncomfortable shuffling of feet. Even David was somewhat stunned by the directness of Miles' orders. But the assurance with which they were delivered indicated clearly that the man would not be misled and that he intended everything to proceed with military precision.

MacDonell called David to his cabin after the meeting. "Grant," he said, "your people want to get to Red River and I want to get them there. We can arrive hale and hearty, or we can crawl ashore in the last stages of the vilest, most painful diseases you can imagine. Cleanliness must be maintained; make it a by-word. You will be responsible for the supervision of all quarters and for the general good conduct of the passengers. How you deal with defaulters is your business. You were in the army, weren't you?"

"Yes, sir! I understand," replied David.

"Have you anyone in mind as an assistant?"

"Probably Gipsy," replied David. "He's wonderful with the children."

"Fine," said MacDonell. "Get him to organize meals, and super-

152

vise the children at play-time. If we are to succeed we must impress on everyone the importance of mutual responsibility. And David," he continued, "be kind but firm. Death is peering over the shoulder of every one of us; starvation, disease, drowning, suicide, are going to be our daily companions; don't let us open our doors wide to them. I'm going to be tough but that toughness is softened by a genuine feeling of love for these poor Highlanders."

When David Grant left Miles MacDonell's presence he knew why Selkirk had chosen him to captain the colonists; MacDonell possessed the ability to organize, the aggressiveness to get things done, and compassion and respect for his fellow beings. David was proud to follow this leader of men. From Miles he would learn the responsibility which each individual must assume for the well-being of the whole. For the first time he understood the significance and loneliness of command. It was a far cry from the warm, neighbourly life of the croft.

Despite the rigid control MacDonell placed on the sanitation facilities and the everlasting efforts of David, the Gipsy and the Braggart, it was impossible to find complete protection against the mounting incidence of lice, skin disease and sea-sickness. Many lay in the sick area while others suffered hopelessly in their dark smelly quarters below decks.

When fever struck Tom McPherson and he raged in delirium they transferred him to the sick area where he died. Fearful that the plague would spread throughout the ship the Captain ordered strict control of the fresh water, stored in casks on the spardeck, and daily inspection of his passengers and crew.

At the short burial service held on the pitching deck, McPherson's niece Anne sobbed silently. She was alone now. Her parents had died on the hungry beaches at Brora and she and her uncle had joined Selkirk with high hopes for a new life in Canada. During the burial service the Gipsy, who had comforted her throughout her uncle's short sickness, took her hand and held it tightly as the body of Tom, in its shot-weighted canvas shroud, went over the side.

Afterwards the two were often seen walking hand in hand around the deck. At night Anne lay on her pallet of straw thinking of the Gipsy and wondering why she had never noticed him before, amazed that no one had taken the time to know him.

She was just a girl when he was found at the innkeeper's door, and while on the Brora beaches they lived at opposite ends of the settlement. He had always been a waif; now she

153

was a waif. But the Gipsy had strength, courage and the will to conquer. He was approaching the New World with hope and confidence. He wasn't like the other men who had been evicted from their little crofts; he had lost nothing of material value, and with only the clothes on his back and the Soldier's pipes, this strange adventure offered him dignity, freedom and opportunity. Now he had fallen in love with Anne and Anne was in love with him.

Eventually the blushing young girl confided her love to the Braggart and Mary. "What shall I do, Mary?" she pleaded, her soft brown eyes glistening with repressed tears. "I love the Gipsy and I know he loves me, but he won't express his feelings. He's been too long an outcast to accept any love I can give him no matter how much he longs for it."

The Braggart's rounded face puckered playfully. "For days we've watched you two love-sick youngsters mooning over each other," he declared. "If you're sure the lad is for you, don't fret any longer, lass!"

The next afternoon when Anne was standing by the rail the Gipsy moved close and folded her in his arms. His face was flushed and his lips were trembling. "Anne," he murmured. "I love you, Anne!"

"How dare you be so forward, sir?" she exclaimed, her eyes filled with mischief, then nestling closer she pressed her lips to his in a long lingering kiss.

While the character of the majority was being moulded and tempered by adversity, others sought to undermine MacDonell's authority and create conflict in the minds of the more timid emigrants. The Mole was defiant. He opposed every order, particularly the rifle drill, which to him pointed out the truth of Donald Sage's contention that they were heading for the Red River as cannon-fodder for the Hudson's Bay Company in its commercial war with the North-West Company.

So the musket drill became a bone of contention that added fuel to the fire of revolt against the unbearable conditions between decks. Eventually the dissenters showed their hand and refused to parade.

"What seems to be the trouble?" demanded MacDonnell as he guarded his musket.

Jimmy Gunn, a reserved lad who seldom spoke, answered, "Damn it, MacDonell, you expect us to drill with guns so we will have some experience to protect our farms, but what are

154

you doing to improve the comfort of the women and children on board this ship?"

There was a murmur of agreement.

"You know that our quarters stink to the high heavens, and the smelly buffalo robes you have allotted haven't added any pleasure, except that of keeping the hungry rats from gnawing us to death. That fetid hellhole, Captain, is worse than sleeping with the pigs my father had before we were evicted. And yet the ship's store-rooms are packed with Hudson's Bay blankets that someone is going to barter to the Indians for more pelts. Now Captain," continued Jimmy, "you supply the women and children with blankets and you'll have no trouble getting us folks to drill; but no blankets — no drill."

General approval greeted Jimmy's appeal. For a moment Miles gazed speechlessly at the bold young man, then he took David Grant by the arm and together they walked away.

Reaching the confines of the Captain's quarters, David opened up. "Jimmy is absolutely right, Miles. It's unreasonable that our women and children should be burdened with so much suffering. Why don't you confiscate the blankets in the name of Lord Selkirk? Not only would you gain the full cooperation of the Sutherlanders, but the women would give you their blessings."

"It shall be done," replied Miles.

Following the delivery of the warm blankets the Mole's disposition improved, but being the Mole, he soon reverted to his former undisciplined ways and David eventually realised that problems with him were more deep-rooted than he had suspected. The matter came to a head one afternoon when in a fit of temper Mole crashed a precious barrel of fresh water against the deck.

It was a day that the colonists would never forget. "All right you . . . " David shouted at the Mole. "Now is the time to decide who is running this ship!"

The excited passengers and crew, gathered in a wide circle. The two bare-footed contestants stripped to the waist and took the measure of each other on the heaving deck.

The voyage had done its best to even out the odds by softening the muscle and generally weakening their physique in such a way that no ship's exercise could attempt to replace. It was obvious, however, that David had the advantage, though age was now against him. Up until the day before sailing, he had worked on the land whereas the Mole had been living a life of enforced idleness on the Brora beaches.

The Mole was wild, and with his youth he quickly rushed David off his feet and cornered him in the scuppers. Blood flowed from David's nose. As he tried to heave himself from the deck, the Mole rained punch after punch on his head and neck while the onlookers gasped with amazement at the cruelty of the attack.

To the Mole it was exhilarating to have authority grovelling on the deck before him. His hatred of all that reeked of discipline or control added power to every blow. He had been the same throughout his life but in the loneliness of the Sutherland Highlands, it wasn't so measurable. The little childish pranks at school and the long record of poaching, stealing and minor assault did not seem so important in the vastness of the heather covered glen, but here in the close embrace of the sea it stood out naked and stark in all its menace and terror.

The challenge had been made and accepted and the bystanders stood in awe respecting the rules of the game. The Braggart and Gipsy watched with clenched fists and flinched physically as each blow struck down on David's blood-drenched head.

But the Mole's very violence, his uncontrolled hatred, was his own undoing. His blows became wilder and in the frenzy of passion he failed to notice that his adversary had regained a sitting position. As David raised himself to full height, the Mole continued his distraught attack against the empty air.

There was a sigh of relief from the crowd and in the intensity of the moment they gave a quick, involuntary cheer when David sent his left fist crashing into the pit of the Mole's stomach and with his right landed a vicious blow on the side of his assailant's bobbing head. The Mole collapsed to the deck. The long hours of caber-tossing and shot-putting had their reward. A fresh, renewing gasp of the salt air cleared David's head and he was ready to assume command. He picked up the Mole by the scruff of his neck and tore the seat out of his pants as he sent him spinning aft to the shattered barrel.

"Get down on your knees and thank God you are still alive," he hissed through aching lips. He gave the dazed man a mighty shove. "Now get that mess cleaned up, then report to me for additional duties. Don't forget that only my regard for your family saved you from being tossed into the Atlantic."

In defeat the Mole was morose and resentful. "I'll get you, Grant," he swore, and during musket drill he continued to grumble about fighting for Selkirk's Empire; but help was to come from an unexpected source.

156

The Mole's wife, who had watched the parade, crossed to her husband's side. "Mole," she shouted at the pitch of her voice so all could hear, "if you don't keep your big mouth shut and stop grumbling I'll hit you over the head with this gun and take your place in the ranks myself. Not only are you annoying our friends, but you're spoiling the entertainment we get out of watching your funny antics. Now make up your mind."

There was a chuckle of relief, and the Mole realized the antagonism he had created. Hatred glinted in his eyes as he shuffled into the rear rank.

For two months the *Prince of Wales* made hesitant progress westward. John Bain, Angus Sutherland, Tom Gunn and Andrew Murray's wife Sarah were given to the sea. Four children died by accident or by fever which was not helped by the putrid, stagnant air below deck. Two women from Clyne died in childbirth.

Some were to carry scars for the rest of their lives. Pretty baby Bannerman would never have a little finger on her right hand. During one horrible night of terror when her mother was forced to devote her attention to a sick brother a rat grabbed it and wouldn't let go. Tommy MacLeod would carry a scar on his face where a falling yardarm slit his cheek from the corner of his mouth to his ear. Thanks to the kindly ministrations of Janet Bain, who had been a midwife in Strath Brora, many of them survived.

Buffeted by the cold Arctic wind, the ship at last headed into the narrow Hudson Strait. The Captain was worried. Ice and fresh snow were gathering on the starboard. Though on one occasion he had been able to sail out of the Bay early in October, he had also experienced trouble escaping a freeze-up in September. The signs now indicated that the Bay would be frozen earlier than usual and the Captain had no intention of being stranded for nine months in this featureless wilderness. His contract with the Company was to unload supplies at Churchill and Selkirk had hoped he could disembark the Sutherlanders at Fort York eighty miles further south on the Hayes River.

The Captain was not a very congenial character. Throughout the voyage he had stayed within his cabin and the wheelhouse and seldom had anything to do with the passengers. At times he tried to interest Miles in a dram of brandy from the secret store he kept to fortify himself, as he said, 'against the cold damp night air' which somehow got at his rheumatism. But the spirits did little to temper the sea water that flowed through his

157

veins. It didn't bother him to make a decision which meant over a hundred miles cross-country for the sixty men and women of Sutherland who were now at his mercy.

"I'm going to unload at Churchill," he informed MacDonell one morning as the low flat mound of the Cape was sighted in the distance. "I can't risk my ship any longer in the Bay!"

"But you must go on to York. There's nothing at Churchill for us."

"I can't help that, sir. By the time I have unloaded, revictualled, and watered, I'll be cutting it pretty thin especially with the Hudson the way she is now."

"These people have nothing — neither is there anything for them at Churchill. Selkirk's encampment is at York."

"They'll make do somehow," cut in the Captain as he abruptly terminated the discussion and ambled off for some renewed fortification from his secret bottle.

While the landing was under way the ship's crew filled their casks with fresh water from the well at the fort, loaded aboard fresh meat and other supplies. Then the sails were set and the *Prince of Wales* headed for England almost before the dazed Sutherlanders knew what was taking place. Thus, in early September 1811, Selkirk's first brigade of Sutherland Highlanders arrived in Canada. They were bewildered, unprepared, and cut off from their supply depot by miles and miles of primeval wilderness.

CHAPTER SEVENTEEN

The Way of the Wild

"When the sky pours down its flaky snow, and the world is silent and dark."

CARTHON

MILES MACDONELL was bewildered by what he found at Fort Churchill. Set in barren country, it provided little solace for him or his followers.

The small fort built by Hudson's Bay Company was staffed by two men, an old Highlander by the name of John Auld, who had joined the company from Glengarry and a Frenchman from Lower Canada. Auld was agent for the Hudson's Bay Company and traded with the Eskimos and Indians. The former trekked down the Bay from the north and from Neultin Lake district each year, and the latter came east from the interior forest. These traders had already been in and had now headed back for their igloos and teepees carrying with them their blankets, knives, beads and cloth. Usually the meeting at Churchill was the occasion for a yearly celebration with friends and relations, but this time, the weather signs were bad and the spirit of the North wind breathed a warning of danger as they headed home with no waste of time.

To the Company's agents the last ship was always important for it carried the trading goods for the new season, thus ensuring a good stock of pelts for the first ship breaking through the spring thaw. It also carried food supplies for the long winter months. But this time the *Prince of Wales* was different. Along with the supplies, she had disembarked more than sixty emigrants who were ill-equipped to challenge the bitter Canadian wilderness.

It was clear to Miles MacDonell that to preserve the sanity and maintain the faith of his flock he had to keep their minds occupied. He prayed to God that his instructions would be given in such a manner that everyone would clearly understand the correct course to follow. His strength alone had supported them through two long, terrifying months at sea. He had earned their respect and devotion and they were entirely dependent on him. Now he had to have time to analyse the present predicament more closely.

"David," he said, "if we don't keep these people occupied we'll undo all the respect for discipline they learned on the voyage. The devil finds work for idle hands and tongues. Send a few men into the tundra to gather moss, sedges and grasses for bedding. They'll find some of these mosses soft and velvety in long mats or hummocks stuck out from among the lichens and sedges. Instruct them to bring back everything that can be used to sleep on. Tell them to pick the driest moss from the top of the knolls and mounds and to watch for bogs and swamps.

"Send as many women as are fit to gather driftwood and anything we can burn. They're not going to find very much — don't tell them that, for driftwood is as precious as gold around here.

"Send five or six men to the bay-shore end of that long mound to scout for large rocks. They'll find many long mounds in this country and there's pretty sure to be a fair showing of broken rock close to the bottom if you can find a cutting through the ice.

"Assign two men and two women under Gipsy to organize the rations. Every piece of food and every drop of water should be divided into batches just large enough for one day's needs. Get them to repack and mark each batch with a number so that only that food will be eaten on the designated day. Let me know how many days' rations we have on hand. While this is taking place, have the Braggart move the remaining women and children over to the lee-side of the factor's hut; afterwards have him work out a plan for the best way to distribute the bedding. The usual Bible meeting will have to be a little later today."

Once again David was grateful for the strength of this man, his quick thinking and his understanding of people. He realized that Miles had the four qualities essential to man. These were the characteristics the old Dominie had instilled in his father Duncan and which Duncan in turn had handed down to his son: the

160

ability to imagine truthfully, to see clearly, to remember accurately and finally, the power to accomplish the utmost.

On his first night in the barren lands of Canada, David was realizing the practical significance of the old Dominie's teachings.

Having issued his orders, Miles now wrestled with the planning of what was to be done to get the Sutherlanders to safety against a cruel winter fast approaching. He had over one hundred miles of bleak, desolate country to cover between Churchill and York. There was no means of transportation. There were few rations left because it had been expected that the landing would be made at York Factory. Many of his people were physically incapable of undertaking such a hard journey.

The eternal wind stung his cheeks as he headed up the slope to the trading post. It was a small building, built of spruce logs floated down the Churchill River from the sparse interior forests. During the three months of summer, an encampment would spring up around the post — teepees, tents, wikiups — but now it was empty and lonely. Only the Factor and his French assistant remained.

Miles assessed the future as he walked along. He had two alternatives — to stay at Churchill, or to move on to York where the accommodation Selkirk had promised must be waiting. If he decided to stay, then he would have to depend on the supplies at Churchill and this was obviously impossible. They had neither the food, accommodation, nor the firewood and other requisites for sixty people. There was only one way out. They had to move across country to York Factory.

"We would be grateful for any help you have to offer, John Auld," he told the Factor after explaining his position. "I'm getting an estimate on our food supplies. In any case at an average of one pound per person per day, there can't be more than enough for five days, and I've calculated we're going to need at least fifteen."

"That means you're going to need 10 days' food for 60 people. Why, Miles, that's ten months' rations for us — impossible, we just don't have that kind of food. We can let you have three days. You'll have to kill game on the way south. We have plenty of blankets and rugs. Sign for them and take whatever you need. Take that pile of deerskins over there — they were left behind by the Captain so you may as well make use of them."

"Most important, Mr. Auld — what can we do in the way of shelter? Is there anything between here and York?"

"Nothing. Your only hope is to make deerskin tents."

Bouchette, the Frenchman, hadn't understood much of the conversation. He had no Gaelic and little English, so he could only guess the course of it by the nods and the pointing at blankets, rifles, skins and food. He understood the signs from Auld's gesticulations.

"Il y a des perches en arrière," he said quickly, pointing to the back of the cabin and Auld recalled that it had been the practice of the Indians to store some of their teepee poles at the post. All they could find were ten poles but they were a valuable contribution to the Highlanders' needs.

As Miles left the cabin he was more optimistic. He was aware of the hardships that lay ahead, and there was no denying that the supplies he had were completely inadequate for such a long trek. Survival lay in his orders being carried through to the letter.

Throughout the afternoon everyone was kept busy fetching and carrying. The women fitted the teepees together and cut and stitched the deerskins to make tents. Others helped Auld and Bouchette move stores around in the cabin to give maximum sleeping area for the children. Both men were models of hospitality and went out of their way to assist at every turn. They knew that lives depended on their efforts.

Auld became the life and soul of the party. He showed the children the old Eskimo game of Cat's Cradle, taught the older ones to throw the harpoon and play kick ball with a grass-packed deerskin laced with hide straps. The women enjoyed his antics, the children hooted and laughed and the cold steely wind echoed with a joy strange to the wilderness. So infectious was the pleasure of the children, so carefree their new freedom that the mothers, huddled with them in their blankets, hummed little native airs and worked their needles with cold-stiffened fingers. It was like a tonic; Gipsy and the Braggart were in the midst of it all. In these first few hours in a cold inhospitable land, the Sutherlanders realized they were not putting in time waiting for death, they were living for these young souls who could find such pleasure in the midst of abounding misery. They were working for the future of their generation — a new life for their people.

Miles was pleased as he listened to the laughter, the singing and the sound of the Gipsy's bagpipes coming from within the cabin. He looked at David. "You know, David, it amazes me how your people can bounce back from the toughest conditions and show feelings to which the heart has long been a stranger."

162

As darkness closed in, the noise and the bustle were stilled. The children, tired and weary, huddled in a corner of the cabin. The others took to separate tents pitched in the lee. Such organization conserved space and was adaptable to the rigours of the trek which was to follow.

Next morning before dawn, David, Gipsy and the Braggart were getting everyone ready for the trail. "Come on, you lazy bones," they shouted. "Let's get moving!"

Their breath billowed out in front of them in the cold morning air as they beat a tattoo on the deerskin tents. In the bitter morning they again blessed Miles' foresight in having the women sew mitts, jerkins, mukluks and hoods of hides on the ship. It had kept them busy throughout the voyage and was going to save many a frostbite in the days to follow.

Jeannie had assembled Mary and other women at the cabin to prepare a steaming breakfast of oatmeal porridge and hot bannocks. The work parties organized by David the day before began preparing sleds and stretchers for the trek. Strips of deerskin formed the binding for the poles and on them were lashed the food, blankets, firewood and implements.

Bouchette had again come up with some more of his 'perches'. He had found long thin poles sealing the gaps between the timbers on the south gable of the cabin and though it meant the hut was going to be more draughty, both men knew that their sacrifice was little compared with the sufferings that the women and children would have to endure.

The brigade was organized in groups so each party had its own particular responsibility. John Gow and the Mole took charge of transporting the sled and litters. Some of the women would carry light hides and blankets. Those without other assignment looked after the children—to shepherd them when they strayed or wandered, carry them when they lagged or became weary, and entertain them at rest periods or stops along the way.

The Gipsy and Anne had no particular assignment. They were the scout patrol, watching for the unusual. The fun they appeared to get out of life under the toughest going had endeared them to all, and their unselfishness and love for each other was an inspiration. Since their marriage by the Captain of the ship, the joy they found in each other brought a tear of pleasure to the eye of the oldsters and a friendly banter from the younger and less serious ones like Jimmy Gunn.

Two tents had been made for the women, two for the men

and a big one for the children. Attached to the children's tent was a small guard tent where on odd occasions parents or married couples like the Gipsy and Anne could sleep alone and at the same time care for the little ones in the big tent.

After breakfast and the short prayer meeting, Miles spoke.

"I don't know fine words like Lord Selkirk and I can't say things the way I'd like to say them, but having watched you live together, share each other's sorrows, joys and miseries I have no fears as I look ahead to the trials and difficulties we are about to face. Before we reach York Factory you'll be forced to use every ounce of that optimism. You're going to have to grin when you stumble, smile when you freeze and laugh yourself to tears when you feel more like dying. With the help of God we're all going to come through, new and better people. Every leader knows his responsibility. Think of the people who are depending upon you to do that job well. You must pay no attention to the cold muskeg you are going to plough through. You must pay no heed to the endless emptiness which will fill the greater part of each day's journey. Shut your hearts to distress and your ears to complaint. Remember only the duty you have to your children and to your neighbour. Without him you are going to die — without you he has little more than a ghost of a chance. May God protect us all!"

As he paused a chorus of "Amen" and "So mote it be" arose from the muffled heads around him.

"The order of travel will be as follows," he continued, "the Braggart's route is charted. He will lead off and keep half a mile ahead of the main body. When they arrive at the first campsite he will set up tents and prepare the fires so that the women can take over as soon as they get there. David Grant will come next with his group and he will be followed by the Gipsy and the children, and the last two groups will follow. Please keep your positions, stay together and don't break the order of march."

The energy of Miles MacDonell seemed to be inexhaustible. He appeared to be everywhere at once — exhorting the people onward wherever he found a flagger. Often he ranged ahead seeking the easiest way across a river or stream. He kept reminding everyone that survival was a full-time job not just one for the moments around the camp fire.

In spite of all their efforts some did not survive.

Andrew Bain was up in years. He came on the journey because his young wife Julie wanted an opportunity for their boys who

164

were now nine and ten. Andrew was spry for his age. His mind was keen and his unfailing courage provided the spirit that kept him going. But the sea voyage struck hard and a bout of the fever was followed by a week in which a racking cough drained every ounce of his energy. The helplessness of the sick in the pitching, heaving hell of the unknown sea appeared to finish the job and though he had kept up his jollity and optimism for the sake of appearance, those who knew him noticed that something had gone from his life.

At sixty he struggled to keep up with the younger and more active men; but each passing mile seemed an eternity and every tuft of sedge a torture to his aching body. To those who urged him on he remained polite, hopeful and full of spirit.

On the second night out from Churchill, Andrew gently kissed his sleeping wife, walked out into the frigid night and was seen no more.

Next morning Julie was distraught as she clung desperately to Peter and Allen. How otherwise could it be? In Andrew's passing she had been denied even the positiveness of his death. Her one thought was that he could still be saved, or that she might lay a soothing hand on his frozen brow. It was no comfort to her that this was the way of the pioneer, the way of the natives. Her blind grief hid for the moment the magnificence of the sacrifice that man is prepared to make for those he loves and cares most for.

Perhaps her grief would have been with her for a long time, had it not been for Jimmy Gunn. As day followed day and danger followed danger Jimmy had grown to understand the meaning of life. He learned to value the example of others and realised how great was his own dependence on others. Andrew Bain in one night had become his hero. To Julie all he could say whilst standing in the cold bleakness of the cheerless mid-day sun was: "I wish he had been my father. The boys must be very proud of him."

The unexpectedness of this sentiment expressed by a young man whom she always regarded as being hard and bitter made Julie realize she had a new responsibility and she determined that Andrew's death should not be in vain and would leave its mark in their lives and in the lives of others.

That evening Julie left the camp with her two boys and Jimmy Gunn. Together they raised a pile of stones in Andrew's memory and placed his tobacco pipe beneath it. When she returned to camp she told David what they had done.

"Andrew would be happy about it," she said. "He told me

at Churchill that Auld had mentioned how Eskimos raised these piles — they call them "inukoks" — to make the barren emptiness of the land look less empty. Andrew's absence makes this land look much less lonely to me now. He's always going to be out there somewhere — and maybe that pile of stones will make the country look a little less forlorn to those who come after us."

The long trek brought more than its share of sorrow and misery. Two of the babies died of exposure to the unseasonable cold and Hugh Bannerman drowned in one of the innumerable water holes between the long fingered mounds which at times cut across their path. Sickness was rife but despite the misery, they drove relentlessly on or were left to die in the wilderness— Miles MacDonell's instructions were quite clear on that point.

But it wasn't all sorrow and misery.

Many's the laugh that burst from cold-chapped lips and many's the song that was sung to the playing of the Gipsy's chanter in the gloaming by the last glint in the firelight. The little guard tent never lacked an occupant. Its calm ruggedness shielded the tender joys of the secret moment. Its cold embrace quenched many a fire in a longing breast.

To Peter and Janet Gow of Strathnaver, their night of solemn reunion in it will go down in indelible memory. To the trekkers it was to remain one of the most unexplained and hilarious mysteries of the whole journey.

Peter and Janet were an oddly matched pair. Janet was the daughter of the teacher in Strathnaver; she was petite, prim, proper and punctilious in everything she did. On the other hand, Peter could hardly have been more different. He had been the innkeeper in the district — big, florid and hearty.

To most people in the Strath, there was always something remarkable in the way he would celebrate well and truly as "Mine Host" on Saturday and pace carefully down the road to the Kirk on Sunday morning in his best breeches. Janet's father's old hat would pop up and down on his head like a jack-in-the-box as he bowed recognition to all his friends.

Poor Janet used to be on sentry duty all through the sermon. His sniffing and snorting were always a thing of great embarrassment to her. An unguarded sniff from the big man at her side would bring an elbow to his ribs and he would go clumsily to his sleeve for the spotless white handkerchief that Janet insisted he should carry for the occasion. Nevertheless, now and again the stillness of the moment of quiet Presbyterian meditation would

166

be shattered by a trumpet of nasal fury when Peter forgot for the time being that he wasn't behind the bar using the big red cotton cloth which always seemed to be dangling from the pocket of his breeches.

They tried hard, however, and their passion for each other was quite evident for in five years of married life they had already added five little Gows to one of the least prolific tribes of the Scottish Highlands.

Throughout the long weeks of the voyage, Peter had never let Janet down. He tried to live up to the dignity expected of him. It was as though his own uncouthness was bowing in reverence before Janet's gentle primness. He wasn't a hen-pecked man, he was rather the devoted slave of propriety. On that cold September evening they both tucked their warmest clothes around them and crawled quietly into the little guard tent.

The evening was moonlit and starry and a cold but gentle wind blew from the east of the Bay. It was one of the few pleasant evenings of the whole journey and Miles and David had selected the shelter of a gravel knoll in which to set up camp. The site was flanked on the north and on the south by water and its eastern end led off as a ridge to the south. For the last two days they had been picking their way through this hummocky, swampy land keeping to the narrow deer paths between the treacherous acres of stagnant water.

The children's tent was to the south and the women's tents had been pitched on the west with the men's tent forming the northern leg of a U-shape open to the east.

The night was still young. David, Miles and the men were sitting around swapping yarns when suddenly the night air was rent by a storm of anguish from the big tent to the south.

Miles and David dashed through the deerskin flaps and gazed in amazement as the little guard tent did a jig in the cold night air, paused for a rest, then flapped frantically. Grunts, groans and gasps came from a bulky figure in shirt tail which hurled itself out through the end wall, catapulted over a rock lying in its path and pitched head-long over the bank and into the water.

Then through the front flap dashed Janet Gow in her thick woollens. "Oh dear! Oh dear!", she whined, "what's gone wrong, Peter? Where are you?"

But all she could hear were grunts, splashes and truly the choicest of bar-room adjectives which she hoped had been left behind for good in Strathnaver some 3,000 miles away. She raced round the tent with Miles, David and the Highlanders close behind her.

She was a gay, spritely figure in her long drawers with the cut-out clearly showing in the seat. But she had forgotten all about this in the urgency of the moment. After all, you don't simply lie still in bed nor do you bother about dressing yourself when your husband suddenly decides to take off in the midst of one of the most passionate, intimate moments of your married life!

For all her sobriety, Janet was like anyone else. Her first concern was for her departed husband. As she whisked around the end of the tent to the mound she gave little thought to the grotesque figure she cut in the barrenness of this Canadian north-land.

She reached the edge just as Peter was pulling himself up the side. He was wet, bedraggled and miserably cold. His teeth chattered, his face and hands were blue and all he wanted was the shelter and warmth of his deerskin. As he raised himself to his feet and saw Janet standing gazing at him in her ludicrous state of undress, his eyes popped from his head.

"God Alm . . . " he gasped, but pulled himself together before offending the ear with such profanity.

He looked at her, this time the incongruity of the situation tickling his fancy. "What on earth are you wearing?"

He stood and chortled. He panted. Then he laughed and the wilderness around echoed back his laughter and everyone saw the funny side. Everyone laughed and Janet laughed and cried simultaneously. Peter picked her up gently and wrapped her in his great hulking wet arms. He carried her to the tent and laid her among the blankets and skins and for a moment he had forgotten his own cold misery.

Peter had been terror-stricken by the flapping wings of a cold, starving ptarmigan that had somehow strayed in under the flaps of the tent. In the dark, close, confines the little bird took on enormous proportions and in Peter's inexperienced mind had become an object of mortal danger. He lashed out at it wildly, heaved himself away from his wife, split the sewing on the eastern side of the tent, tripped over the rock and landed in the miserably cold, water-soaked mud.

The experience taught Janet the essential part of the process of living in such close dependence on others. For the first time she had been able to take a good look at herself and laugh. She was at last equipped to be a pioneer in a rough, relentless land.

168

The final twenty miles to Selkirk's depot were the most difficult. The settlers had floundered so long through deep snow that their tired bodies and hearts would gladly have settled down to die had not Miles and David pushed them on.

On the fifteenth day temperatures began to rise and snow fell heavily. Great white flakes blanketed the land and blinded the marchers. This was followed by a rising wind that lashed the snow mercilessly against the ranks. Again MacDonell's trail sense came to their aid. He had given specific instructions to the Braggart that when the weather showed signs of changing for the worse he was to back-track until the entire body was united. This accomplished, the Sutherlanders closed their ranks and with heads down struggled into the blinding blizzard.

"This is not what we bargained for when we left Cavaick," David commented one night to Miles as they sat chewing frozen ptarmigan legs.

Miles grinned. "I didn't promise you this either, David, but you still have more than you had living under the heel of the Countess."

"It seems to me, Miles, that all you had to offer was freedom to freeze to death in this wilderness."

"Or freedom to live a life of respect and dignity," retorted Miles spiritedly. "There's only twenty miles to go. The battle's almost won. Let's continue to fight and suffer for another three days. The snow musn't hold us back. We must drive on to the Nelson. We must keep moving."

It was on the second night after the snows that the Mole went missing.

Since the fight, he had continued to be morose and whenever he could get someone to listen, he became argumentative and quite objectionable. Bitterness against David still smouldered within. Though he did his part in the daily routine he contributed nothing to the success of the trek.

It was with many misgivings that David and Braggart headed back through the snow and bitter wind to the ice-scarred granite rocks where Mole had last been seen. On the northern edge, frost had dug deep into the cracks and crevices and wedged out great blocks which now lay half-hidden in the snow. They circled round to the southern edge calling, "Mole!" as they went. But there was no reply. The biting wind whipped their voices into silence.

It wasn't until they had reached the north side of the rock that they found him — a black shadow against the whiteness of the snow. He had fallen from the slippery rocks and struck his head. Fortunately he had come to rest part-way under the shelter of the rock but his foot had caught in a cleft and his ankle injured. Now he lay head-down in the darkness oblivious to the discomforts of the night.

"Why not leave him?" howled Braggart into the wind. "Miles has shown us that we can't afford to be handicapped with anyone who will be a drag on our progress."

"We can't leave the bugger," snapped David. "He can still fire a rifle."

"You should be the last one to lift a finger to help him."

"Maybe," returned David. "Now give me a hand to get him out of here."

They were standing together howling against the fury of the wind. David gesticulated violently to enforce his point. After a tussle the Mole was hoisted onto David's shoulders for the journey back to camp.

In the barren Canadian northland, Braggart had learned the first law of the wilderness. Top in order of survival stands man the hunter, the provider, the defender — without him there is little chance for survival of wife, children or grandparent. Without the able-bodied settlers there was no hope that any of them would reach the Red River.

No matter how he might distrust this man, no matter how much he resented his efforts to undermine the discipline and authority of Miles and himself, David knew that they needed every pair of able hands that they could muster. His personal feelings or those of the Braggart had to be set aside in the interest of the majority. As they staggered into the camp and laid Mole under the pile of blankets and deerskins in the men's tent, everyone knew that they were witnessing another inevitable law of this relentless new land.

Throughout the following day David stayed with the Mole and helped him hobble along behind the others. When he suggested that because of his injury Mole should stay behind with one of the tents, he gratefully accepted. Arrangements were made to return from York Factory to pick him up, while his wife and children moved ahead with the brigade.

Next morning when told that this was the final day of the trek, some wanted to leave their tents and travel light to Fort York where they expected that Selkirk had prepared for their arrival. Miles refused saying: "In this country you don't leave

170

valuable equipment lying around. You've carried it all the way from Churchill. You can carry it the last few miles."

As they moved out Mole stood by the door of his tent.

"Grant," he said, "have you a minute?"

David stopped and accepted the hand that was thrust towards him in silence.

"Thank you," said Mole. "I won't forget."

"It's nothing," said David. "We need you around a little longer. We'll be back in a couple of days to pick you up."

The column moved forward and by mid-afternoon they saw the Hudson's Bay Company flag flying from Fort York. The shouts that echoed through the cold still air resembled the joy of castaways who had spotted an island in the distance. Those who could, ran down the hill anxious to feel the warmth of a fire and the comfort of a cabin wall. The others plodded doggedly after.

In place of a commodious fort they found only three small shacks half-buried in the snow. They were frozen, empty and there was no evidence of the supplies that they had been promised and so desperately needed. Snow was still falling and it was well below zero.

"Where do we go from here?" asked David. "How far are we from Red River, Miles?"

"About 700 or 800 miles," MacDonell replied. "It's too late in the year to move inland. We'll have to winter here. At least there is some sign of life."

He gazed through the large flakes at a tall, dignified figure dressed in a black buffalo robe and wearing a headdress. He strode forward and spoke in a language that none of the settlers understood.

"He's a Cree Chief," he explained to the awed settlers. "His tribe are camped a short distance away. He said the factor of the depot went inland with the fur brigade after the pick-up ship sailed. We'll have the place to ourselves."

Grumbling broke out. This was the last straw.

Miles sensed trouble and decided he had to keep the Sutherlanders busy. He raised his voice for attention. "Don't waste your time complaining. You are men of Sutherland and it matters not at this moment what promises were made. From the time you were born your lives have been a continual struggle for existence. On the trek from Churchill you've shown that determination and courage can win. Surely you haven't lost your guts now! There's room in the cottages for the women and children. You have tents and there's probably more in the shacks."

"MacDonell is right," David sang out. "We've come this far and I'll be damned if I want to quit now. Come on, let's get to work. Braggart, Gipsy, follow me, we'll make something out of this nothingness."

The days that followed were filled with feverish activity. MacDonell arranged with the Cree Chief to have his braves help set up the wigwams, teepees and wikiups while the friendly squaws were everywhere encouraging the men, suggesting faster and better ways to repair the poorly-built shacks and to make the women and children comfortable.

They had found saws and axes in the factor's cabin. They filled the cracks between the logs with clay and moss cut from the frozen ground and thawed out in front of the campfire. Large rocks from the riverbank provided fireplaces. Fortunately there was a good supply of driftwood cast on the shoreline. This had drifted down the Nelson and the Hayes from the scrub forests of the interior.

By the end of October the cabins had been rebuilt and the settlers were lodged in units with their own family responsibilities. For the present they were protected from the snow and the cold, and the chances for survival looked better.

During the construction period the Gipsy and the Indians had become friends. For one thing, the sound of his bagpipes had aroused their curiosity. Often, within the wigwam which they had specially built for the Gipsy and Anne, the Indian tom-tom beaters attempted to synchronize their rhythmic cadences with the Gipsy's music as he piped the Highland marching airs.

When the Cree hunters made a kill they shared their meat with the white settlers. On these occasions the carcass would be roasted over a huge fire on the earthen floor of a teepee. This was a rare treat for the Sutherlanders. As time went on the meetings between Crees and colonists took on the atmosphere of a Highland *ceilidh*. Before long the Sutherlanders, as well as their children, learned many of the habits and hunting tricks of their wilderness companions. The natives taught them how to judge the depth of the ice on the lakes and streams, how to draw maps and make signs on the bark of trees for those who were to follow. They also learned the ways of the beaver, the moose and other animals and great was the jubilation the day David Grant tracked down a deer and killed it with an arrow.

172

Soon the brigade, by sign and language, were able to convey to the red man some idea of the unhappy circumstances that had brought them to the shores of Hudson's Bay. By the same means they learned that the Indian totem was the emblem of each tribe. The totem might consist of a turtle, a buffalo, an eagle, a bear, a moose, or some special symbol.

"Aye," declared the Gipsy as he unclasped the silver crest from his tattered bonnet. "We have totems, too. This, my friends, is the totem of my people." He handed his 'Sans Peur'* crest to the Chief who in turn passed it among his tribesmen.

The shining ornament was quick to attract the fancy of the natives. The chief was so taken with it that he produced a robe of white ermine and offered it in exchange to the Gipsy.

The Gipsy made the trade. "This will make a New Year's present for Anne," he declared.

With the coming of the New Year MacDonell ordered the snow cleared from a large oval in front of the campsite. The Chief and his warriors supplied pine torches to outline the area and light up the night's festivities. Never was Hogmanay celebrated in a more primitive and colorful manner. The Cree warriors, bedecked with multi-hued paint and head feathers, performed their dances to the beat of the tom-toms, presenting a strange and colorful contrast to the Sutherlanders hopping around the compound to the tune of the Gipsy's lively reels and Highland flings.

As the merrymaking increased the natives attempted to imitate the dancing and exultant whoops of the Highlanders. At the hour of midnight ranks closed to sing 'Auld Lang Syne'. Red hands joined white hands in a great circle of friendship. Thus was the fateful year of 1812 welcomed by the Sutherlanders at Selkirk's remote wilderness depot.

---

* "Sans Peur" (Without Fear) — the motto of the Sutherland people.

CHAPTER EIGHTEEN

West to Red River

"Let thine arm reach to the renown of they fathers. Be thy course in the field, like the eagle's wing. Why shouldst thou fear death, my son? The valiant fall with fame; their shields turn the dark stream of danger away."

LATHMON

ONE MORNING in late spring, David Grant was roused from his sleep by a series of sharp staccato noises, followed by a thunderous roar that shattered the stillness of the Nelson River Valley and brought the settlers scurrying from their bunks into the early dawn.

In the compound, sounds of excitement mingled with shouts of delight arose from men and women who ran from their cabins and tents to gather in chattering little groups.

"What's all the din about?" demanded David of the Braggart.

"Ice is breaking on the river! David. Isn't it a wonderful sound? The hardship we have suffered since leaving the Highlands will soon be behind us."

David placed his hand on his friend's shoulders. "It's great news, Braggart. Can I tell you now how proud I am of you? You have given strength, courage and hope to our people." He hailed Miles MacDonell as he saw his muffled figure wading through the snow.

"How long, Miles, how long will it be before we are on our way again?"

"It's hard to say. It all depends on the weather and how much ice must be moved. Warmer weather will hurry the flow along. You are soon going to find it uncomfortably hot in these parkas."

The Mole, now completely recovered from his fall, stuck his head from behind the moosehide drape that covered the door of his wikiup. "What's all the disturbance?" he shouted.

"You ignorant goat," jested the Gipsy in the Gaelic. "Don't you know that the breaking of the ice is the first sign of spring?"

All winter David and the colonists had been busy fashioning river boats from huge logs that Selkirk had delivered to the settlement prior to their arrival. Four of the boats were now ready, and with the sound of break-up, and warmer weather in the offing, efforts were renewed to finish a further eight boats required to take the first brigade up the river and over the divide to their journey's end.

Each lengthening day, as the ice flowed past the encampment, hearts and tasks became lighter. With renewed diligence, the ship-building continued. The boats were heavy and ugly but Miles insisted they would be a safe means of transportation.

In the wake of the vanishing ice came the Saskatchewan fur brigade, a collection of canoes and buckskin-dressed trappers who shouted, laughed and strutted among the fascinated settlers. The Hudson Bay factor was with them. After greeting the colonists, he stored the trappers' furs and placed them in the shacks the Sutherlanders were preparing to evacuate.

Early in July, the Sutherlanders broke camp in a manner again characteristic of the discipline and efficiency drilled into them by Miles MacDonell. The flat-bottomed boats were skidded to the river bank, launched and loaded. Winter furs, blankets, tools and food were carefully stored aboard. They donned their tattered Highland regalia and followed the Gipsy's skirling pipes to the embarkation point. The women and children went aboard the boats while the men slipped into birchbark canoes that MacDonell had purchased from the Indians.

Only the Mole seemed to get started on the wrong foot. When his canoe was being launched, it upset, tossing him into the icy river. He emerged, dripping and dishevelled. "It's an ill omen," he spluttered as he staggered up the riverbank. "Bad luck!"

"You're raving like an idiot!" his wife scolded. "You've always bragged about being tossed into the stormy waters of Loch Brora from your mother's wash tub. Now you whimper like a whipped puppy because you made a fool, a clumsy fool, of yourself by upsetting your canoe. Shame on you, man."

175

"Hold your blathering tongue, woman, or I'll throw you in," blustered the dripping Mole.

There was no time for doleful predictions. Seven hundred miles of hazard-filled wilderness lay between them and their destination and all were anxious to get underway. The oarsmen soon discovered that their winter in camp had not prepared them for such an arduous task. Muscles began to ache and arms and legs grew tired. Soon their hands had blistered and were bleeding from the friction of the oars, setting poles, and towing ropes. But with the passing days they toughened; the pain went out of their backs and legs and the flesh grew firmer, the blisters turned to callouses and tiredness vanished. Their movements became fluent and economical — muscular bodies rising and falling in rhythmic time.

Their skill and dexterity grew as they poled through the shallows or bent their backs to track past the rapids. They became accustomed to the hurried unloadings and reloadings and the backbreaking effort across the portage with the heavy loads.

At times the bleak waste stretched into emptiness; then the gloomy vastness would change into black precipices, yawning gulfs and towering rocks whose naked backs had withstood the storm and ice of centuries. When they came to a narrow gorge the lazy Nelson would become a thrusting, swirling cataract rampaging in foaming flood over ragged elbows of rock that jutted above the torrent's surface. Only the extraordinary skill of the oarsmen could guide their heavy craft and canoes past the dangers that lurked above and below the turbulent surface.

David Grant enjoyed battling the river. As the convoy progressed from rapids to deep water to narrow canyons and back to wide open stretches, he relaxed in the changing panorama. The days were pleasant and grew warmer as the party moved upstream away from Hudson's Bay. Jeannie rested in the warm sun in a cozy corner of the river boat, and the children, Fiona and Joseph, squealed with delight at the fish the men caught or at the sight of the moose and bear on the river bank.

The Grants travelled in the same boat as the Gipsy and Anne and as the weeks rolled on it became evident that the marriage consummated on the pitching deck of the *Prince of Wales* was about to produce its first fruit.

Before leaving the encampment it had been arranged that a dark shirt would be hoisted over the boat if the expected child were to be a boy, and a white shirt if a girl.

176

Now as the brigade entered the rapids above Mossy Portage, the Mole pointed to the boat and shouted, "Look, there's the black shirt. It's a boy!"

The colonists yelled a welcome. The Gipsy stood up to play a reel for the new arrival and almost fell overboard as the boat lurched suddenly into foaming rapids. But soon the flotilla was out into the calm waters of Swampy Lake and Miles MacDonell signalled them into a quiet backwater.

The crafts were beached and the settlers crowded around to see the Gipsy's baby feeding lustily at his mother's breast. The birth of the child was a tonic to the Sutherlanders; he had brought them new life — hope for their future.

MacDonell's voice boomed out: "Men and women of Sutherland, may I have your attention? It's only fitting that the first white child born in this land should be baptized in a way that we'll all remember. We'll have a baptismal service and celebrate the christening with a festive supper."

The assembly cheered. "Everyone will do his part. The Braggart and the Mole will shoot a couple of calf moose. The women will prepare a few delicacies that I have stored away, and the rest of you can set up camp and build fires. There's enough rum to provide a dram for all!"

When the fires were roaring and the moose were being barbecued, MacDonell had Anne, the Gipsy and the baby brought before him. Scooping a horn of water from Swampy Lake he stood on a boulder facing the travellers.

"Men and women of Sutherland, since you left your homeland you have faced many stern tests and disappointments, yet you have survived. The child before you in his father's arms is living proof that not all the terrors we go through can stop this regeneration of our people. In this child's eyes we see hope; his presence gives us courage for our future. Without a minister to attend to the living and to the dead your problems have multiplied. But God is with us, watching over this baptism as though it had been performed at home in our church."

As he sprinkled a few drops of water on the child's head, MacDonell intoned: "In the name of the Father and the Son and the Holy Ghost, I name you Donald Gipsy MacPherson." He turned to the festive group. "To the best of my knowledge this is the first white child to be born in the territory."

John Bannerman moved forward and handed Miles his old family Bible. "I'd be proud to have the name of the Gipsy, Anne and Donald enrolled with my kin in this Holy volume. The records go back for over two hundred years but never would the entry have been so well deserved."

A mighty cheer greeted the old man's words.

Miles made the entry. "I think it's time for a drop of Selkirk's rum," he commented, as he closed the Book and turned to broach the keg. "Come on, Gipsy! On with the music!"

The Gipsy exchanged his baby for his pipes and struck up a lively Highland reel. Immediately, the men and women were dancing on the rocky shores of the wilderness lake. Their wild hurrahs and 'hoochs' awoke the echo until it seemed that the huge dark rocks around were all singing in chorus. Every now and then they paused to enjoy a slice of moose meat and a wee noggin of rum.

Near dawn, when the perspiring Sutherlanders lay down to rest their tired bodies on the banks of Swampy Lake, little did they realize that a horrible danger, more distressing than they had ever encountered, lay ahead.

It was late afternoon three days later when Miles beached the convoy and made arrangements to portage. Further navigation at this point was impossible. Although the boats proved cursedly heavy and unwieldy to carry, and progress had become slow and rough, spirits were still high. It was a welcome change from the river and there was plenty of game to supply them with food. It was hot by day, but the nights were cool and it was a well-earned pleasure to rest weary limbs around the campfire flames and fall to dreaming — dreaming of the reality that awaited them in the promised land.

"Thank God!" sighed John Bannerman, his chest heaving in its ancient frame. "The seven hundred miles to Selkirk's Red River Valley are gradually becoming shorter. A land waiting in all its virgin richness, a land where we can enjoy the results of our toil, the creations of our ingenuity, the product of our hands, where we can cultivate, build homes, raise cattle and where we'll all prosper — a land where a man can work and have pride — a land where none shall call another master. Praised be the Lord!"

"Amen," came the chorus.

The way became swampy and the sun that burned and scorched and shot its rays into the heart caused a dank, damp, soul-pervading humidity — so intense and fierce that to breathe became laborious and to move, a hardship. Even thinking was an effort.

178

The shrubs were hot and clammy. The earth was mucky, steaming. The air they inhaled stifled and suffocated, and memories of the clear, fresh breeze of the hills at home haunted them like evil chimeras that mocked their present plight.

Then came the pestilent hordes: nurtured and propagated by the heat, humidity and the leafy density, these bloody parasites— mosquitoes, black flies, clegs — filthy objects and merciless opponents beset the Sutherlanders.

There was no escaping the onslaught. It came at them from everywhere and despite the curt oaths and sharp slaps as men, women and children flailed themselves in a vain attempt to destroy the blighting things, the bloodsucking devils continued to attack their aching, sweating limbs.

Their plight became so severe that travel was impossible and Miles, in desperation, ordered the winter clothes unpacked.

Beneath the scorching sun and swaddled in the heavy hides of winter, the colonists struggled on. The little ones were driven to a point of insanity; their faces and every exposed part of their bodies were swollen and bloody. To make matters worse, the soil had become so boggy that they had to cast aside their tattered shoes and plough bare-foot through the endless marshes.

Before continuing the portage, Miles told them that the pests would be with them for two more days. "They have their own plan of attack," he said, "like the women, the female is the deadliest. Her sharp beak pierces the skin and before you know what's happened she has siphoned out her meal of blood and she's gone, leaving you with her itching, pricking punishment. They dash through the smoke of camp-fire or strong tobacco like a foxhound through bulrushes; they will creep under veil or glove like a ferret in a rabbit-hole; where they can neither dash nor creep they bide their own time with the pertinacious cunning of a red Indian. They'll creep in single file up the seams of your gloves and try each stitch in succession until they find an opening — God help you then. I know it's going to be most difficult but try to avoid scratching. Try to keep your clothes from touching the knee or elbow closely."

The following morning it was obvious that no one had slept. They had lain awake swatting their vicious enemy. Inability to resist the urge to rub and scratch was evident from the blotched, patchwork mass of inflamed, swollen eruptions on arms, legs and faces, crimson-streaked with bloodmixed pus, repulsive and loathsome.

"Oh, God!" sighed a Highlander, "it would have been better if I myself had gone with the hundred smokes up the chimney. Then at least I would have died in peace amidst my native hills."

David glanced around in answer to a mournful cry from Jeannie. She was looking down, her face curling in disgust. A black fly, a bloated thing, stomach distended, clung to her ankle. She jerked her leg — it fell to the ground heavily saturated — too full of human blood to fly. David, grinding his heel upon it, could almost hear the brittle crunch and squelch as its glutted body mingled with the sodden ground.

The Gipsy, fetching water in a goat-skin bag, recognized on every face the lines of despondency and despair. He heard Anne choke back a sob as she suckled her babe. "Poor lass," he thought, as he approached to comfort her.

"Miles," said David. "Did all of these pests simply arrive with us from Sutherland? In my little cottage at 'Cavaick' Colin Robertson spoke about the beasts, fish and richness of the country but only now do we learn about plagues of insects that could wreak more havoc in a few weeks than the worst of the Countess' evictions."

"Well, David," replied Miles with a wry grin. "No one expects to find perfection in man, beast or Countess. Once you get settled in the Red River Valley, all this suffering will be forgotten by the blessings you'll find there. When we reach Lake Winnipeg the going will become more comfortable. Meanwhile, let's all pull together; let's keep faith."

The three lakes, Swampy, Knee and Oxford, proved more enjoyable; the worst of the mosquitoes had been left behind. On the lakes the men raised rough sails over the river boats and as the wind scudded them ahead the rowers had a chance to relax. Beyond Oxford Lake, the flotilla entered a narrow gorge between precipitous cliffs known as Hell Gates, and from then on they pushed down through a chain of small lakes and connecting streams until at Painted Rock Portage, they reached the summit of the slope drained by the Hayes River. They followed the Echemamish to Hairy Lake, then by Blackwater Creek to the Nelson River again and on to Lake Winnipeg. The huge body of water seemed so enormous that David thought they had reached the seas on the western shores.

A few days later they arrived at the mouth of the Red River and from here they continued to its junction with the Assiniboine. On August 30, 1812, a year and thirty-five days after leaving the Highlands, the weary but hopeful Sutherlanders reached the land they would now call home.

As he stepped ashore David Grant scanned the wide empty meadows beyond the river bank. "There's nothing here," he declared in amazement. "Didn't Selkirk promise homes and equipment!"

"Something unexpected has prevented his lordship from carrying out his plans," was all Miles could say.

Jeannie looked at David.

"We've been deceived again," she murmured, her eyes full of tears.

David put his arm around her. "Aye, lass, but we're here now and this looks like a fair and free land. God's help is all we need." He knelt down and dug at the soil with his hands. It was black and rich, so different from the rocky ground that he had worked all his life in the Highlands.

MacDonell called for attention in order to make one last announcement. The warm prairie sun beat down on the assemblage. In the distance a slight breeze ruffled the leaves of the trees on the river bank, where birds chirped cheerfully and the Red flowed sluggishly by.

"People of Sutherland," he said, "I know that each of you must feel bitterly disappointed to find nothing but barren prairie to greet you after such a long journey. From the size and loneliness of this land you must appreciate how difficult it would be for Selkirk to fulfill his promises in so short a time. There is nothing to gain standing here like the sheep that replaced you in the Highland glen! If we make the best of what we've got you'll become successful, land-owning farmers. Let us get down on our knees and thank God for what He has already done for us. Let us ask His protection in the days ahead."

After the service David spoke: "Fellow Sutherlanders, we should thank God for Miles MacDonell. He trusted Lord Selkirk as we did, but he kept his promise and brought us safely to the most fertile soil that any of us have ever seen. I, for one, intend to make my home here." He turned to his wife. "Jeannie, have you got the heather?"

Indeed, she had. Through the many weeks at sea, fighting the frozen wastes along Hudson's Bay and across the lakes region to the Red River, Jeannie had carried her tiny root of heather, wrapped in a small bag. Often it had been protected by the warmth of her body, under her petticoat. Now as she drew it

181

tenderly from its moss and woollen wrap, she wondered if the little bit of Highland life had survived.

"Look at it, David!" she exclaimed excitedly. "It's still alive! It will grow!"

"This is a momentous occasion, Jeannie! Gather the children together, get some water from the Red River and we'll plant a little piece of Cavaick."

David unsheathed his dirk and dug a hole in the black loam. Taking the plant gently in his hand, he placed it in the soil. He stood and spoke. "This sprig of heather I give to the rich soil of our new country. May this be a sign that we have come to stay. Let us hope that along with our people, it will thrive."

The spot where David had planted his heather was two miles from Fort Gibraltar — the local headquarters of the North-West Company. John Willis, the commandant of the fort, had earlier called to introduce himself. Even though he realized that the settlers were sponsored by Selkirk, the rival Hudson's Bay Company, he welcomed them and gave the women and children temporary accommodation in the Company buildings whilst the men-folk set to building new homes in the valley.

MacDonell named the new settlement Colony Gardens.

Each man was given ten acres on the river bank and included in it were the rights to the rough scrub forest which had rooted itself by the river. David built close to the spot where he and Jeannie had planted the heather.

By the end of September he had completed a sturdy log cabin with a sod roof, and with his family, had moved in and started to work the land. There were no oxen or horses and no farm implements. Their only tools were a few spades, hoes and axes that they had managed to obtain from Gibraltar or had brought with them from Selkirk's depot. It was too late in the season to plant crops and a few weeks after the colony had begun to settle down, fate was to decree that they must move again.

One evening, Miles called at the Grant cabin. Jeannie left her cooking pot to greet their visitor. "It's buffalo stew. Will you stay to supper?"

"I'll be most happy to. You are lucky to have buffalo meat; most of the settlers are without."

"I was able to get a haunch from one of the Indians. If there's no meat, a hungry winter is in store for all."

"That's what I came to talk with you about. There is no place to get enough food for the sixty people in the settlement. We've

182

got to get them to Pembina where the Company's hunting parties live during winter. It's the only place we will be able to find food and shelter."

Jeannie was startled. "Oh, Miles," she protested. "We've been travelling for so long; can't we stay here? This is our home."

MacDonell smiled sympathetically. "Of course this is your home, Jeannie. And you'll come back to it in the spring. If we are going to live through the winter we must follow the buffalo." He turned to David. "Pembina is seventy miles from here and it's imperative that we get the settlers moving; they must pack without delay."

"That won't be easy," replied David. "Most of them have their cabins built and the last thing they want is to move again. I'll see what I can do."

The Sutherlanders grumbled, but they had become accustomed to change and hardship and although the weather had turned bitterly cold and snow was falling across the prairie, they moved out into the wilderness once more.

The Fort at Pembina provided accommodation for the women and children. The men lived with the French and the half-breeds while they built their own shelters. The floors were of clay and the windows were filled with straw to keep out the wind, but they had food and shelter and that was most important for the moment. David, the Braggart, the Mole, and the Gipsy joined buffalo hunts and learned how to ride Indian ponies bareback on the snow-drifted plains. The closeness of the chase tended to foster warmth and understanding between the races and it was with regret that they parted when the Sutherlanders returned to Red River in May of 1813.

Colony Gardens remained as they had left it. The cabins had wintered well and the men immediately turned their attention to preparing the soil for spring planting. They tilled with spades — long, laborious work — but the land was rich and easily broken. It was remarkable how well the small supply of wheat and oats, purchased by Miles from Fort Alexander on Winnipeg River, multiplied in the warm moistness of spring.

Unfortunately, however, blackbirds and pigeons, passing over the colony on their way South during the harvest ate over eighty percent of their crops. Another bleak hungry winter was in store for them. Fish was scarce. Roots and berries they had valued as food were not plentiful. Their only means of survival was a harsh and tasteless wild parsnip which grew in abundance and a plant called Fat-Hen, similar to a nettle, which they ate raw or boiled.

Winter again found the colonists on their way to Pembina. This time things were entirely different. The cabins they had built the year before were now occupied and the buffalo had moved further away into the open plains. Pembina had less to offer than the settlement they had just left.

In a temperature well below zero the suffering from cold and hunger was beyond human endurance. They knew not who would be the next to die or from where the next food was to come. Had it not been for an Indian who agreed to take them to the camp of his people, it is doubtful if any would have survived. There the Sutherlanders were received with great kindness. They were provided with food, clothing and shoes and shared the already cramped quarters with the native people.

At least they had found a haven of refuge for the winter, but they were not experienced hunters and knew little of the dangers of the chase. Neither had they anything with which to purchase provisions. They were as poor as the Indians themselves, for everything they could spare, every article of clothing not on their backs, had already been bartered away to sustain life. They had to become the drudges of the camp, slaves of the slaves, while the natives went hunting.

When the Sutherlanders returned to the colony they were in great destitution and so discouraged that they resolved never to return to Pembina. Fate, however, was shaping new complications for their life in Colony Gardens.

In the fall of 1813 when the colonists had moved to Pembina, Miles MacDonell had been appointed Governor of the District of Assiniboia for the Hudson's Bay Company. He had also been nominated by Lord Selkirk to superintend the colony. Motivated by a sincere interest in the well-being of all and determined to protect the Sutherlanders against want, he issued the following proclamation in the early months of 1814.

Whereas the Right Honourable Thomas, Earl of Selkirk is anxious to provide for the families at present forming settlements on his land at Red River, with those on the way to it, passing the winter at Churchill and York Factory in Hudson's Bay, and also those who are expected to arrive next Autumn, it becomes a necessary, indispensable part of my duty to provide for their support. In the yet uncultivated state of the country, the ordinary resources derived from the

184

buffalo and other wild animals hunted within the territory are not deemed more than adequate for the requisite supply. Therefore, it is hereby ordered, that no person trading furs or provisions within the territory of the Honourable Hudson's Bay Company, or the North-West Company, or any individual, or unconnected traders, or persons whatever, shall take any provisions, either of flesh, fish, grain or vegetable, procured or raised within the said territory, by water or land carriage, for one twelve month from the date hereof, save and except what may be judged necessary for the trading parties at this time within the territory, to carry them to their respective destinations; and who may, on due application to me, obtain a licence for the same.

The provisions procured and raised as above shall be taken for the use of the colony; and that no loss may accrue to the parties concerned, they will be paid for by British bills at the customary rate. And be it further made known that whosoever shall aid and assist in carrying out, or attempting to carry out, any provisions prohibited as above, either by water or land, shall be taken into custody, and prosecuted as the law in such cases directs and the provisions so taken, as well as any goods and chattels, of what nature soever, which may be taken along with them, and also the carriages and cattle instrumental in conveying away the same to any part but to the settlement on Red River shall be forfeited.

Given under my hand, at Fort Daer (Pembina) the 8th day of January, 1814.

Signed, Miles MacDonell, *Governor,*
By order of the Governor.

When the North-West Company at Fort Gibraltar received the news, fast canoes were dispatched eastward and a few weeks later a hardy coureur du bois slipped into the offices of the North-West Company in Fort William with a copy of MacDonell's proclamation. The news evoked from the North-West traders the bitterest of outcries against the colonists and set off a chain of events that had been feared, even expected, by the Sutherlanders.

"Lord Selkirk must be compelled by law to force MacDonell to rescind this order," thundered William MacGillivray, the chairman, at a directors' meeting.

"If I know Selkirk, legal means will have no effect," disagreed another director.

"That's right," said another. "By the time the law acts, Mac-Donell will have cut off our pemmican supplies and isolated us from our western branches and depots. We must use force to protect ourselves."

At Colony Gardens the Sutherlanders were ignorant of the evil forces Miles had inadvertently set in motion. They were too busy cultivating the land, extending their cleared areas, sowing grain and vegetables and looking forward to their first abundant harvest.

It was at this time that Duncan Cameron, a Gaelic speaking Highlander, who had replaced Willis as factor at the North-West Company fort at Fort Gibraltar, arrived. He strode boldly from the river in a red military coat, sword swinging by his side, and nailed his notice of appointment to the gates of the fort so that all could read of his authority. For the first few days he assumed a friendly air with everyone; he visited among the colonists and having the Gaelic, he was immediately accepted, especially by those who had just arrived with the second brigade of settlers.

Many of these were from Sutherland and a few from Ireland. There were Gunns, Bannermans, McKays, Smiths, Stewarts, Mc-Beths and Sutherlands. Jeannie and David remembered many of them and spent hours catching up on the news from Brora where many hundreds still lived in misery on the beaches. Public opinion, however, had called a halt to the Countess' evictions.

They had been told glowing stories about the first settlers and they had expected great things. But if it were possible, they were even more disappointed than the First Brigade when they reached the Red River. Their discontent was ripe for Cameron to exploit.

It was evident to David that his plan was to weaken Selkirk's colony by inducing the settlers to join his North-West Company.

"Hello, David," he remarked affably as he stopped to have a chat one afternoon. "I'm having a little celebration at the Fort tomorrow night; I'd like you and Jeannie to come."

So the Grants, Gipsy, and Anne and many more at Colony Gardens accepted the invitation.

Cameron feted them well. They had roast duck, deer meat and strong whisky and after the banquet they enjoyed the dance while fiddles and bagpipes put out one lively reel after another.

"Oh, David, I'm having so much fun," Jeannie remarked. "It's such a long time since we danced."

David enjoyed the evening, but he was disturbed. A new-comer, George Campbell, had formed a very close friendship with Cameron. Moving from one group to another the two of them eventually came to David and the Gipsy.

186

"David, my boy, how are you enjoying yourself?" Cameron asked in the Gaelic.

"I'm grateful to you, Duncan. We're having a wonderful time."

They discussed the crops, the hardships of the country and the likelihood that it could be a hungry winter.

David did not encourage conversation so Cameron continued. "You should go to Eastern Canada. The winters there are much warmer."

"That would be foolish," replied David. "We've built our cabins and I'm sure the crops we are about to harvest are going to enable us to enjoy prosperous times in the Valley."

"We'd have the struggle all over again if we went East," added the Gipsy.

"No, this is not true," Cameron remarked. "Did you know that the North-West Company is offering free grants of land and will provide settlers with implements and supplies?"

The Gipsy's eyes widened. "That sounds good."

"Hold on, Gipsy," David interjected. "Selkirk promised us the same, didn't he? You know that promises have a way of being broken?"

"You can believe the word of the North-West Company," Cameron said reassuringly.

"That's right," Campbell agreed. "I believe them. I've had enough of Selkirk and MacDonell and the empty promises they've made. I'm throwing in with the Nor'Westers."

"I like it here. This is my home," David retorted.

"And I feel the same," declared the Gipsy. He turned to Campbell. "You can go on any wild goose chase you like, but I'm staying right here."

"We musn't leave the ladies alone too long," remarked Cameron. "David, do you mind if I dance with your wife?"

"Not at all." He stood aside so Jeannie could follow Cameron onto the rough plank floor, where she was led into a lively Highland reel.

Next morning David told Miles MacDonell what had taken place at the party.

"So I understand," said Miles. "Cameron has employed Campbell to sow dissension among the colonists. There's nothing I can do to prevent them from going anywhere they wish. However, I have the authority to curb the North-West Company's influence in this valley and I intend to do it. This letter will be delivered to them today." He handed a paper to David.

187

To Duncan Cameron, Esquire,
Fort Gibraltar,
Red River Territory.

Dear Sir:

Acting on behalf of your landlord, the Right Honorable Thomas, Earl of Selkirk, I do hereby give you official notice that you and all your associates of the North-West Company must quit the post and premises you now occupy at the forks of the Red River within six calendar months from the date hereof. Penalty for failure to accede to these directives will result in the confiscation of all your goods and the imprisonment of yourself and your employees.

Miles MacDonell,
Governor, Red River Colony.

"That means Cameron must be out of here by mid-April," David commented.

"Yes, by next spring we'll be rid of his interference!"

"He'll probably find a lot of sympathizers among the settlers. He's wined and dined them, speaks their language and he's very well liked."

"I doubt that he's won over too many," MacDonell retorted. "Many will stand firm."

"He's not only trying to get them to move east, but he wants to hire men to work for the company here," pointed out David. "He's offering good pay and accommodation to anyone who'll work for him."

"This notice will drive him out and put an end to his persuasion," MacDonell retorted.

MacDonell was wrong. Cameron and his new friend, Campbell, continued to work among the settlers, promising help and assistance in re-locating in Canada or high pay for working with the company.

When spring cultivating was ready to start, about one-third of the settlers had thrown down their hoes to accept Cameron's offer. Among his recruits was the Mole.

This success prompted the Nor'Westers to flout MacDonell's warning. The Metis were on their side and over the signatures and marks of Chief Cuthbert Grant, Bostonais Pangman, William Shaw and Bonhomme Monjour, a mandate was delivered to the settlers early in March. "All settlers shall retire immediately from the River and no appearance of the Colony shall remain."

The battle lines had been drawn and a new stockade called Fort Douglas was quickly built for the settlers.

188

CHAPTER NINETEEN

Faster to Kildonan

"But silence, for many dark-brown years, had settled in grassy Rath-col; for the race of heroes had failed, along the pleasant vale."

CATHLIN OF CLUTHA

MORE AND MORE armed men were arriving from the plains and Eastern Canada to bolster Fort Gibralter, and the turncoats from Colony Gardens were adding to this total. Eventually all friendly contact with the colonists was broken, and MacDonell's ultimatum set the stage for the armed clash that followed.

When Miles MacDonell left Colony Gardens for a visit to Fort Daer Cameron chose this opportunity to make his first aggressive move. He gave George Campbell a letter to deliver to Archie MacDonald, who had been left in charge of Fort Douglas.

"What do you want?" demanded MacDonald when Campbell entered his office.

Campbell tossed Cameron's order on the table. "Read it, MacDonald."

I have authorized the Nor'Westers in my employ to take possession of Selkirk's two field pieces. This action is not for the purpose of using the guns against the colonists, but only to prevent MacDonell from making wrong use of them. I trust that you will not be foolhardy enough to put up useless resistance, especially since we Nor'Westers wish to do no harm either to you or to your people.

"Well," growled MacDonald. "What are you waiting for?"

"I'm taking the field pieces."

"Like hell you are. Where does Cameron get authority to write a letter like this? Get out before I string you up from the nearest tree."

Campbell blanched, hesitated for a moment and left. David met him as he strode angrily through the door.

"What was on Campbell's mind, Archie?"

"Read it." MacDonald handed him Cameron's ultimatum.

David felt a surge of alarm as he read the curt order. "I don't like it. When will Miles return?"

"Within the week, but Cameron wouldn't dare make such a dangerous move. He's pulling a bluff."

MacDonald was wrong. Next morning a band of armed men marched through the gates of Fort Douglas and entered Mac-Donald's office.

"Hold it," ordered George Campbell levelling a musket. "We have come back for the cannon and ammunition."

"I'll be damned if I'll surrender any weapons to you and your gang of cut-throats," was MacDonald's angry reply.

"I wouldn't be a hero," Campbell smirked. "You, the sheriff and the other inmates of this fort are now my prisoners. Don't be foolish. We mean business!"

Archie walked into the yard where other Metis were holding his men at bay.

"All right," Campbell commanded. "Take their guns and ammunition." He kicked at a small cannon that MacDonell had set up inside the fort. "Never mind that junk, it's not much good for anything."

They arrested MacDonald, the patrol commander, and the company storekeeper and headed North to Gibraltar.

When Miles MacDonell returned he found only a few nervous settlers. David Grant explained what had happened.

"That man Cameron must be mad," Miles declared. "Surely he knows that his actions are a prelude to open war!"

David was startled. "War?" he blurted. "We don't want war, Miles. Besides, who would fight it?"

"Anyone who wants to protect his land," Miles snapped back. "You've got guns and by this time you should know how to use them. We'll organize a militia and demand the release of MacDonald and the other prisoner. If they refuse we'll drive them out of Gibraltar."

190

But it was too late. Scouts had already been posted by the Nor'Westers and hardly had MacDonell entered his office before a strong body of armed Metis under Cameron arrived at Fort Douglas. Cameron dismounted and stepped briskly up to MacDonell.

"MacDonell, I have a warrant from Montreal charging you with stealing property belonging to the North West Company. Some of your people are presently under arrest in my fort."

"What right have you to make arrests, Cameron? This is Lord Selkirk's territory. I'm the governor here."

"You were the governor," Cameron retorted. "I have my orders, Miles." He handed a document to MacDonell.

The Governor reached for the warrant. As he read, his mind was racing furiously. He knew that if he offered resistance Cameron would not hesitate to use force and there would be much bloodshed. With his weapons and men gone, resistance was out of the question.

The compound was hushed as Miles shrugged his shoulders in resignation.

"All right, Cameron. There will be no resistance."

Cameron smiled. "I'm sorry it had to end this way, Miles. You of all people must realize that the very existence of the North-West Company depends on getting the settlers out of the valley. It's a matter of life and death for my company."

"I understand. We both have a duty to perform. At this particular moment mine is to protect the colonists. God knows they have had more than their share of suffering." He stiffened his shoulders and raised his head. "What do you want me to do?"

"Order the settlers to make ready to move to Upper Canada without delay. No long-winded explanation is necessary," Cameron counselled. "Tell them that their coming to the Red River Valley was a mistake. Assure them that they'll be escorted safely east to Selkirk's settlement at Baldoon on Lake St. Clair. After they've gone, give yourself up to me at Fort Gibraltar."

"Agreed," said MacDonell with a sigh. He moved away, then turned around and said loud enough for all to hear. "Far better that I surrender than have the valley strewn with the bodies of my defenceless people. You have won the first round, Cameron."

"I'll not leave like a craven coward," snorted the Braggart. "My wheat is almost ripe and it looks like a bountiful crop."

"You're right," acknowledged the Gipsy. "We'll stay and fight for our farms. God knows we've earned the right to own them."

191

David Grant raised his arm. "Friends, I'm afraid we must leave."

"Leave? What do you mean?" demanded Geordie Gow.

"We have no other choice."

His words were lost in the angry mutterings. David called for quiet.

"Most of you, who arrived with the first brigade, came because we believed in Miles MacDonell and in what he told us. It's true that things were rough at times but he warned us of that. He has always shown his understanding of our problems and has done everything he could to keep us alive," he continued. "MacDonell must be facing fearful odds or he would never ask us to leave our homes and crops. You heard him tell Cameron that he would surrender himself. What better evidence have we of this man's courage?"

David paused. All was silent. He glanced over the river to the flat fields and clumps of trees stretching away to the horizon. His heart was heavy as he concluded. "I've grown to love this land. I hate to leave it just as much as you do but what else is there for us? We're outnumbered and unarmed. The Metis and the Nor'Westers are spoiling for a fight. We'd have no chance against their armed strength." He paused, "I suggest we go peacefully."

Having declared his position, David took Jeannie by the arm and walked slowly towards their cottage. Joseph and Fiona tagged behind, sober-faced and pale. They, like the other children, knew what moving meant.

At the cottage, Jeannie collapsed into a chair; David sat beside her. They looked around the cabin — not elaborate by any means but one of the best in Colony Gardens. Most of the settlers had built cabins with only two rooms, but David had extended his to four. He had added a verandah where they sat on a summer's night, when the day's toil was over. Whitewash brightened the interior, to somewhat atone for the lack of light through the hide windows. David had built tables, chairs, beds and other furniture and Jeannie with her dainty touch had added curtains and frills, pleasant reminders of home. Now, they had to leave it all.

"Oh, David, I'm so tired. When will we ever find peace?"

"Hush, Jeannie. Pack what we can carry and leave the rest here. I know we'll be back. Miles mentioned that Selkirk would send armed relief when news of our eviction reached him."

192

"You didn't tell the people that," Jeannie said accusingly.

"I didn't want to raise their hopes. I don't really know whether reinforcements will come or not." He rose to his feet. "Come Jeannie. We had better start packing. We'll leave in the morning."

Joseph helped his father gather up tools and other implements and store them in the shed. Fiona and Jeannie folded blankets and placed them neatly on a shelf. Then mother and daughter packed some food for the journey ahead.

"Where are we going, father?" asked Joseph.

"To Norway House at the end of Lake Winnipeg. The Hudson Bay factor will provide shelter and food there."

David gazed proudly at his son who had grown into a straight, long-limbed boy. Joseph held a bow and some arrows, fashioned by a Metis who had taken a liking to the sturdy lad. As he watched David thought sadly of the young Grants who had been so confident at this age, yet who later faced such bitter disappointments. He remembered the stories about his grandfather, Duncan, who had been born during the massacre of Glencoe and killed at Culloden. Then he thought of his father, Duncan, a refugee from Cumberland's slaughter, driven into exile in his last years. Now he was being forced to flee again. Was Joseph, the only male heir to the long Grant line, ever to have a chance to find peace?"

Jeannie entered the cottage.

"I was taking a last look at our crops. The vegetables are beginning to fatten, the kernels of wheat are starting to form."

"Aye, we'd have a good crop this year," said David without looking up from his packing.

"But I don't understand why my heather won't grow," she mused. "When we planted it on the river bank I was sure it would; though it seems to have taken root it's not showing any signs of life at all."

"Aye, you nursed the plant halfway round the world. When I was in the Cape I heard that heather once removed from its native heath wouldn't live."

"I'm not going to give up hope," Jeannie declared. "Sometimes plants look dead, but often there's still life in them. Maybe I'll prove your friend in the Cape was wrong and some day my heather will bloom again!"

That was a figurative wish which passed through many minds as once more the Sutherlanders left behind the fruit of three years labour. What was to happen to the settlement no one could guess. It was unlikely that the wilderness would be allowed to reclaim its own. More likely roving bands of Indians would take over, strip the colony of anything valuable and use the huts as a staging camp in their interminable wanderings after buffalo and furs.

The settlers could carry only what their canoes would take, and some of their implements — spades, hoes, axes, adzes — and building materials, which had been purchased on credit from the Hudson's Bay Company, were left behind. Their cherished possessions were still those little items which had come all the way from the County of Sutherland. The chief one — the family Bible — had seen a great deal of use in the new land. No minister had yet been sent out to join them and their Christian needs were still being ministered to by those they had chosen as leaders of their church, among them David Grant.

They boarded their canoes for the long two-hundred-and-fifty-mile trip to Norway House. There were twenty-two in all — the remnants of the first brigade who set out from Sutherland more than four years before.

David Grant had always been a leader, but now for the first time, he had sole responsibility for the Sutherlanders who had stuck with Miles MacDonell and had resisted the solicitations of the Nor'Westers. He alone was to lead to safety the few who were left.

As he settled down in the canoe, he raised a hand in salute to that staunchest of all leaders whom they had come to respect and to admire. Miles stood silently on the grassy slope and watched what he believed to be the last act as the curtain fell on his settlement in the Red River Valley. He could not bring himself to feel bitter about the lack of support which had brought it to this end. Nor could he feel personally resentful toward the enemy who had dealt him the last blow. His feelings were for the people who had resigned themselves to their fate and once again had become pawns in the never-ending challenge of history.

As he watched the settlers crowd into the canoes, Miles stood thoughtfully dedicating his last few moments to a silent prayer that time would heal the gaping wounds which had been left in their hearts and that one day they would find peace and prosperity in the haven of this new land. He watched John and Mary Bannerman, two of the older settlers and now the last to leave the colony, come slowly down the slope.

John was a fine, upstanding man with a mane of white flowing

194

hair that stirred gently in the breeze. His ruddy complexion was in sharp contrast to the pale whiteness of Mary clinging to his arm.

In his right hand John held a long staff which prodded the hill at his feet with a sureness and dexterity born of many hours of shepherding in Strath Brora.

John and Mary reached the pier and paused for a moment to look back at Colony Gardens. Then, side by side, they knelt on the green turf, John with his eyes raised heavenward and his staff upright in his hand, Mary with head bowed in reverence.

Silence prevailed on the boats and the shore line. The vast emptiness of the morning became suddenly filled with meaning when they saw their old leader walk slowly across the hill and kneel quietly behind the Bannermans. It was a call to supplication and rededication and within minutes the canoes were empty and every man, woman and child was united in prayer by the river.

David felt strangely confident as he picked up his paddle and headed up the river. As he turned into the bend he raised his hand in farewell to the lonely figure of Miles MacDonell who stood on the jetty watching the string of boats move north.

Five days later the flotilla arrived at the mouth of the Winnipeg River. Here David was surprised to see canoes pulled up on the lakeshore near several campfires. As he drew close he observed a large body of white men watching his approach.

"My God," he exclaimed. "That's Colin Robertson!"

"Colin," he hailed. "What are you doing here?"

"David," came back the echo. "David Grant! You're a sight for sore eyes."

Grant still remembered Colin from the recruiting campaign in Sutherland and the next moment he was wading ashore to grasp his hand. Meanwhile the women and children piled out of the boats and swarmed around as the members of the armed brigade made them welcome.

David Grant could hardly believe that the long awaited help had arrived.

"My God, we're glad to see you, Colin," he called joyfully.

"What on earth are you doing here?" demanded Colin.

"We're on our way to Norway House," David replied. "We've been driven out by Cameron and his half-breeds. He has threatened to arrest or kill us if we return."

"Let him threaten all he wants. I've got two hundred men with me and I can assure you that they are a match for five hundred of Donald Cameron's. What happened to Miles?"

David's face clouded. "He was arrested by Cameron. I understand he is now on his way to Fort William. Did you meet the North-West party along the way?"

"No, they could have taken another route. This is a big country."

Hope was reborn in the heart of the unfortunate Sutherlanders. "Now we can return in time to harvest our crop," remarked John Gow.

"What's the sense in returning when we haven't seen the tools and provisions Selkirk promised us?" the Braggart demanded.

"You'll get them before the winter sets in," Colin promised. "There's another brigade of settlers on the way to the Red River with enough supplies for everyone. We're also putting an armed schooner on the lake for protection. Lord Selkirk is coming out to you next year and the Hudson's Bay Company are sending a new Governor called Semple to take over the administration of the colony. That's not all. To honor the men and women from Sutherland, his Lordship has decided that, hereafter, Colony Gardens is to be named 'Kildonan'."

An enthusiastic cheer went up from the weary wanderers as they crowded around Colin seeking news of home.

Sellar and his cronies were still administering the affairs of the county from Dunrobin and while the evictions had stopped, the plight of the outcasts who had remained on the Brora beaches was still pitiful. Many had died. Starvation and exposure had taken a heavy toll and those still alive were existing under the most wretched conditions. Selkirk's recruiting scheme was becoming more and more successful.

"Oh, for a cup of usquebaugh," exclaimed the Braggart.

"I have the answer," laughed Colin going to his canoe. He returned with a small keg. "Here," he called as he broached the cask. "I knew you Sutherlanders would be thirsting for some clynelish so I brought this little fellow along for your special entertainment."

Laughing and shouting the settlers gathered around the cask. Gipsy brought out his bagpipes and soon they were dancing merry jigs and reels on the beach.

At dawn the settlers boarded their canoes and followed Colin Robertson's boat down Lake Winnipeg. They who had paddled morosely north with their Indian guides now laughed and sang and worked furiously at their task of getting home before the crops spoiled in the fields.

In spite of the gaiety around him, however, Colin Robertson

196

was sorely troubled. He knew how ruthless the North-West Company and the Hudson's Bay Company could be. The struggle for control of the fur trade was a battle for high stakes and neither side was willing to give up the rich returns that would come from its successful exploitation. As long as the settlers remained in the Red River Valley they threatened the lines of communications which the North-West Company had strung across thousands of miles of wilderness from their base of operations at Fort William to the Rocky Mountains. By fair means or foul he knew the Nor'Westers would stop at nothing to drive the settlers out.

He looked around. The canoes were strung out on the smooth bosom of the lake in the warm afternoon sun. No one seemed concerned at this moment about what lay ahead. In the distance he saw the recess in the trees which marked the broad outfall of the Red River. "Faster," he yelled, digging his paddle furiously into the water, "Let's move ahead to Kildonan."

CHAPTER TWENTY

No Defense

They who defended Oithona fell by the gloomy chief;
What could I do? My arm was weak. I could not lift the
spear.

OITHONA

A s soon as the canoes were beached Jeannie and David hurried to their home. Everything seemed in order. Nothing had been disturbed in the cabin and the crops were standing ripe and ready to harvest.

"Thank God," Jeannie cried, clinging to her husband's arm. "Now we'll have plenty of food for the winter. There will be no need to go to Pembina."

But not all the settlers were so fortunate. In the short three weeks during which the colony was vacated, some of the cabins close to Fort Gibraltar had been burned by the Nor'Westers and the Metis had trampled the crops with their ponies.

In the midst of the harvest Selkirk's fourth brigade arrived and everyone left the fields to welcome the new settlers. Among them was Donald Bain who explained to David that the Countess had imposed such high taxes that he had to give up his croft.

The gay chatter changed into a hurrah when Colin Robertson announced, "Let's all go to the fort and celebrate."

Colin was as good as his word. He rolled out several casks he had brought with him, rounded up two fiddlers, an accordion player and the Gipsy. The celebration was well under way, when emergency rations were brought out for the occasion.

In the midst of the festivities another canoe pulled in at the jetty.

"It's the new governor," someone shouted.

Colin hurried to the river. Seated amidships in the canoe was a corpulent man dressed in tight breeches, a tailored coat and a plumed hat. As the Indians beached the canoe, two of the occupants assisted the richly dressed official ashore.

"I'm Governor Semple," he announced pompously as he straightened the ruffles of his shirt and pulled at his coat tails.

"I am Colin Robertson, sir. At your service. This is David Grant, one of the original settlers."

Semple ignored the introduction.

"Well, Robertson, we've had a difficult voyage," he said. "This is Dr. Wilkinson who will act as my secretary. Lieutenant Holt has come to command the armed schooner on Lake Winnipeg and Captain Rogers will take charge of our troops and explore this area for minerals." He turned to a thin-faced man who was standing behind him. "This is Dr. White who will be surgeon of the colony."

While Semple arrogantly minced his way toward the fort the colonists formed two lines and stood proudly at attention. The Governor, however, passed between the lines without a nod or a greeting.

"Did you ever see such an arrogant popinjay?" the Braggart whispered. "The stiff-necked bastard didn't have the courtesy to acknowledge the homage we paid him."

"He's tired after his trip," David commented. "Anyway he won't win much popular support by the way he carries the plume in his bonnet."

"Who is he anyway?" Geordie Gow asked.

"I hear he's a New England royalist who has no frontier experience. But he must have some ability or the Hudson's Bay Company wouldn't have sent him here," replied David.

"I don't like what I've seen of him," the Braggart muttered. "His interests seem confined to his own lordly personage. I'd say there's a cobble full of trouble brewing beneath those fancy feathers!"

The Governor pleaded fatigue. When asked to join the party he retired to his private quarters, heedless that his cold arrogance had completely dampened the happy spirits which were the culmination of a successful harvest and a spirited reunion among old and new friends.

Next morning Semple called Robertson to his office. "Start

building a palisade," he ordered. "It's our only protection against sudden attack. I'm leaving tomorrow for Pembina. The refinements of civilized society will provide a much needed rest."

After the Governor left the colonists continued to speculate on the future, and an uneasy fear plagued Kildonan.

Meanwhile Duncan Cameron had returned to Fort Gibraltar and found to his surprise that the settlers had returned to their homes and a palisade was being built around Fort Douglas. He could no longer delay his plans to eliminate the settlement.

The following night an Indian appeared with a letter from the Mole. Enclosed was a copy of the latest dispatch Cameron had sent to the principals of the North-West Company.

> We at Fort Gibraltar are about to commence hostilities against Selkirks' colonists in the Red River Valley. You can be certain that we will do our best to maintain what we consider to be our rights in the interior. Undoubtedly some serious casualties will occur because our objective will be the complete annihilation of Selkirk's colony. By the time you receive my next dispatch I expect that our problem with the settlers will be solved."

The Mole was a troubled man. He had not joined the Nor'Westers to fight his own kith and kin. "Mary," he confided. "I could never take up arms against David, Jeannie and our other friends."

Mary was just as apprehensive. "We should go back." But he would have none of it. He had made his decision and he refused to jerk back and forth like a rabbit in a snare!

The Governor was quite unconcerned when Colin showed him Chief Peguis' warning and Cameron's dispatch. "Governor Semple," he said, "the palisade doesn't offer enough protection. I also hear from our friend Chief Peguis that the Nor'Westers are arming the half-breeds and Indians. If the settlers could take shelter in a defensive position, we might, with the support of our cannon, still hold the Nor'Westers off."

Semple snorted derisively and dabbed at his lips with his lace handkerchief. "Robertson, my naive young man, someone has evidently planted unfounded rumours in your stupid mind. I came seventy-five miles downstream from Fort Daer without hearing a whisper or seeing any indication of the hostile activities that the crazy Indian reported to you! As for the dispatch, it is nothing but a fake. Where's Cameron's official seal?"

Colin gritted his teeth. "This is not the original order, but a copy, sir. Kindly refrain from referring to Chief Peguis as a

200

crazy Indian. I knew him in the Norway House Territory; I have earned his friendship."

The Governor frowned, rose to his feet and crossed to the window, then turned back toward Colin. "Would it be presumptuous as Governor to suggest that I'm much better informed on the Nor'Westers than your Indian friend? If there were any evidence of danger my secretary wouldn't be packing my bags, would he? I'm leaving on an inspection tour of all company forts in the Assiniboine territory. I'd suggest that while I'm gone, you leave well enough alone and try not to provoke hostilities."

The Governor's curt reply and abrupt departure left Colin in charge but without the authority to take the precautionary measures he felt were necessary. In desperation he decided to visit his old friend, Joseph Lajimonière, who lived in a small cabin farther down the river. When he arrived at Joseph's door a beautiful French-Canadian woman with black eyes and a soft voice greeted him. "Glad to see you, Colin."

"Marie, it's been a long time. Is Joseph at home?"

"Yes, he's resting. He'll be glad to see you. Please come in."

Marie was about to call her husband when he appeared at her side. He smiled broadly and held out his hand. "Welcome, Colin. "It's a long time since we've seen each other."

"Yes, Joseph, it seems to take an emergency to bring us together. May I talk with you alone?"

Joseph nodded. "There's a little shed beyond the clearing. We can talk there." Lajimonière was reputed to be the foremost voyageur in all the west. He had roamed the plains from the Missouri to the North Saskatchewan and from the Red River to the foothills of the Rockies. For many years Colin and Joseph had been friends. Today, however, he hesitated to ask a favour which would take Joseph fifteen hundred and fifty miles to Montreal, along trails closely watched by Indians and Nor' Westers. But he had no choice. Only Lajimonière could get through with his message.

"Joseph, you're already aware that Selkirk's colony is menaced by the Nor'Westers."

"Colin, you don't have to tell me how serious the situation is. I know the Nor'Westers are determined to drive you out."

"The Earl of Selkirk is expected to arrive in Montreal in about six weeks; could you deliver this dispatch to his lordship when he arrives? I am asking a tremendous favour, I realize."

As he spoke, Colin drew from the inside of his deerskin shirt a small waterproof pouch.

Lajimonière whistled. "It's no easy matter to travel twenty-five miles a day through that wild country at this time of year!"

Colin agreed. "I don't want you to take the risk without realizing the danger. If you are caught by the Nor'Westers with my dispatch in your possession, you'll have a difficult time explaining."

Lajimonière laughed and placed the pouch inside his beaver skin shirt, his strong hand clasped Robertson by the shoulder. "My friend, danger is my business. I'm honoured that you chose me to make the journey. I have a friend who'll go with me."

"This is an immense relief, Joseph, and I thank you. We'll provide Marie and the children with food, and if they want to stay in the fort we'll be glad to have them."

That night Lajimonière slipped silently out of the cabin and headed east.

Next morning Colin summoned his council. He relayed the information he had received from Chief Peguis. "For months Cameron has been whipping up hate against us. The Indians and the Metis are thirsting for our scalps; they're supported by MacGillivray and the other North West officials at Fort William."

"But isn't MacGillivray a Christian man?" David asked. "I met one of his kinfolk on the boat. He said his uncle was carrying out religious work among the heathens."

"It's true that MacGillivray talks with a scriptural tongue for half an hour each Sunday," Colin retorted. "But the rest of the week it becomes a slippery, malicious implement provoking hatred against us. He'll fill the Indians with whisky, then incite them to strike with such ferocity that we'll be forced to leave the Valley."

"I can't believe that all the Indians and Metis are depraved and bloodthirsty," the Gipsy remarked.

"Many of them are as human as we are," said Colin, "but when they are being told that we are interlopers who have driven the buffalo from the hunting ground they have lived on for generations, little wonder there is no room for friendship."

He paused for a moment to let his next few words register clearly with his listeners, "I've ordered the Hudson's Bay Company at Fort Daer to attack the North-West Fort at Pembina. We're going in tonight."

202

"My God," gasped David. "You've set a fuse to the powder keg!"

David was silent. Colin Robertson was a brave man, but was he an impatient and foolish one? Surely he realized that any attack on the North-West fort would invite immediate retaliation and the colonists would be in the midst of it. David shuddered at the thought. It was five years since he had come to this valley and for the first time prospects were good, the land was bearing abundant crops and Jeannie, Fiona, and Joseph were looking forward to a secure future. This time he had to fight for his land.

"I'll stick by you. I'll defend my land and my family," he declared. "I think as you do. Striking first is better than waiting to be scalped. Come on, Gipsy, Braggart, you don't want to be driven out! Let's fight, I say."

"Right you are," said the Braggart as he hurried away to prepare the colony for action.

It was midnight when Colin Robertson, leading a platoon of armed men, crashed through the doors at Fort Gibraltar taking Cameron completely by surpise. On his desk was an unfinished letter to Cuthbert Grant of White Horse Plains, with a footnote stating that the time had come for the Indians to attack Selkirk's settlement. They also found copies of similar letters to North-West agents throughout the territory.

"It seems we arrived in the nick of time, Cameron," said Colin triumphantly, "a few more days and you'd have aroused the Indian tribes to our massacre."

"You'll regret this, Robertson," Cameron shouted. "Only a madman would dare to attack this Fort."

As they left, David recognized the Mole. He bore little resemblance to the blustering character who had challenged his authority on the *Prince of Wales*. Their eyes met in friendship and David sensed that the Mole wanted to speak to him, but the pushing and shoving of men moving through the compound broke their contact.

When Governor Semple learned what Robertson had done he broke into a towering rage.

"Robertson! You're a stupid fool!"

"I resent that, sir."

The Governor shook with indignation. His face was livid. "You've jeopardized the life and limb of everyone in the colony by your unwarranted attack on Fort Pembina. To top it all, you've arrested Cameron."

Colin bit his lips. The frown that passed over his face showed the tumult of fierce emotions raging within him. He struggled to remain calm.

Semple waved his hand affectedly. "You seem to have forgotten, my man, that the Hudson's Bay Company represents the government of this country and I am their appointed representative. In my absence you usurped my authority when you took it upon yourself to raid Gibraltar and arrest Cameron. I also understand that you sent a messenger to meet Lord Selkirk. How could you be so stupid as to imagine any courier would reach Montreal before his lordship gets there? You've now ordered the colonists to arm and have made a sanctuary of their church for women and children. Even your dull mind must recognize that your flagrant bungling is an act of open aggression. All I can do now is hasten to make amends."

As Semple spluttered and coughed into his lace handkerchief, Colin took up his own defence.

"Governor Semple, you must remember you left me in complete charge. I raided the fort and arrested Cameron when I heard he had received orders to organize an attack on the settlement. The orders came direct from MacGillivray at Fort William."

Semple gave a snort of disgust. "My job is to prevent bloodshed and retribution," he growled. "I've ordered Cameron's release."

"You have what?' Colin demanded rising from his chair. "You stupid fool! You want him to continue his plans to drive us from the Valley?"

"Cameron isn't that kind of man," retorted Semple.

"Take care that you don't end up making the biggest mistake of your life," Colin raged.

Before Semple could reply, he tossed a batch of letters on the plank table. "These letters are bonafide proof that the action I took was no error! Go ahead, read them! You'll find that Cameron instructed Alexander MacDonell to lead the Metis from Qu'Appelle in an attack on this settlement. The same letter indicates that William Shaw has already received instructions to encourage all those Indians and Metis along the Saskatchewan to arm themselves and follow him to a rendezvous at Frog Plain, just down the river from here. This letter instructs Cuthbert Grant to take command at White Horse Plains."

"What difference does it make?" Semple demanded. "You made the first belligerent move by attacking the Nor'Westers!

204

What did you expect them to do, treat it as a trivial matter? How can I explain your offensive actions to my company, the British Government, and the authorities?"

Colin continued as if he had not heard Semple. "We also found on Cameron's person a letter from Alexander MacDonnell." He unfolded a sheet of paper. "Listen to what this says:

> The warriors of the new nations have taken up their war hatchets and are rallying behind their chiefs. Soon they will be advancing to the Red River Valley to clear, from their hunting ground, the paleface settlers who have no right to lodge thereon."

As Colin paused for breath Semple blurted out, "It makes no difference what the letters say. History will prove the Nor'Westers acted in self defence. How can I justify your action?"

"It doesn't matter whether you can or can't. Your chief concern should be the salvation of the settlement. It's true that I sent Lajimonière with a message to Lord Selkirk. I knew his lordship was on his way to Canada. I suggested that he come with sufficient men to protect his property. I have no doubt that Lajimonière will reach Montreal. My only fears are that Lord Selkirk will not arrive in time to protect us."

Semple adjusted his coat and ruffles. "Robertson," he said sternly, "if your action was an effort to undermine my authority, I like it not. Nor do I deem your excuses reasonable. I must remind you that I was appointed by His Majesty. I am the law in this territory. You, Mr. Robertson are merely an employee under my direct command. Furthermore, your insulting words prove you're a bigger fool than I thought you were. You may withdraw!" concluded the Governor with an imperious wave of his jewelled fingers.

When Chief Peguis again warned Colin of the impending disaster he strode determinedly back to the Governor's quarters for a showdown. The Governor was busy. After a two hour wait Colin was finally admitted.

"What is it now, Robertson?" Semple demanded.

"Governor, I've been waiting for over two hours to report to you the grave danger that threatens the colonists. Chief Peguis confirmed Duncan Cameron's intentions. The Nor'Westers at this very moment are assembling at Frog Plain. They are armed and preparing to attack. We are indeed in a serious situation and need your support."

The Governor threw up his hands in annoyance. "I have heard the rumour. Do you think I'm not aware of what's taking place? There is nothing I can do to prevent them assembling. Do you expect me to tell them to disperse?"

"May I remind your lordship that the North-West directors have already issued an ultimatum to their factors. They have been quite open about this. I have a copy of a letter circulated to Cameron and other officials. Listen to what it says: "Nothing but the complete extermination of the settlers in the Red River Valley will satisfy us.""

Robertson paused, then added: "If that isn't clear enough. I don't know what is."

Semple's heavy lips curled into a sardonic smile. "When the attack comes, you'll find that I have sufficient military intelligence to know what to do. It will be my pleasure to order the slaughter of as many of the Nor'West rabble as they care to send against us."

"Sir," Colin thundered, "we're outnumbered ten to one! If we must fight, let it be from behind barricades and trenches that will afford us some protection."

The Governor hesitated. An uneasy feeling was creeping over him. He couldn't lose his dignity in front of his aides and Colin Robertson. There was no evading their keen scrutiny as they anxiously waited his decision.

"Robertson, I was honoured with this position of trust by His Majesty King George II. I must make my own decisions. However, to ease your troubled mind I shall personally survey the situation. Captain Rogers, bring a telescope and follow me."

Accompanied by the Captain and Robertson, Semple minced across the compound and mounted the ladder to the catwalk of the stockade. From here he could look far out in the direction of Frog Plain. He then looked west, south, and then across the river. The warm, hazy summer day obliterated the view and no evidence of war preparations was evident. He handed the telescope to Rogers. "I see nothing unusual. Look for yourself, Captain."

The Captain swung the glass in a hasty arc along the horizon. "Everything appears normal, sir."

"If the North-West forces are as well prepared as your savage friend suggests, Robertson, there should be some sign of activity," Semple remarked smugly. "Since there is nothing, I have no fear of losing England's dominion over the colony. I'm certain that God will protect our rights without the assistance of barricades and trenches."

"Governor Semple," Robertson said with finality, "I came here not to bandy words but to warn you of impending danger. I must request that you make defensive preparations against the attack that is sure to come. Otherwise, you are an incompetent military nonentity who has neither the resolution nor the wisdom to take the rudimentary steps necessary to protect the settlement. Since you persist in doing nothing, I beg to inform you that I must disassociate myself from any connection with your affairs."

"That is your privilege and is of no consequence," Semple replied.

"In that case I shall leave at once." He turned to go, but paused at the door. "I only hope that Selkirk's reinforcements will arrive in time to save these defenceless wretches from your stupidity."

CHAPTER TWENTY-ONE

Uprooted Heather

Whence are thy beams, O sun! thy everlasting light?
The oaks of the mountains fall: the mountains themselves
*   decay with years;*
The ocean strikes and grows again: the moon
*   herself is lost in heaven;*
But thou art forever the same; rejoicing in
*   the brightness of thy course*
When the world is dark with tempests; when
*   thunder rolls and lightening flies;*
Thou lookest in thy beauty from the clouds,
*   and laughest at the storm*
Exult thee, O sun! in the strength of thy youth!

                                        CARTHON

COLIN's departure for Churchill was a severe blow to the morale of the colonists. David Grant was working in his field when he saw him striding through the grain.

"Hey, you've trampled down a bushel of wheat," he said jestingly as Colin stormed up to him. Seeing the angry Highlander's face he asked anxiously, "What is it, Colin?"

"That fool. That damned fool," Robertson exploded. He raged and stormed. "It's that empty-headed pompous dolt Semple. I'm leaving for Churchill."

Gradually the story of the Governor's obstinacy came out. David was alarmed. He knew that without Colin there would be no leader bold enough to stand up to the Nor'Westers.

It almost seemed as though Colin was reading David's thoughts. "You'll have to take charge, Grant. The welfare of the colony is in your hands. Organize patrols and some method of defence. Otherwise you may all be slaughtered while you sleep."

"But I'm not a soldier," protested David. "I'm a farmer. All I want is to be left at peace with my family and my land. You are the man for the job. Must you go?"

"I had no other choice," remarked Colin, holding out his hand. "It's up to you now. I'll see what I can do for you. Good-bye and good luck!"

David stood like a sentinel and watched his friend stride towards the river, slip his canoe into the water, and paddle silently away.

Later that day David explained to the colonists that Colin Robertson had left because Governor Semple refused to comply with his recommendations to defend the colony.

A committee was quickly formed. David was named the chairman. Among the other members was the Braggart and Geordie Gow.

Among the first resolutions passed was the organizing of a night patrol and a decision that during the daylight hours, only the work necessary to bring in the crops would be permitted.

Semple sneered when he heard what action the colonists were taking.

"Those crazy settlers!" he laughed. "No one will dare attack while I, the representative of His Majesty the King, am in charge. I told Robertson that he was an hysterical fool," the confident Governor exclaimed to his aides.

Tensions began to ease as days passed without any hostilities. The Highlanders, after their day's toil, gathered in the long summer evening to compete in putting the stone and tossing the caber. Many a typical Highland *ceilidh* was enjoyed, when they gathered to sing and tell stories of the old days in their homeland.

Below them, stretching as far as the eye could see, were fields of ripening wheat, oats and barley. The bounteous crops and the fields of potatoes and other vegetables brought a feeling of prosperity. The land was rich and the air warm. It was difficult to believe that the morrow might bring death and destruction.

West of Fort Gibraltar, Mole sat in his lonely bivouac. It was customary for him and Duncan Cameron to keep watch on the activities at Fort Douglas. Since his office had been raided, Cameron had kept his own counsel and relentlessly pursued his plans to drive the Highlanders out of the valley.

Alone in the enemy camp the Mole was suffering the torments of hell. He knew that hostilities would erupt at any moment. He must warn his friends. Since he had left the settlement, he and Mary had no further contact with David and Jeannie. This troubled Mary more than it did the Mole. She liked the Grants. She had been their neighbours before the evictions. Now she kept urging her husband to go back to his farm and to resume his contact with the settlement.

As he tossed in his bivouac he knew he had to act quickly or he would be an eye witness to the annihilation of the people that had been his kith and kin for generations. He closed his eyes and in his disturbed mind he pictured Mary and his child lying scalped on the prairie and around them he imagined the mutilated bodies of his old friends.

The strains of the Gipsy's bagpipes drifted up the river and the Mole nostalgically recalled the heather-covered hills of home. His panic abated. It was his duty to warn the Sutherlanders.

Quietly he rose from his twig mattress and moved into the night, to picket lines posted by the Kildonan settlers. The Braggart was alerted. "Who goes there?" he shouted into the darkness.

"It's me — the Mole," came the Gaelic whisper. "I must talk with you, Braggart. Shoot me afterward, if you must, but for God's sake listen to what I have to say."

"Put your hands above your head and move slowly forward. You sound like the Mole — but I must be sure. Keep to the path and stop when I order you."

With the soundless gait of a hunter, the Braggart concealed himself in a thicket.

The Mole reached the path and stopped.

"Where are you, Braggart?"

Hardly had the words passed his lips before the sharp tip of a bayonet was pricking the back of his neck.

"Stand still."

"I have no weapons."

"Let me decide that. Turn around," barked the Braggart. "What brings a cringing coward like you to our picket lines?"

"I'm no coward, Donald. I have come to warn you that Cameron and Cuthbert Grant have completed their plans. They'll attack at any moment. You must flee while there's still time."

210

"It's the Mole."

"The Mole? What in hell's he doing here?"

"He says an attack is imminent. Cuthbert Grant has mobilized his forces. I'm taking him to David Grant. Be careful, Geordie, and keep a sharp eye open."

The Braggart and Mole hurried across the pasture fields. A moment later they were knocking on Grant's door.

Jeannie slowly opened to them. "What's the trouble, Braggart?" then she saw the Mole and demanded, "What's he doing here?"

"There's no time for talk, Jeannie. Where's David?"

Jeannie was not to be put off. "Where's Mary? Where's your

"Mole, is this a trick?"

"It's no trick, Braggart. I implore you. Believe me. You're confused because I deserted, Donald. I don't blame you but . . ." He slowly raised his right hand. "On my respected mother's grave, I swear I speak the truth."

The knowledge that a Highlander did not swear lightly on his mother's grave gave the Braggart confidence in the message the Mole had brought. He took him by the arm. "We'll go and see David Grant."

Reaching a grove of poplar trees they found the second line of defence, Geordie Gow was on picket duty.

"Braggart, who's with you?"

family?"

"They are still at Fort Gibraltar, Jeannie."

David appeared at Jeannie's elbow. He was puzzled by the sudden appearance of the man from the enemy camp. He stared accusingly at the Mole. "What does it mean?" he asked. "Did Cameron take over while I slept?"

"No, David, no one has taken over, but they will very soon if we don't hurry. The Mole came to warn us that the Nor'Westers are forming ranks. The attack could come at any moment."

David scowled. "If this is a trick, Mole, you'll answer at the end of a rope," he warned.

"That's the chance I took," Mole replied. "There's no time now to argue rights and wrongs. It's a true emergency David. Let's have a *ceilidh* and decide how we're going to protect the settlement!"

Dawn was breaking as the colonists hurried from their homes to the church where all the meetings of the settlers were now held. Their *ceilidhs* had taken on a new meaning. They were no longer social gatherings. Instead they had become forums for the general expression of opinion. At these sessions they were able to decide on common laws and precepts of behaviour which would guide their actions both in the Fort and outside. They had passed through the stage when they depended solely on the promises made by others. They had seen these broken so often by others that now they realized that only in their own united endeavour lay their strength.

Silently they took their seats in the little church. David walked to the front with the Mole.

"Settlers of Kildonan," he said, "the Mole has brought us extremely bad news. We're in grave danger. Cameron and his followers are massing their forces to attack Fort Douglas. During the past few weeks it has seemed that all danger to the colony had faded. Now the enemy is at our door. We must decide what action we are going to take. Do we quit the soil and the crops we've worked so hard to harvest, or do we stay and defend our land and our homes?"

"It seems the Reverend Sage was right after all," someone shouted. "I say, let's get out of here before we're all butchered."

"What do you say, David?" asked another.

David was reluctant to tell them that he was a simple farmer and not a leader of men. He recalled the times his people had meekly accepted oppression at the hand of the Countess. But that was past. They were no longer living and suffering as individuals. They had come to depend on others and had learned to live and work as a group. They were united and ready to fight.

"We shall stay and fight," said David. "Mole says we're outnumbered, but what we have to fight for and the spirit we fight with, is what counts. Where could we find land so well worth fighting for? Tell me where we could watch the warm winds of freedom dance more gaily over our wheat fields? We of the first brigade have suffered seven years of despair, doubt, and fear. By right of settlement and occupation we have earned this land. We have nurtured every blade of grass with our tears and sweat. We have fought for every acre with toilworn hands. We have the right to protect it against attack from outside or from folly within. If we run now we will never stop running. Governor Semple must be made aware of his responsibility to defend our rights."

The colonists stood up and shouted their support, and as his countrymen crowded forward to shake his hand, the great loneliness and responsibility of command weighed heavily upon him.

212

He led them from the church and across the compound to Semple's quarters. The rising sun was casting long shadows over the fresh countryside. Birds had begun calling to each other in the trees and somewhere near the outbuildings a cock crowed.

At the door of the fort they were challenged by Dr. Wilkinson.

"We've come to see the Governor," David stated. "It's an emergency."

"It is impossible to see the Governor at this hour!"

The Highlanders were in no mood for refusal. They pushed their way into the Governor's bedroom.

Semple was startled. He rubbed his eyes and sat up. "How dare you ruffians invade my privacy in this manner?" he demanded angrily.

"The attack of the Nor'Westers will be no respector of privacy either," announced David.

Semple grunted. "Has Colin Robertson returned? It sounds as if he has been inciting you again."

"This has nothing to do with Colin Robertson. We're in serious trouble."

"I'll see you in my office. Now leave my room!"

The Governor was a frustrated man when he seated himself in a chair behind his desk. Taking out a white handkerchief he blew his nose fastidiously and folded the silk into his pocket.

"What is it?" he asked curtly. "State your reason for this intrusion."

"Governor Semple, your complete refusal to prepare defences against the hostile Nor'Westers left us no alternative. We are here to ask that you take immediate steps to protect the colony."

"Ha! ha," laughed Semple. "So the tenant peasants are so bold as to question my judgment on military affairs! Imagine that, Wilkinson."

The doctor winced but made no comment.

"With your approval, sir, we could have barricades within an hour. If you deny us this protection you will force us to take the law into our own hands."

Semple exploded. "I've heard enough of this balderdash," he shouted, banging the table. "You hear a stupid rumour and you want to make preparations for a major war! It is my responsibility, Grant, to evaluate all truths and rumours and observe them in terms of the overall situation. I have reliable information that so long as we have our cannon, Cameron and his cowardly half-breeds will not dare attack. I'm also convinced that the presence of the Nor'Westers at Frog Plain is just a bluff to frighten chicken-hearted wretches such as yourselves. You may inform the settlers that I will provide adequate protection when it is required."

Semple paused. "Now that we understand each other will you be good enough to get out of here."

"Are we to take that as final, Governor?"

"Show them out, Wilkinson. And don't dare invade my privacy again with your fears and stupidity."

Early that afternoon when the sun broke through the mist, Cameron's moment arrived. When he learned that the Mole had disappeared he surmised where he had gone. Grant, the shrewd energetic Metis, who had been given command of Fort Gibraltar's armed employees, ordered all to deck themselves in feathers and daub their faces with warpaint so that in their buckskin suits they looked like Indians.

"We don't want the North-West Company involved. It must look as if the Indians went on a rampage," he explained to Cameron as they marched over to a knoll called Seven Oaks.

His drunken half-breeds had fortified themselves with long swigs of fire-water from the kegs Cameron had provided. The disguised horde then shuffled into position, many with their flint locks or rifles couched in the crook of their arm while they scraped off rust or worked the action frantically to make sure it wouldn't fail at the last moment. Only the native Indians who had thrown in their lot with the Nor'Westers sat tall in the saddle and added dignity to the massacre which was to follow.

As the Mole patrolled the fringe of the settlement, the glint of a bayonet sent him hurrying to David Grant, and set in motion the last act of Semple's folly which was to be remembered among the Highlanders in song and story for many generations to come.

At Fort Douglas, David found him supervising the packing of his baggage. His aides lolled at ease in the warm sun. David looked aghast at the scene. "Are you preparing to leave, Governor?" he enquired.

"I don't think it's any business of yours," came the caustic reply, "but if you must know, I'm going to Fort Daer."

"You're mad," exploded David, unable to control his wrath. "An army of Nor'Westers are heading this way and you have nothing better to do than ruffle your lace and preen your feathers for a pleasure trip."

214

The Governor overlooked the insult in the shock of the moment, as the warning bell of the church pealed out and the scurry of settlers bore witness to a new danger that must be faced.

The Fort was suddenly a beehive of activity and officers scrambled for their weapons and headed for the gates.

"Halt!" the Governor ordered. "Assemble your platoon with loaded muskets and follow me."

His plump figure bounced across to the watchtower of the bastion, closely followed by the Captain. He panted up the ladder and stared breathlessly through his field glasses in the direction of Seven Oaks. "They're there all right," he muttered handing the glasses to the Captain. "They seem to be waiting for us to make a move."

He flicked his lace handkerchief up to his nose, dusted an invisible spot from the shoulder of his velvet coat, and fluffed up the ruffled lace of his shirt front. He sniffed. He coughed. He was a nervous and perplexed man. Beads of perspiration rolled onto his collar. He was obviously pondering his next move. At the bottom of the ladder, Lieutenant Holt was awaiting orders with a squad of thirty armed men.

"I'll have a talk with them," said the Governor in a tremulous voice. "When they realize I'm the King's representative they'll soon disperse."

As Governor Semple strode across the prairie to face the menacing Indians and Metis, the factor, Alexander McLean, walked in the lead, bearing the Hudson's Bay Company banner high over his head. Behind McLean marched Semple, Wilkinson and White. Then followed Captain Rogers and Lieutenant Holt and his platoon. Behind the platoon walked David and Pritchard, a settler who had recently arrived from Montreal.

They marched up the open trail that led across the uncultivated land towards Seven Oaks. To David it was evident that the Indians and Metis outnumbered them ten to one. He grew tense and his heart began to pound. He glanced back and forth and noted that many of the colonists had taken protection behind the palisade of the Fort. To him it seemed woefully far away.

Midway between the fort and Seven Oaks the Governor ordered a halt and raised his telescope to survey the enemy. "Looks as though we are up against a formidable force," he remarked to Captain Rogers.

"Certainly seems so, sir. In addition to those in the open, there's a large number taking cover in the thicket."

"Perhaps we'd better make a show of strength," the Governor suggested. "Send Grant and Pritchard back for the cannon."

David heard the order with incredulity. He hastened to obey, and as they headed back he could visualize the 'show of strength' thirty men would make with a rusty cannon, surrounded by five hundred blood-thirsty and fearless Nor'Westers. David was glad to get away from this man whose strange brand of authority was leading them nowhere but to certain death.

Meanwhile Cuthbert Grant decided to strike. Setting spurs to his horse he moved his troops out quickly and encircled Semple's party. He stopped about two hundred yards away and sent one of his Lieutenants forward with a message.

"What do you want?" the Governor demanded.

"I've been instructed by Cuthbert Grant to ask that you surrender peacefully."

"Tell Cuthbert Grant that I am the Governor, the representative of the King. Tell him to come out and lay down his arms. I have no intention of surrendering." He grabbed at the bridle of the man's horse. Startled by the sudden action the horse reared into the air.

In alarm the messenger reached for his gun. A shot rang out and he dropped from his saddle, a red blotch spreading suddenly on his buckskin shirt.

David Grant and Pritchard turned at the sound of the shot and stood rooted to the spot.

Both the Nor'Westers and the Governor's party opened fire. Lieutenant Holt, shot through the head, fell to the ground at the first volley. Governor Semple was wounded and collapsed beside him. A dead soldier fell on top of him, but Semple pushed him off. Other soldiers were falling dead or wounded and groans and screams of men and horses filled the air. Those who remained after the first few rounds massed in a group and discharged a concentrated volley into the hordes advancing on them. Several Indians and Metis tumbled from their horses.

"Run for it. Save yourselves!" the Governor shouted hoarsely, but it was too late to run. Another volley cut down the remaining troops like a scythe going through a swath of standing grain. Captain Rogers, wounded in the chest and thighs, fell to his knees. Struggling to hold his sword in a defensive position, he was disembowelled by a half-breed. The howls of suffering of the wounded and dying men mingled with the neighing of horses and the war whoops of Indians. It was a horror not to be forgotten.

216

From a distance David saw Cuthbert Grant's drunken half-breeds running amok among dead and wounded, slashing and stabbing with their long knives. Another Indian, who had scalped a dying soldier, danced around in a circle with the bloody scalp held high in the air. All of the brave men who had marched out with Semple were dead or dying.

Cuthbert Grant himself was appalled at the fury he had unleashed. He stood over the wounded Governor and knocked Indians aside who tried to get at his scalp.

"Stop, you drunken fools," he bellowed. "Stop it, you crazy bastards."

He herded the Indians and Metis back from the dead and wounded, but they still milled around, hooting and shouting and firing their weapons into the air.

When the carnage was over Governor Semple looked up with dazed eyes.

"I appreciate your protection," he gasped. "Are you Cuthbert Grant?"

Grant nodded.

"I wasn't prepared for this slaughter," muttered the Governor.

Grant, stunned by the sudden fury of the battle gave a bitter grimace. "Nor was I."

"Will you get me safely back to the fort?"

"Carry the Governor back," he ordered.

As Grant turned away, another half-breed rode up. Before anyone could stop him, he levelled his gun at the Governor's chest and pulled the trigger.

The shot that killed Governor Semple aroused David and Pritchard. They raced frantically toward the fort. There was no pursuit.

Throughout that night and the next day the stillness of death lay over the valley. The settlers, too terrified to leave the palisade, waited for the next move from the Nor'Westers. On the open prairie the bodies of Governor Semple, his aides and soldiers bloated in the blistering sun. Nothing more could be done.

It was on a June day in 1817 that Lord Selkirk met with the settlers on the bank of the Red River. Behind the gathering that waited his arrival, the open prairie stretched into the distance for over a thousand miles, beckoning more and more colonists. The palisade and towers of Fort Douglas stood over to the east and on the opposite side of the river, Fort Gibraltar was forlorn and empty. To the west the settlers' homes and outbuildings extended along the river that flowed sluggishly toward Lake Winnipeg, and was completely heedless of the exciting things that were happening on its banks.

Everyone who could travel was there. The Metis and Indians came out of curiosity, the soldiers out of boredom and lack of anything better to do. Two hundred ragged settlers — men, women and children — had gathered, tired and weary, but still defiant and ready to fight for the land they had found so difficult to conquer.

No one could guess why the Nor'Westers had failed to follow up the advantage that their bloody treachery at Seven Oaks had given them. Though the colonists had waited day and night in helpless terror nothing had happened. Both sides had seemed sated by the horror of the engagement and it was as though a silent handshake of mutual revulsion had passed between Fort Gibraltar and Fort Douglas.

Three hundred miles to the east Selkirk's reaction had not been so silent, nor had the hand of his anger been so easily stayed. As his heart bled for the people of Red River he turned his mercenaries against Fort William and quickly subdued this key fort of the Nor'Westers. The speed of his retaliation shocked the Metis at Fort Gibraltar still further, and a few days later he had taken over the North-West posts in the Red River Valley without a struggle.

Now Selkirk was making his way towards the speaker's platform. His countenance was drawn and haggard, and there was every indication that the long journey from his comfortable home on St. Mary's Isle, with its trials and disappointments, had left their mark on the great nobleman who had given so much of his time, finance, and energy to foster a better way of life for the outcast Sutherlanders of new Kildonan.

Deep within his tall, calm and dignified frame, there lay a sincere remorse for the manifold wrongs that the Highlanders had suffered as the result of his plan. It was a remorse he had now tried to allay by travelling these many thousands of miles to recruit an expensive army of mercenaries for the defense of a people for whom he had the deepest regard and in whose future he had the greatest faith.

Few men really knew or understood this man, yet his arch enemy, Alexander MacKenzie, was later to say of him: "There

218

were times when I would like to be his friend, and share with those who stood by him, his courage, energy and convictions."

Before he had reached the steps, many a rough hand had grasped his, and many a buffet and malediction had been cast on him. Yet it was when he stood before them on the flag-draped stand, that the tumultuous joy of the Selkirk settlers drowned out the taunts and gibes of the Nor'Westers who had suffered at his hand.

Boldly and with confidence Selkirk spoke of his faith and his hope that they would find peace and contentment in the land and make it great. He told them that he had ordered the erection of a school for their children and a church and, when someone asked what had happened to the Reverend Donald Sage, Selkirk promised he would send a new minister.

"I know what hardships you must have suffered," he said. "Many of your homes and holdings have been lost. I have personally arranged to finance the building of new homes and outbuildings, and the replacement of your tools, equipment, arms and other necessities of life. You are also going to have a mill to grind your grain. We're going to construct roads and bridges so that you can travel through this great country. Let us pray and ask God to bless this land that we may live here in peace."

After the meeting, David and Jeannie walked slowly home through the waving fields of grain. They were silent. Each was thinking of the common hopes and dangers that had united their people on the banks of the Red River. They thought of the evictions, and the hopelessness of life on the Brora beaches. They recalled the long voyage to Hudson's Bay, the bitter cold winter in the rude shelters at Churchill and York, and the long, hard, overland journey to their new home.

Now they knew what their new way of life really meant to them. Here the miles were longer and distance greater than they could ever have dreamed of in the narrow Highland glens; many had to have faith in the few; the feeble could place trust only in the strong; and some made continuing sacrifices for the good of all. At home on the croft the helping hand held out to the unfortunate neighbour was small and puny compared with the one held out by Andrew Bain when he walked off into the night or the one offered by Lajimonière as he pushed relentlessly through the wild forests to Montreal.

Religious belief and faith meant something different to them now. It was still nurtured on the strength of their old church at home but they saw clearer than ever that by God's will nothing could really be changed. The comfortable seclusion of the wee kirk at Brora where the treacherous Countess knelt to pray as she planned her tyranny was a long way from the fearsome grandeur and inspiration of God's new land.

Through it all they had faced unexpected situations and dangers. They had met and were forced to live with strange peoples and had had to assume a great new responsibility — the responsibility of law and government. "Yes," thought David, "we are a new people."

He clasped Jeannie's hand and knelt in thankfulness at the jetty where John Bannerman had asked for God's blessing, and where the emptiness of that morning had become suddenly filled with so much meaning.

"Jeannie," he said, "Selkirk never saw the Red River Valley until a few days ago. Now that I've heard this man, I can understand how the words of Colin Robertson in the Dillon Hotel, Montreal, awakened in him a vision of greatness far beyond even Colin's wildest dreams. That was the day Selkirk heard the cry of a virgin land, weary of waiting for its future — calling, pleading:

> Send me the best of your breeding,
> Loan me your chosen ones,
> Them will I take to my bosom,
> Them will I call my sons."*

"We used to blame him, criticise him, and call down the Wrath of God upon him when things went bad with us. But I'm sure that if he thought we were to be abandoned in Churchill he would never have sent us."

"He saw success and a future to this country, Jeannie; he saw nothing but failure and misery on the beaches at Brora. How could we blame him for not getting us our supplies, our accommodation, or tools, — he was a lone voice in a big company. He wasn't running a croft. He had a long, long chain of command and he had to depend on others who were not as interested in us as he was."

Jeannie listened thoughtfully and then asked: "You mean the Hudson's Bay Company failed Selkirk and did not send the food, shelter, equipment and stock he promised us?"

"That's right, Jeannie. With all his faults there stands out one great quality that should make his name remembered among the

---

* No words could express David's feelings better than these few lines written by Robert W. Service many years later.

220

people of Sutherland. Giving was for him the easiest of all duties and from his appearance today, in addition to his great wealth, he has almost given his life to bring us here, the first colonists in this vast territory."

"Whether he goes down in history as a 'saint' or 'scoundrel' as Colin used to say, we were honoured to shake his hand this morning. He has given us a purpose in life and a pride in accomplishment."

"I have a peaceful feeling; we've come home at last," David remarked.

"Oh, David, I was thinking the same thing. I feel at last we have found a real home."

David smiled. "For as long as I can remember, our clan has fought and died for freedom but never have I felt so calm and certain that our days of conflict are over! To live without fear and to work with God's blessing is to realize our fondest hope."

He noticed that their cabin needed a coat of whitewash. He would start on that tomorrow. Later he would build another storage shed to hold the grain which had been ripening while violence and death had held the centre of the stage such a short distance away.

When they reached the cottage, Jeannie suddenly dropped on one knee.

"Oh, look, David, look! My heather is going to bloom!"

Sure enough, the sprig of heather that Jeannie had set into the soil on their arrival was sending forth new shoots rugged and strong.

"It has taken root," he murmured. "And so have we. God has, indeed, watched over the children of our tribe."